The Dalit Brahmin and Other Stories

Sharankumar Limbale is one of Maharashtra's foremost writer-activists, and the author of more than forty works, including novels, poetry, short story collections, and essays. Best known for his autobiography *Akkarmashi*, translated into several Indian languages, and in English as *The Outcaste* (2003), his other works include *Tale of Untouchables* (2017), *White Paper* (2017), and *Hindu* (2010). *Towards an Aesthetics of Dalit Literature* (2004) was the first critical work on Dalit literature to appear in English. He lives in Pune.

Priya Adarkar is a writer, critic and translator of repute. She has translated the works of iconic Marathi writers and playwrights such as Vijay Tendulkar, *Silence! The Court is in Session* (1979) and three other plays; Satish Alekar, *Mickey and the Memsahib*, in *Collected Plays of Satish Alekar* (2010); and Vishnubhat Godse, *Adventures of a Brahmin Priest: My Travels in the 1857 Rebellion* (2014). She lives in Hyderabad.

Anand Teltumbde is an award-winning bilingual writer, civil rights activist and political analyst who writes extensively on issues relating to peoples' movements and Dalits. He is the author of several books including *The Persistence of Caste: The Khairlanji Murders and India's Hidden Apartheid* (2010); *Dalits: Past Present and Future* (2016); *Mahad: The Making of the First Dalit Revolt* (2016); and *Scripting the Change: Selected Writings of Anuradha Ghandy* (2012).

The Dalit Brahmin

and Other Stories

Sharankumar Limbale

Translated from the original Marathi by

Priya Adarkar

With an Introduction by

Anand Teltumbde

Orient BlackSwan

THE DALIT BRAHMIN AND OTHER STORIES

ORIENT BLACKSWAN PRIVATE LIMITED

Registered Office
3-6-752 Himayatnagar, Hyderabad 500 029, Telangana, India
e-mail: centraloffice@orientblackswan.com

Other Offices
Bengaluru, Chennai, Guwahati, Hyderabad,
Kolkata, Mumbai, New Delhi, Noida, Patna

First published 2018
Reprinted 2025

041712

ISBN 978-93-5287-294-7

Typeset in
Cambria 11/13.8
by Le Studio Graphique, Gurgaon 122 001

Printed in India at
Avantika Printers Private Limited, New Delhi 110 020

Published by
Orient Blackswan Private Limited
3-6-752, Himayatnagar, Hyderabad 500 029
e-mail: info@orientblackswan.com

Contents

White Paper

Sharankumar Limbale

I do not ask
for the sun and moon from your sky.
your farm, your land,
your high houses or your mansions.
I do not ask for gods or rituals,
    castes or sects
Or even for your mother, sisters, daughters.
I ask for
my rights as a man.
Each breath from my lungs
sets off a violent trembling
in your texts and traditions,
your hells and heavens
fearing pollution.
Your arms leapt together
to bring to ruin our dwelling places.
You'll beat me, break me,
loot and burn my habitation
But my friends!
How will you tear down my words
planted like a sun in the east?

My rights: contagious caste riots
festering city by city, village by village,
   man by man
For that's what my rights are—
Sealed off, outcast, road-blocked, exiled.
I want my rights, give me my rights.
Will you deny this incendiary state of things?
I'll uproot the scriptures like railway tracks.
Burn like a city bus your lawless laws.
My friends!
My rights are rising like the sun.
Will you deny this sunrise?

Translated by Priya Adarkar

From *Poisoned Bread*, ed. Arjun Dangle, 74–75, 2nd edition
(Hyderabad: Orient BlackSwan, 1992; 2009)

Translator's Note

Priya Adarkar

My first introduction to Dalit literature was through a memorable Sunday supplement in the *Times of India* in the mid-1970s. The paper had published a powerful selection of Marathi Dalit writing translated into English. It was a long time since I had been so stirred by the written word, taking me as it did into a different world hidden away from the average literature of the day.

Was it shock? Was it fascination? I only felt that the publishing company I worked for (Orient Longman, now called Orient BlackSwan) must publish writers like this in book form. It was surprising, I learned, how much had been written in Marathi and for how long, by Dalit writers, and how little was available in English. The only answer, to start with, would be a representative anthology of the various forms: poetry, prose, short story and the most publicly lauded form, autobiography.

The company readily agreed and we embarked on a long odyssey of finding a suitable Dalit writer/scholar to be the general editor of the anthology. We finally agreed upon Arjun Dangle. The ensuing journey saw us corresponding with a battery of writers and translators, inching towards pages of manuscript. Although over eighty writers were ultimately represented, we were obliged to leave out some more that we would have liked to include. Reasons ranged from a total lack of response to our approaches, to expectations of payment too high for anthology compilers to meet.

As time went on we had a large corpus of texts, some well-translated and some unrecognizable as versions of the original. It had become important to aim at last at a publication date. So a few of us put our backs to the struggle and started reworking matter and translating the new matter that Arjun kept sending us.

This was how I met, not in person but on the page, Sharankumar Limbale. I knew of him as the author of the famous *Akkarmashi*, since published as *The Outcaste*. It was my good fortune that one of the texts that fell to my lot to translate was his outstanding poem 'White Paper'.

The sheer number of writers included in the anthology made it impossible to include more than a fragment of a single writer's work. *Poisoned Bread*, as our Dalit anthology was named, therefore contained only 'White Paper' to represent Sharankumar Limbale when it was published in 1992.

But that did not matter. In the years since its publication in *Poisoned Bread*, 'White Paper' has flown around the world, and earned Limbale admirers in many countries. (See pp. *vii–viii* for 'White Paper'.)

It was a pleasure to be asked by Orient BlackSwan to translate his *Dalit Brahmin*. I now had a very helpful and cooperative author to work for, and it really helped that I so admired his work!

This collection has some stories that are painful to read, and some that are intensely lyrical. They show the author's versatility in his mode of conveying the Dalit experience, for all the stories, whether lyrical or not, have at their core a deeply felt pain. Professor Anand Teltumbde has, in his introduction to this book, discussed the contents of these stories in detail.

Discrimination, scorn, exploitation, disillusion and humiliation: one might feel that there may exist in so many stories on similar themes some sameness, some repetitiveness. But Limbale's stories have a vigorous variety and newness, and reflect Dalit life in different spheres, in town and country, among young and old, students and labourers alike. So the work of translating them was with each of them a new experience. Each story had a different focus, and the style of language, too, was so varied that at times one almost heard the different voices of the narrators. The levels of Marathi used vary with the character who speaks or narrates. It is, of course, not always possible to convey the effect of dialect in the original, when it moves to a different language. One just has to approximate it with simple, less sophisticated words. Translating these stories has, as with other Dalit writing, enlarged my vocabulary, as there are a number of words in them that do not feature in standard urban Marathi, as well as my awareness of different practices (e.g. the Dhadka).

Introduction

Anand Teltumbde

Why do you call this literature?
These are people burning!
In huts engulfed by fire
A smouldering scream
In the grip of four demons
A suffocating cry
Lost in assaults of the goons
A pitiful howl
For a handful of water
A scream of agony
Tell me, tell me O Gandharvas,
To which scale do these *surs* belong?

These lines by Sharankumar Limbale were written in response to the Dhoki massacre wherein caste Hindus had set a hamlet of Pardhi people (a tribe) on fire. Such were the questions posed by Dalit writers to the Brahmin literary establishment that dismissed what they penned as 'literature'. Gone are those days. Rather than craving recognition from Brahminical hegemons of the literary world, Dalit writings occupy a central place in literary discourse today, not only in Maharashtra but far beyond. It is an established genre reverberating in most universities of the world.

The history of Dalit writings, as the experiential narrative of Dalit lives by Dalits themselves in writing, goes back to the Tamil Siddhas (6th to 13th centuries C.E.) and Bhakti saints; since many of them were Dalits, it is probable that their oral verses were committed to writing for their aesthetic and spiritual value by others. But true oral tradition is rooted in storytelling which is common to all poor, labouring people as a cathartic device for enduring their hard life. They are seen in the form of folklore, parables, anecdotes and proverbs.

Modern Dalit writing, a product of the consciousness created by the Ambedkarite Dalit movement and the spread of education among Dalits, adopted the natural genre of short story. The first of Dalit writings—that made their author Baburao Ramchandra Bagul (1930–2008) the father of Dalit literature—was a collection of short stories: *Jenvha Mi Jaat Chorli Hoti* [When I Stole My Caste] published in 1963, followed by his second collection, *Maran Swast Hot Aahe* [Death is Becoming Cheap] in 1969. They were not actually the first to be published, but the first to raise the flag of rebellion in breaking all norms of conventional story writing in Marathi, and inspired others to follow suit. Bagul was a prolific writer of the most powerful short stories, novels, poems and thought-provoking articles. Around the same time many Dalit writers came into being with the Little Magazine movement of 1950–1970. At least two names come to mind: Shankarrao Kharat (1921–2001), whose short story collection *Bara Balutedar* (1959) rather predated Bagul's, and Bandhu Madhav who wrote a short story *Vikhari Bhakar* [Poisoned Bread], which would become the title of the collection edited by Arjun Dangle in 1993.

The Little Magazine movement that gave space and voice to many budding writers and poets, and had a natural rebellious tendency, was not confined to Marathi, but it was particularly strengthened by the context of a larger popular movement called the Samyukta Maharashtra movement for creating a state for Marathi-speaking people with Mumbai as its capital. Spearheaded by communists and socialists, and later joined by Ambedkarite Dalits, the movement had a pro-people progressive stance which necessarily reflected in the pages of little magazines. The beginning of the Little Magazine movement is approximately marked by a cyclostyled publication of *Shabda* in the mid-1950s by Dilip Chitre, Arun Kolatkar, Ramesh Samarth and their friends. It spread like wildfire with the emergence of hundreds of ephemeral to relatively longer-lasting magazines such as *Vacha*, *Bra*, *Bharud* and *Rucha* among others. It brought forth a new generation of writers who were dissatisfied with the established Marathi literature, which they saw as bourgeois, Brahminic, moribund and orthodox. It ushered in modernism in Marathi literature and significantly became one of the catalysts of the Dalit literature movement.

One name that represents a confluence of these three movements—Samyukta Maharashtra movement, Little Magazine movement and Dalit literature movement—is comrade Annabhau Sathe (1920–1969). Born a Mang, a Dalit caste far more oppressed and miserable than the Mahar, Annabhau walked four hundred kilometres with his father from his village Wategaon in Sangli district to Mumbai in search of livelihood. He settled into a labour colony, joined the Communist Party and produced a treasure of literature spanning multiple genres, novels, plays, travelogues, ballads, and of course short stories, portraying the incessant struggles of the downtrodden. Annabhau's stories were testaments to Dalit self-respect and resistance. He thought that Dalit literature and 'Dalit writers are entailed with the responsibility of liberating and shielding Dalits from the existing worldly and Hindu tortures as the long standing conventional beliefs cannot be destroyed instantly.'[1] Annabhau represented the rustic Dalit in his writings, powerfully exposing caste, class and gender oppression, and he saw a universalist solution.

While the Little Magazine movement might have provided a spark to the accumulated Dalit anger of millenniums, it was not capable of containing the vast energy that the explosion would unleash. When the avalanche of Dalit literature broke out in the post-1960s, the short stories were nearly eclipsed by poems. Poetry was perhaps found to be more suitable a genre for the expression of misery and rage. It was certainly more economical than a story; just a few lines could contain a universe of emotions. It also had to do with the Black Art movement that erupted in 1965 in the United States, of which the literary component was overwhelmingly dominated by poetry. Poetry has been the forerunner of Black literature, going back to the eighteenth century when African-born slaves worded their agonies in the form of ballads and verses. Lucy Terry Prince (1730–1821), an African-born slave, became the first known Black poet as her ballad, 'Bars Fight', is the earliest known poem by an African American. It describes an Indian raid on Massachusetts settlers in 1746, and was not published until 1855. The first published book by an African American, Phillis Wheatley, was *Poems on Various Subjects, Religious and Moral* in 1773. Born in Senegal, purchased at the age of seven or eight and brought up by a kindly master and mistress in Boston, Wheatley wrote herself to freedom, modeling her verses after those of Milton, Dryden and Alexander Pope (as was the fashion of her times) and, as a representative of colonial culture.

The next genre of slave literature that followed was dominated by autobiographical-spiritual narratives. The Harlem Renaissance of the 1920s was a time of flowering of literature and arts. The Civil Rights Movement of the 1950s and 1960s was a radical influence as Black activists were pushing to end segregation and racism and create a new sense of identity and Black nationalism. In the 1970s,

African-American literature reached the mainstream. As part of the larger Black Arts movement, which was inspired by the Civil Rights and Black Power movements, African-American literature began to be defined and analysed. Dalit literature also reflects the same trend, but at a much lower scale. Dalits began to narrate their discriminated selves through poetry and autobiographies. After the poetry and autobiographies established Dalit literature as a separate genre, other genres like short stories, novels and plays followed and began to receive critical attention and appreciation.

The present collection of twenty-eight stories by Sharankumar Limbale, an acclaimed name among contemporary Dalit writers, is a notable contribution to the genre of Dalit short fiction. Limbale's literary journey confirms the development of Dalit literature. Coming into the limelight with his fiery poems, published as a collection titled *Utpat* [Disorder] in 1982, he became famous with his autobiography, *Akkarmashi* [The Outcaste], which proved to be a landmark in Marathi Dalit literature when first published in 1984. Its English translation came out in 2003 and catapulted him to fame. He was an Akkarmashi, a casteless one, being born as an illegal son of a Lingayat Patil and a poor, landless Mahar mother. His mother lived in a hut, his father in a mansion. His grandmother, whom he would project as his guardian, lived with a Muslim. It was this mindboggling complexity embodying caste, class and gender dynamics embedded in Indian society that *Akkarmashi* explored, shattering the sensibilities of the world. Thereafter Limbale wrote short stories, some of which have been presented in this collection. His critical work, *Towards an Aesthetics of Dalit Literature* (2004), is also considered a seminal work.[2]

Poetry provided the most economical medium for pouring out emotions ranging from pathos to revolt, and had therefore become popular among Dalit writers. Under the guise of defying convention, anything and everything written became poetry, and its writer, a poet. Some Dalit writers, however, realised the limitations of poetry. Its emotion-centricity lacked the capacity to sketch and narrate their lives the way a story could—storytelling alone could constitute memory. The tale rooted in oral tradition and the sketch, manifested in the written form, are precursors of the story. The tale was a medium through which a culture spoke to itself across time and thus perpetuated its own values and stabilised its own identity. The socialisation of the young took place through tales. The sketch, by contrast, communicated across spaces, depicting some phenomenon of one culture for the benefit or pleasure of a second culture. Factual and journalistic, in essence, the sketch was generally more analytic or descriptive and less narrative or dramatic than the tale. Progenitors of the short story, like Nikolay Gogol, Nathaniel Hawthorne, E. T. A. Hoffmann, Heinrich von Kleist, Prosper Mérimée, Edgar Allan Poe combined elements of the tale with elements of the sketch to create the genre of the modern short story in the nineteenth century.[3]

Stories were the real scaffoldings of memory through which one communicated about the self and the world. As Milan Kundera says in *The Book of Laughter and Forgetting*: 'the struggle of man against power is the struggle of memory against forgetting.' Stories help people crystallise their experience, communicate it to others, and make others do the same. They thus represent the social dynamics of the period they are cast in. As a repertoire of experience they provide the insight to articulate ways of changing the dynamics. I have always been troubled by the question as to why the African Americans made more progress than the Indian Dalits, and was never satisfied by the stereotypical rhetoric about the viciousness of caste over race. One of the reasons appears to be the stories of the African Americans that were born out of their confrontation with racism. The Dalit universe did not have these stories as it took its suffering in its stride as the natural life-world. The African American stories are built around the content of their lives, content that comes from pain, shock. In the life-world of Dalits that embedded their exploitation, oppression and humiliation, there was no shock and therefore no stories until the last century that awakened them from their stupor.

Limbale's stories, located in the larger narrative frame of the Dalit experience, open up a brutal and cruel world conditioned and sanctioned by the caste system. They may have been based on the India of the 1960s through the 1980s, as experienced by the author, as the book itself was first published in 1984. The settings range from feudal villages to modern cities; the characters range from bonded labourers to feudal lords and slum-dwellers to middle classes, and their responses range from meek submission to violent revolt. Irrespective of their settings and situation, his stories expose the underbelly of an Indian society structured by illiteracy and superstition, exploitation and oppression, class, caste and gender violence, trickery and hypocrisy, duplicity and betrayal, dejection and desperation. They present a kaleidoscopic account of Dalit lives in post-Independence India. Almost all the stories have the Ambedkarite movement as a prominent backdrop, particularly its socio-cultural dimension of conversion to Buddhism. The Buddhist identity the Mahars of Maharashtra wore after 1956 certainly lent them a new confidence, and also brought them into conflict with the larger society that construed it as their defiance. If we take what is portrayed in this collection to be representative of the state of Dalits in contemporary India, one wonders how to assess the changes that the Constitution of India, architected by Babasaheb Ambedkar, has ushered.

Limbale handles every story with dexterity and presents it with commensurate creativity to produce a compact unified effect, as ordained by Poe's thesis on the short story.[4] The short story, it says, presents a single significant event or scene involving a limited number of characters who are revealed through an action or a dramatic situation. Its form encourages economy of setting, a concise narrative and the omission of a complex plot; character is disclosed in action and dramatic encounter, but is seldom fully developed. The short story is noted for its focused nature and swift narrative style with a pre-conceived ending, which may be abrupt and inconclusive but never sans the desired impact. Because of its format, it demands both creativity and craft. Dalit literature may have discarded the ideological and normative structure of Marathi literature, but it still qualifies the universal criteria for each of its genres. Limbale impresses one in superbly handling his craft and displays ingenuity, originality, compression and a touch of fantasy, which have been noted as the ingredients for successful short story writing.[5]

However, Limbale himself sets the 'test' for the aesthetics of Dalit literature elsewhere, viz., the authenticity of experience, the generalisation or universalisation of those experiences and their ability to inspire a yearning for an egalitarian social system. He further regards that Dalit aesthetics manifests itself as an expression of the cardinal values of Independence, Justice, Equality and Fraternity, and that Dalit literature be studied from this perspective rather than as 'caste literature' or something else.[6] Each of the stories in this collection passes these tests with flying colours.

It is intriguing that Limbale titled this collection *Dalit Brahmin*. Although it does not reflect the major theme or the dominant character of his protagonists, the oxymoron 'Dalit Brahmin' has a profound sociological significance in terms of the class transformation of a section of Dalits post-Independence. Whatever the accomplishments of the Dalit movement may be, it has certainly produced 'Dalit Brahmins'—as the urban-educated Dalit middle class is disparagingly termed by the community-oriented activist section of Dalits. They are accused of looking down upon their own folk much as the Brahmins do. The term was first coined by Baburao Bagul, but made famous by Arjun Dangle through his anthology, *Poisoned Bread*. Describing the attitude of these educated Dalits towards the Dalit literature movement, Dangle writes:

> ... some educated people from amongst the Dalits too viewed Dalit Literature very negatively. They wanted to forget their past, could not face the harsh social realities surrounding them and were filled with an inferiority complex. They took all the benefits of the concessions resulting from Dr. Ambedkar's movement, but the movement made no impact on them. They believed that with their individual prosperity, society had also prospered.
>
> These Dalit Brahmins felt (and feel even today) that Dalit Literature was something dirty which had tarnished the image of their society. They wanted to speak, write, and live like Brahmins and missed no opportunity to ridicule Dalit Literature.[7]

Dangle's description of the Dalit Brahmin as one who seeks to distance himself from the political progress and cultural expression of his caste community drips with disdain. Dangle's Dalit Brahmin is educated, yet beset by an inferiority complex. He is opportunistic, and unmoved by the communal spirit of freedom and struggle of the Dalit movement. Dangle continues, 'When one examines the views of these "Dalit Brahmins" who equate the depiction of the pitiable conditions of the Dalits with their derogation ... one gets an idea not only of their middle class attitude, but also of their mental impotence.'[8]

This passage suggests a kind of intolerance for criticism and debate over the nature of Dalit literature and narrative representations of Dalit life. Dissenters are viewed as enemies, as threats to the collective consciousness, and are isolated with epithets like 'Dalit Brahmin'. This essentialism in defining a concept of Dalit consciousness is problematic in the context of a changing society. Inasmuch as this consciousness is sourced from Ambedkar himself, any insistence on *the* definitive interpretation may be contentious in view of the inconsistencies in Ambedkar's own thinking. It must be appreciated that it is difficult to neatly sift Ambedkar's thoughts from the context-laden polemics. Babasaheb Ambedkar himself did not believe in such a construction as he followed a doctrine of pragmatism imbibed from his teacher, John Dewey, which relies on successive principles rather than any universal theory. The insistence on an essentialist definition of Dalit consciousness evidences the identity orientation of a section of middle-class Dalits which would rather exclude the 'other' that disagrees with it. It is true that there are well-placed Dalits, the beneficiaries of reservations, who would prefer not to relate with their larger community. Ambedkar himself experienced this self-centredness and ingratitude of Dalit bureaucrats who personally declined to help him in his need.

Ranajit Guha provides a somewhat universalistic explanation for the above to suggest that among subaltern societies, any member of the community who chooses not to 'continue in such subalterneity' or does not embody a commitment to the collective subaltern in their own self-consciousness is seen as an enemy of the collective. 'The task of the "consciousness" of class collectivity within a social field of exploitation and domination is thus necessarily self-alienating.'[9] So, in Dalit society, anyone who does not espouse the normative demands of exhibiting a carefully defined Dalit consciousness is rigorously secluded from the public persona of 'Dalitness'. The bitterly ironic 'Dalit Brahmin', for example, is a common epithet for Dalits who try to distance themselves from their caste identity, or who put more emphasis on personal material success than community betterment, thus perhaps espousing a middle-class or elite-class position. This phenomenon foregrounds the extreme opportunism of Dalits to the extent that those who swore by Dalitism and castigated others as Dalit Brahmins and betrayers of the Dalit cause have themselves acted against the interests of Dalit masses while still flaunting their Ambedkarism. What would one call those Ambedkarites in active politics who have gone over to the ranks of rightwing Brahminical parties like the Shiv Sena or the Bharatiya Janata Party?

This embodies a larger problematic that belies the core representational logic of Babasaheb Ambedkar. He believed that Dalits in legislative bodies or bureaucracy would protect and promote the interests of the Dalit masses. In this regard, the folly of political reservations was a bitter experience for Ambedkar in his repeated defeats by political pigmies. His experience with Dalits in bureaucracy was no less painful; he himself lamented their selfishness. They formed a thin class layer over the vast mass of Dalits that erroneously represented Dalit progress. Aspirationally, they look upwards and fear to look downwards to their origins, except for projecting their own 'greatness'. They are largely indifferent towards ordinary Dalits and rather expect them to pay their obeisance to them. One may certainly lament the Brahminic traits in this section of Dalit bureaucrats, but when it is a rampant phenomenon, it warrants a critical probe. The answer lies in comprehending the process of class transformation. A Dalit, once lifted from his socio-economic locale, undergoes a class transformation that hinders his identification with the masses he came from. Derogatory epithets like 'Dalit Brahmin' push people to cling harder to the very notions and biases that produced it. It is the same when Ambedkarite Dalits self-righteously castigate those who speak of material interests of the Dalit masses as Marxists. This, however, is not reflected prominently in any of the stories in this collection except for a passing reference in 'The Life Lived', where Kale, a Dalit professor, gets infuriated with the protagonist when he hears Advocate Bandsode's name, calling him a Marxist. He reasons it out, saying

Babasaheb opposed Marxism. This obsession with identity has splintered the Dalits into innumerable factions, which they refuse to acknowledge.

***

The stories in this volume reflect varied experiences of Dalithood and are not amenable to easy categorisation. However, for the sake of convenience we could club them into the following five categories:

1. Experience of the Dalits with Brahmins and upper castes: 1. The Weevil, 4. Sudha Dear, 6. Son-in-law of the Government, and 21. The Steps
2. Experience of the Dalits with their own middle class: 2. A Life Lived, 3. Enlightenment, 5. Dalit Brahmin, 7. Ganpati Bappa Morya!, and 23. The Procession.
3. Experience of the Dalits with upper-caste women: 8. Madhavi, 9. Sujata, 10. Niloo, 11. Sunita, and 12. Rajani
4. Experience with/of Dalit women: 13. Soni, and 14. Ratna.
5. Experience of the Dalits with feudal oppression: 15. Womb of Darkness, 16. The Yeskar's Bhakri, 17. The Saintly Man, 18. War, 19. Caste, 20. The Harijan Master, 22. Cobra's Head, 25. The Mausoleum, 26. Sir, I Salute You, 27. Vows, and 28. Sunflower.
6. Outlier: 24. Cow Slaughter.

In the first category of stories, varied experiences of Dalits are depicted mostly in modern urban settings, attempting to characterise the intriguing nature of Brahmins, their doublespeak, prejudices and cunning. For instance, in the first story, 'The Weevil', Khanolkar, an established figure in Marathi literature, is shown stealing the life story of the protagonist, a Dalit student who seeks his guidance in writing. Dalits tendentiously look at Brahmins with respect as benign and progressive, but when it comes to observance of the caste code, they do not measure up to their expectations. When Dalit students present Khanolkar with Ambedkar's statuette as a memento, and expect to see it in his drawing room, they are disappointed to observe, 'No matter how progressive a high-caste man may be, he still swears by caste in his house.' The story projects Brahmins as hypocritical, unethical and amoral, and Dalits as gullible and innocent.

In 'Enlightenment', a budding Dalit poet faces the typical Brahmin abhorrence and fear of any subversiveness which threatens the status quo, and thereby Brahmin power and prestige. We see the trajectory followed by his newly published collection of poems, which he gives to Professor Khanolkar for his feedback, on account of its purported obscenity, the book lands up in a waste paper depot. While it is universally true that the entrenched classes do not like any kind of subversion, the story establishes it through the professor's wife, who shields her daughters against obscenity out of motherly concern. The question is what is 'obscene', and how does the poet's Dalitness influence her perception of obscenity.

The third story in this category, 'Sudha Dear', paints an upper-caste professor, Avinash Swami, in similar colours. How he intrigues against the protagonist, a Dalit professor, admonishes him for teaching a Dalit poem in class in a 'casteist' manner, and assigns the poem to be taught by an upper-caste teacher instead to humiliate him into submission is depicted beautifully. The upper-caste professor also abuses his authority to indulge in sensual pleasures with girl students. In the next story, 'Son-in-Law of the Government', Brahmins abuse their authority to exercise their cultural hegemony, until resisted. They hold Lakshmi pujas and Satyanarayana pujas in office, in contravention of the Constitution, but resist the Dalit demand for celebrating secular events like Ambedkar Jayanti. The story also subtly and brilliantly depicts the undercurrents within the Dalit movement.

A similar amoral, criminal and vicious character of a Brahmin high school headmaster, fortifying himself with authority, is portrayed in 'The Steps'. Here, a Dalit teacher is hired as mandated by the rules, but at a grade below his qualification. When he demands his grade, he finds himself trapped in a series of false charges. Cornered from all sides and driven against the wall with no hope of redemption in sight, he retaliates.

The next category of stories depicts experiences of/with people of the Dalit middle class. In the first story, 'A Life Lived', a Dalit youth aspiring to make it big with his autobiography is shown seeking guidance from various people, perceived to be established in literary circles. It portrays how middle-class Dalits reflect the Brahminic vices of hypocrisy, double speak and lies in addition to their traits of jealousy and rivalry. They malign and speak against each other: Kamble against Khanolkar as a Brahmin, Bandsode against Kamble as a Hindutvawadi, and Kale against Bandsode as a Marxwadi, although all of them are in the end found seeking Khanolkar's favours at the latter's residence.

The next story in this category, 'Dalit Brahmin', and the title story of the volume, characterises a typical middle-class Dalit who tries to show off as a Brahmin. While living in the Dalit colony, he enjoys the visits of his Brahmin friends as they add to his social prestige. He leaves the colony as advised by his Brahmin friends and relocates to a middle-class locality. He adopts Brahmin ways of life, performs Satyanarayana pujas; his wife goes to *haldi-kunku* ceremonies of the upper-caste ladies. If Dalit activists come home, he pays some donation or buys some publication from them, but avoids any further engagement. He wears intellectual airs and furiously talks about revolution and changing the system, but when asked to come for a march, excuses himself with a sense of self-importance, saying, 'the activists have to fight; we just supply them with a provision of thought.' He speaks softly, strives to sound balanced and accuses Dalit writers of being sectarian. He enjoys being invited to the RSS functions and attends them with pride. He enjoys being hosted by Brahmins at their homes, not having an iota of suspicion that even in their show of affinity and affection they could be still observing the caste code. It requires a Dalit activist, Dinesh Kamble, who is used as an antithesis of the Dalit Brahmin, to remind him, 'Do you know—all the utensils you used were kept separate. All the clothes you used have been taken and given to the laundry.'

Another story in this category, 'Ganpati Bappa Morya', is in some way an extension of the 'Dalit Brahmin'. Here, a Dalit middle-class employee makes compromises for living in an upper-caste neighbourhood, unlike the Dalit Brahmin who tries to wear his new identity. Not to be singled out for harassment, he pays contributions for Satyanarayana pujas and participates in Hindu festivities, but is still seen with jaundiced eyes by the others. When Samir Joshi, his Brahmin friend, is attacked by thugs, Joshi's family attributes it to their friendship. Joshi is called a 'Jai Bhimwalla' by the Brahmin colony, and he as a Hindutvawadi by the Dalits. It echoes another dilemma of radical Dalits: they are called communists by the Dalits, and Ambedkarite by the communists! When his daughter is harassed by some workers of the Ganapati mandal, he ignores it, but his son intervenes and gets beaten up. His family regrets: 'Let us go back to Maharwada. We don't want this daily torment.' When he asks Joshi to intervene, Joshi backs out saying, 'I am not a spirited person, I can't fight. I won't come.' He regrets his friendship with Joshi. Annoyed with this harassment, when he tries to speak out his anger, a riot breaks out. Joshi hides, but Dinesh Kamble descends with his dagger drawn and scares all away. While the story powerfully portrays the plight of a middle-class Dalit employee facing upper-caste prejudice in his attempt to be integrated, the picture of Dalits coming to his rescue is too far-fetched and romantic. Dinesh Kamble's character reminds one of Ayyankali who at the dawn of the last century, much before the advent of Babasaheb Ambedkar, won many liberties for his people using the intrinsic strength of the Dalits—their bodies.[10]

'The Procession' depicts the process that sucks in even the idealists among Dalits to become part of the very establishment they wish to fight. Diwakar, a Dalit youth who is the first to get to college from his village, decides to fight casteist oppression. He organises a resistance with the help of his college friends. They decide to install a statue of Ambedkar and unveil it with a procession on Ambedkar's birth anniversary. The caste Hindus decide to counter this by celebrating Shivaji Jayanti and stage a play in the path of the Ambedkar procession on the same day. There is a clash injuring many, and the Ambedkar statue is broken into pieces. Next day, the newspapers cover the clash, projecting Diwakar as a leader. Enthused by this fame, Diwakar stands for assembly elections as the Republican Party of India (RPI) candidate, but is defeated by another Dalit candidate fielded by the ruling party. Diwakar introspects his defeat, and joins the party in power to win the by-election. When his victory procession with saffron flags and throws of vermilion reaches his basti, his mother nostalgically remembers the earlier procession. It highlights another dilemma posed by the prevailing political system: if Dalits stick to their identity they can never win an election; and when they win the election they have to align with the ruling powers and forget Dalits.

While the phrase Dalit Brahmin could be problematised as done before, it marks a serious paradox of the Dalit movement. Babasaheb Ambedkar imagined that a few Dalits endowed with higher education would rise and take care of the Dalit interests. But this process has produced 'Dalit Brahmins' who distance themselves from the Dalit masses and instead of challenging Brahminism, who themselves adopt it. It also exposes the deep-drawn inferiority complex of the Dalits, both the common masses as well as the middle classes, in their valuing their association with upper-caste/class people.

The Dalit experience with Brahmin/upper-caste women, which forms the next category, is represented by five stories, viz., 'Madhavi', 'Sujata', 'Niloo', 'Sunita' and 'Rajani', that portray them with a broad brush as the daughters of well-to-do parents either in mutual love with or only loved by the protagonist. They are insensitive, selfish, narcissist bodies that lure Dalit youth and become the cause of catastrophic devastation of the entire Dalit community. Madhavi, a Patil's daughter, is in love with the protagonist Dalit boy. His building a pucca house becomes the cause of gruesome atrocity that devours the entire Dalit basti and takes a Dalit's life. Madhavi is taken away to Delhi and married off to a man from her own caste. Shalan, a Dalit girl and Madhavi's friend, a witness to the affair, also suffers in the atrocity. Finally, the protagonist marries Shalan, who makes him see the world differently. In 'Sujata', the slum-dwelling Dalit protagonist is in love with an upper-caste girl who stays in an adjacent bungalow. He imagines her occasional sightings at the window to be her response to him. But the real relationship between them is marked by his mother and sister working as maids in her house. When the municipal squad comes for demolition, people resist. The basti is razed and people are rendered homeless to make space for a garden. Sujata remains unperturbed through it all, and goes on drying her hair. The window that frames Sujata serves as a metaphor for the upper-caste/class world which now appears like a villain's eye.

In 'Niloo', the theme is repeated with a slight change of locale and occupations of the protagonist and the girl. They are shown as sportspersons in friendship, but he imagines it to be mutual love. She finds his Dalit colony dirty. Their worlds are contrasted by the fact that his mother is a scavenger in Niloo's colony. In Niloo's wedding procession, his mother carries a gas lamp on her head. The gas lamp explodes, his mother dies, but the procession continues with another Dalit woman replacing her. Like Sujata, Niloo also represents the insensitive upper-caste/class world. In 'Sunita', the Dalit protagonist falls in love with the daughter of the upper-caste village deputy sarpanch. Their love affair becomes an excuse for the villagers to 'teach Dalits a lesson' by unleashing destruction and butchery on the entire colony, their reason being: 'Today one girl from the village has lost her caste. Tomorrow, the village itself will lose caste.' Sunita retracts her love and calls it a mistake. He finds 'Sunita even crueler than the murderers'. The story ends with the protagonist taking up a blue flag, swearing to fight injustice. 'Rajani' explores the inter-caste marriage of the protagonist's parents. His mother is a Brahmin and his father a Mahar. In the middle-class father's house, 'Ambedkar's photo and Ambabaichi parade (the basket of Ambabai, a relic from the pre-conversion era) both co-exist.' The last one is 'Rajani', in which the protagonist is a Dalit from a well-to-do middle-class family that represents the most advanced end of the cultural continuum, its past represented by his grandfather and great grandfather, rooted in a typical Dalit milieu. His mother, a Brahmin, having experienced the cultural chasm herself, is not in favour of her daughter marrying a Maratha lecturer. As for Rajani, despite the protagonist's hopes of marriage, she declines, mainly citing the reason that her father was an orthodox Hindu.

The portrayal of these women in Limbale's stories is sans empathy. His depiction of them is typically patriarchal, making them beautiful bodies, mere objects of desire, objectifying the pride and prestige of their community and hence meant to be vanquished. Limbale does not consider granting them subjectivity, agency and the right to make choices. In each of his stories a Dalit boy desiring to marry an upper-caste girl ends up in disaster. It is attributed either to insensitivity or insincerity or outright casteism of the girl, but not to her compulsions or rational choice. When Rajani decides to be friends but not to marry, it is easily attributed to the caste factor but not appreciated as her rational choice which is also corroborated in a way by the protagonists' own Brahmin mother, opining against her daughter marrying her Maratha colleague, after having herself lived through the experience of inter-caste marriage. Most stories depicting love disasters have glaring class differences marked by a stark relationship such as owner and servant. While Limbale excels in painting the protagonist's love for the girl with poetic flourish, he fails to convince when he attributes the failure of these love affairs, mostly one-sided, to the girl's caste prejudice. The material circumstances that placed them at two extremes are not paid attention in allocation of the blame. His only defence may come from the format of the genre that expects him to create a unique impact, which he chooses in terms of targeting only caste.

The next category dealing with Dalit women has two stories: Soni and Ratna. Limbale overcompensates his lack of empathy for Brahmin women and the tendency to caricature them as sex objects. Soni is a Dalit who follows her mother into prostitution out of sheer hunger and destitution. Her mother was thrown out by her husband for bearing her, a female child. Out of penury, she becomes a prostitute. She marries off her daughter Soni to an elderly man, Babu, as his third wife. His first wife had committed suicide, and the second had run away. Babu suspects Soni, burns her. She comes back to her mother and inevitably becomes a prostitute. Their Dalit neighbourhood does not take them kindly. When she becomes pregnant, she wants to abort and have a family planning operation to get some money as per the government scheme. When the protagonist decides to marry her, he is mistaken as a customer and the police take them away. It is a powerful portrayal of the pathos of Dalit life that represents the intersectionality of caste, class and gender in its heady mix.

The next story is that of Ratna, a Dalit girl staying with her mother in the village; her father is an army man. She and the protagonist grew up together but because of a family feud would not marry. A village goon, Gana, takes a liking for Ratna and begins to harass her. Such was his terror in the village that no one would dare stop him. One day, the protagonist and Ratna decide to run away and meet at the river bank. When he reaches the spot, he finds Gana beating her. He cannot control his anger and runs into him with full force and kills him. He throws Gana into the flooding river. The story depicts Ratna's helplessness before the overtures of the caste Hindu goon despite her father being an army man. It also illustrates that the perpetuation of injustice to Dalits is in large measure due to the absence of resistance from them. Resistance may not succeed every time, but it never goes in vain. Even in defeat it has a message to an adversary that his misdeeds would not go unanswered. When the protagonist takes Gana head on, he proves to be not as invincible as was made out to be.

The category of Dalit experience of feudal oppression contains the maximum number (eleven) of stories. They depict the village situation as of course might have been experienced by the author in the 1960s through 1980s. They may also appear distant enough in the past to be of relevance to us. After all, it is difficult to reconcile that feudal India post-Green Revolution of the early 1960s remained untouched and the servitude of the Dalits post-Ambedkarite awakening remained unaffected. We do get glimpses of such a bygone past, however, in the wake of every notable atrocity. The narrative of the cases may change, but not necessarily their essence.

The first story in the category is 'Womb of Darkness' that depicts the agony of a Mahar, Bali, a wood chopper, who learns about his pregnant mother being buried alive in the foundation of the Patil's mansion at the instance of a tantrik. The Patil, father of the current one, had given his father a piece of land and managed to put a permanent lid on it. Burning with the fire of vendetta, Bali decides to kill the Patil's daughter Varsha, who is about to deliver her baby. On the penultimate day, as he has finally run to the door where Varsha was, he hears the cry of the newborn baby. He drops his revenge and disappears into the darkness. A captivating and moving narrative creatively presented, it depicts the desperate lives of the Mahars who were made to slave for the village lords in exchange for their leftovers. The story also highlights the contrasting morality of the exploiters and the exploited. While the Patil cold-bloodedly kills Bali's pregnant mother, Bali's humaneness prevents him from killing Varsha, mother of a newborn.

The second story, 'The Yeskar's Bhakri', is equally moving and depicts how the sheer destitution of the Dalits fuels rivalry among them, to the glee of their tormentors. Nama Mang is the Yeskar, the village watchman. The story shows how Dalits have completely internalised their oppressed status. Nama wants to be remembered for his honest work. Paradoxically, he recounts, 'When the Marwari Ranglal died, the whole village wept. When Ambya Mahar died, everyone abused and cursed him.' There is a burglary at the Marwari's house. Patil takes Nama to task and accuses him of colluding with the thieves. He gives him a week's time to retrieve the stolen goods. Nama searches around every Mahar and Mangwada, but fails to find any clues. After a week, he is summoned by the Patil and mercilessly thrashed. Interestingly, his thrashers are Dalits. With remorse for having got a bad name and fearing he would be thrashed again, Nama hangs himself, pushing his family into destitution. The Yeskar's staff is passed on to one Lavha Mahar. The story powerfully brings out the internal dynamics of Dalit lives that perpetuates their slavery.

The next story, 'The Saintly Man', is similar to 'The Yeskar's Bhakri' in portraying the divide among Dalits. The protagonist's father is jailed for cutting down a tree in the moneylender's field. His family is driven to dire destitution. Bajya Nana, the moneylender's Mahar, is the culprit who reports about the tree. For want of food, Dalits wait for cattle to die, or poison them. The protagonist poisons the moneylender's buffalo. The moneylender's men round up the entire Mahar population to the village square and mercilessly flog them. Mahars hate Bajya for acting against his caste, and poison him. After Bajya, it was the turn of the protagonist's father to be the moneylender's Mahar. He is freed from jail and appointed in place of Bajya. The family swiftly forgets the moneylender's atrocities and considers him a saintly man. The story powerfully brings out how hunger drives the Dalits to desperation and how the economic structure of the village keeps them on tenterhooks sans any options to survive except relying on the pittance from upper castes.

'War' is about a Dalit who suffers horrific punishment for challenging the village Deshmukh, but does not give up the fight. Bhagwan, an army man who was wounded in the Indo-Pakistan war, gets a job in a bank and some land. He tries to seed self-respect among the Mahars and trains school children in discipline. He stops his father from working for the Deshmukh as Mahar. Bhagi, his sister, however, continues to work in the Deshmukh's house. She becomes pregnant by his son. He takes her into the Deshmukh house and leaves her there as Deshmukh's daughter-in-law. Deshmukh issues a verdict to remove the thorn of Bhagwan. The entire caste-Hindu village backs him and decides to teach Bhagwan a lesson. They drag Bhagi out of the house and parade her naked in broad daylight to the Maharwarda. They set Bhagwan's hut on fire, burning his father and wife to cinders. They gouge out Bhagwan's eyes. The story ends with Bhagwan rising and commanding the school children gathered around him for a war.

The 'Caste' exposes how deep caste-consciousness is embedded in the Indian social psyche that it overrides all secular feelings and emotions of love and affection. It is told through the friendship of two students studying in a Sholapur college, one belonging to a Lingayat caste and other, Hanmya, a Mahar. When the Lingayat boy goes to Hanmya's house in the village for attending Hanmya's sister's marriage, the entire Mahar community is overwhelmed by the obligation to provide for an upper-caste boy. However, when Hanmya visits his friend's house, he is made out to be a Dhangar so as to be acceptable to the Lingayats. The Lingayat boy's mother falls sick and is hospitalised. She fondly remembers Hanmya. Just when Hanmya is to give her blood, she learns his caste and suddenly all her fondness, love and affection is overtaken by anger for polluting her house, and the threat of her body being polluted.

'The Harijan Master' highlights how a Mahar teacher coming to a village school faces discrimination. He has to live in a dharamshala in Maharwada. He is shown to be a good teacher, but nobody from the upper-caste village respects him. Eventually, he asks for a transfer.

'Cobra's Hood' exposes how the existing feudal order neutralises the constitutional reservations for Dalits in politics. As it happened all over the country, the feudal masters managed to maintain their fiefdom by becoming people's elected representatives in the post-colonial parliamentary regime. In the story, a Patil of five villages is the MLA of the area. He designates his faithful Mahar, Kondiba, to be his personal assistant. When his constituency is declared a reserved constituency, he fields Kondiba as the candidate. However, the twist in the story comes through Kondiba's son, Daulya, who is a close friend of the Patil's son. While Patil's son goes to college, Daulya has to discontinue his education. He gets married and lives in town with his father-in-law, an RPI leader, as the resident son-in-law. Daulya files his nomination as the RPI candidate against his father. Patil tries bribing Daulya for withdrawing his candidature, but he refuses. They forbid him from entering the village. When Daulya comes to the village, they set the Mahar colony on fire and grievously injure him. The story ends with the court acquitting all innocent. The story, with multiple strands to expose various vulnerabilities of Dalits, shows how the new constitutional institutions have been easily subverted by entrenched interests to perpetuate their control.

In 'The Mausoleum', the Dalit Kotwal, Ambadas Sabne, who is at the forefront of the Dalit struggle for self-respect, is brutally murdered by the caste Hindus in a temple, and is projected as the saint for his extraordinary devotion to God. In a simple plot Ambadas Sabne, who takes the lead in installing a statue of Ambedkar in the village, is killed in the temple where he had come to take shelter from rains. It depicts how even a rebellion can be subverted, neutralised and co-opted in service to the status quo.

'Sir, I Salute You' is set at the intersection of Warkari and Ambedkarite consciousness. The Mahars of Lonkheda village refuse to drag dead animals. The villagers set fire to their huts. They leave the village and come to the town. A boy, the protagonist, makes his livelihood by stealing the footwear of people coming to visit the temple and selling them. Later, he graduates to an organised service to look after footwear for a small fee. He is happy as it fetches him good money. Even degree-holders crave a job and do not get any, he thinks. He develops an interest and puts in hard work into this service. One day, he suddenly finds his father caught stealing chappals. The story ends with the boy throwing all the footwear in his care, perhaps conveying the plight of the Dalits, that howsoever they conduct themselves their woes do not leave them.

'Vows' depicts the hold of age-old customs even when they entail risk to life. In a moving narrative, the destruction of a Dalit family which had made good by moving to Mumbai during one of the droughts, is shown happening at the altar of the village goddess, Mahishasuri. A Dalit, named Parsya, goes to Mumbai during the drought and makes a saving, which would not have been possible staying in the village. His family, wife Subhadra and son Mhasha return to the village to fulfil the undertaking to the goddess by making his teenage son take a *dhadka* (a forceful strike against the temple wall).

Mhasha takes dhadka and dies instantly. Mhasha's mother Subhadra cannot bear the loss and bangs her head against the temple wall. Overtaken by grief, she herself takes dhadka and collapses to the ground in a pool of blood. Such is the force of custom that villagers worry not about the deaths of a mother and son in front of them, but about the curse of the goddess incurred by a woman's dhadka, which was not allowed by custom. Parsya is shown going mad at this loss. He runs in rage into the temple, climbs upon the goddess's head and begins stamping and dancing. A rebellion born out of agony is very creatively portrayed in the story.

The last story in the collection, 'Sunflower', portrays a similar awakening dawning on a fifteen-year old Mang boy, Trimukh, who is journeying to Banaras to consign his mother's bones to the Ganges. His father, Sambha, is Shivaji Patil's Mang. When defeated in election, the Patil attacks the Maharwada through his goons as a punishment for voting the opposition candidate, and kills one Dagdu Mahar. In consequence, he loses his post of Patil, which goes to Dagdu's son. Unable to stomach the ignominy, the Patil gets Dagdu's son murdered by Sambha. Sambha goes to jail. His wife Saraja slaves for the Patil, and becomes pregnant by him. She is disposed of, having died of a snake bite. Patil sends Trimukh off on a journey to Banaras. Walking to the nearest railway station, Trimukh has several brushes with death because of hunger. He gets to eat his first meal in an Ambedkar Jayanti celebration. On the way, he picks up some animal bones from a carcass. He sells them, supplemented by his mother's bones, for a rupee. He wants to donate it to the fund being collected to install a statue of Babasaheb Ambedkar. The story depicts the germination of new consciousness in a Mang boy. Ambedkar was considered by Mangs as a Mahar leader, but he transcends that identity barrier. Also, it depicts an enlightenment against blind rituals that needlessly put people to hardship.

The story 'Cow Slaughter' is an outlier in this collection because it does not have caste as a central theme. Mhadba sells his unproductive cow to Yakub, a butcher. While taking away the cow, Yakub is accosted by Shekhar, Mhadba's son. A scuffle between Hindus and Muslims breaks out, injuring people on both sides. The matter spreads and Shekhar becomes famous for having confronted his father for the cow's sake. The voices against cow slaughter disturb the beef-eaters, Muslims and Mahars. They murmur, 'Cow may be mother to you, but it is our food. What kind of ban is this on our food?' The impact of all this makes cow slaughter and beef eating surreptitious. Yakub brings in animals at night from outside and slaughters them early mornings. Those who eat beef take the meat away. Shekhar announces a fast unto death demanding a ban on cow slaughter. Meanwhile, the barren cow dies. Mhadba calls Ganu Mahar to take her away. Shekhar feels bad but rushes to the district headquarter to sit for the fast. Soon Shekhar gets a ticket for the Lok Sabha election and withdraws his fast. All the clamour over cow slaughter was thus only for political gain. It is an apt comment on the contemporary turbulence created by the Sangh Parivar over cow slaughter.

Notwithstanding his masterly handling of the craft of short story writing, Limbale's engagement with the Dalit universe appears tunnelled insofar as he either does not confront the complexity induced by capitalist development that has been taking place since the last century, or notes it but prefers to drive past it on the preconceived caste road. All these stories tend to see the woes of Dalits either due to casteist prejudices of the upper castes, whether in the classical feudal realm of rural India, or the semi-feudal (if one may call it so) realm of urban India, or in the disunity of Dalits, often induced by the dominant castes. While this approach serves its purpose in exposing caste oppression, undoubtedly still prevailing in India in varying forms ranging from its most hideous version in the rural interiors to subtler forms in corporate-dominated urban India, it fails to locate it in the contemporary world with its precise coordinates. While many of Limbale's stories reflect class-caste and even gender issues, he appears obsessed with caste and refuses to engage with the other two. If he had engaged with them, the world with a new array of forces and myriad struggles against them would have been uncovered before him. After all, caste, being the life-world of the people for millenniums, is going to linger on for many more years, and would also serve as a conduit or a fault-line for new non-caste contradictions to manifest. The question to engage with is to know the dominant contradiction.

Class-caste duality, I have always maintained, is an unfortunate product of the dogmatic vision of the communists and the misconceived internecine contention of the two streams, Ambedkarite and Marxist. It is related to the conception of classes in the given Indian context, which was admittedly unique enough to invalidate the use of readymade moulds that worked elsewhere in determining classes. To be consistent with the Marxist schema of class struggle being the motor of history, the classes had to be properly conceived. If castes were India's pervasive social reality, classes could not exclude that reality. Classes, therefore, would necessarily incorporate castes and internalise the anti-caste struggles as an integral part of the class struggle. No society emerges from a vacuum and conforms to conceptual models in theory; it always comes variously contaminated with traces of bygone modes, and any revolutionary struggle will necessarily have to confront them. They just cannot be wished away. The consequence of this miss has been the obsessive divergence of the Ambedkarite Dalit movement and the Marxist communist movement. This obsession has inevitably affected all spheres of life, including literature. Limbale's refusal to engage with Dalit life in its entirety is not a disconnected phenomenon.

Consequently, he always makes his protagonists veer round the blue flag that symbolises the Ambedkarite rebellion for him. He rightly notes the bankruptcy of the Ambedkarite Dalit movement, its leaders being only interested in collecting contributions and not engaging with the real struggles of the masses. In the conflict between the Dalit and other employees over the celebration of Ganeshotsava in office, the Dalit employees approach the Dalit Panther leaders, but they just dodge it. Again in 'Sunita', the Dalit leaders are shown collecting funds in the name of atrocity, making speeches and going away. If this is the state of the Dalit movement, what is the meaning of Dalit protagonists lifting the blue flag as a symbol of revolt? Is that not an identitarian consciousness, a false consciousness, being perpetuated even in literature? Limbale tends to see the consciousness dawning on the non-Mahar Dalit castes to unite under Ambedkar's blue banner, but does not engage with the harsh reality of Mangs and Mahars (or for that matter Malas and Madigas in Andhra and Telangana, Pariah and Chakliars in Tamil Nadu, or Holayas and Madigas in Karnataka and the most and next most populous castes of Dalits everywhere), separating with their respective icons, reservations serving as the main rouse, of course, amplified by the ruling classes.

The other question to engage with is why, even after seventy years of Independence and the Constitution being laid down, the Dalit situation remains much the same as existed a couple of centuries before. Limbale's stories rightly corroborate this. What precise changes has the conversion to Buddhism brought into Dalit lives? Why has it failed to appeal to Dalits other than Mahars or their equivalent (most populous Dalit caste) in other states? Some of the stories do point to the new dynamics unleashed by electoral politics (like 'The Cobra's Hood'). Has it not become the main prop for caste today? Why lament over the betrayal of political leaders or the behaviour of the Dalit Brahmins without also problematising the reservations that produce them? There are numerous such questions that should impel Dalits to introspect. Perceptive writers like Limbale have a definite role to play. They are not expected to provide answers; their role is to hold a mirror to society.

Notwithstanding these issues, which, it must be admitted, are far from settled even in theory, this collection of short stories succeeds in effectively and powerfully presenting the darker side of Dalit lives in contemporary India, that aspires to be the world superpower. They are without doubt a vital contribution to Dalit literature. The English readership will surely welcome these stories as it did the author's *Akkarmashi*.

Endnotes

[1] B. N. Gaikwad, 'Manifestation of Caste and Class in Anna Bhau Sathe's *Fakira* and Baburao Bagul's *Jenvha Mi Jaat Chorli Hoti*', *The Criterion*, Issue 12 (February 2013). http://www.the-criterion.com/V4/n1/Baliram.pdf. Accessed 16 January 2018.

[2] Jaydeep Sarangi, *Subaltern Speaks*: *Selected Essays on Sharan Kumar Limbale* (Allahabad: Cyberwit.net, 2015), 166–171.

[3] Kathleen Kuiper (ed.), *Prose: Literary Terms and Concepts* (New York: Britannica Educational Publishing, 2012), 135.

[4] James Cooper Lawrence, 'A Theory of the Short Story', *The North American Review*, Vol. 205, No. 735 (February 1917), 274–286.

[5] Brander Matthews, *The Philosophy of the Short-Story* (New York, London and Bombay: Longmans, Green and Co., 1901). https://archive.org/stream/philosophyshort01mattgoog/philosophyshort01mattgoog_djvu.txt. Accessed 16 January 2018.

[6] Sharan Kumar Limbale, *Dalit Sahitya Ka Saundaryashastra* (New Delhi: Vani Prakashan, 2002).

[7] Arjun Dangle, 'Poisoned Bread', in Arjun Dangle (ed.), *Poisoned Bread: Translations from Modern Marathi Dalit Literature* (Hyderabad: Orient Longman, 1992), 249–250.

[8] Laura R. Brueck, 'Making the Boundaries of a New Literary Identity: The Assertion of "Dalit Consciousness" in Dalit Literary Criticism', in Steven E. Lindquist (ed.), *Religion and Identity in South Asia and Beyond: Essays in Honour of Patrick Olivelle* (London: Anthem Press, 2011), 357.

[9] Gayatri C. Spivak, 'Subaltern Studies: Deconstructing Historiography', in Ranajit Guha (ed.), *Subaltern Studies* (New Delhi: Oxford University Press, 1985), 342.

[10] Anand Teltumbde, *Mahad: The Making of the First Dalit Revolt* (New Delhi: Aakar, 2016).

1

The Weevil

It was becoming a custom to go to Professor Khanolkar's house in the evenings. Khanolkar Sir used to teach us Marathi. The entire class would be engrossed while he taught us. Though I was his student, I didn't know him very well. There was a talk by the Professor at the college hostel on the occasion of Sixth December. I myself was the organiser of this programme; I was president of the hostel students' association. Khanolkar Sir was the chief guest for Babasaheb Ambedkar's Memorial Day. The programme went off very well. I had personally gone in a rickshaw to collect him and afterwards, to drop him home. Both times, I was treated to tea at his house. Sir's daughter, Aparna, who was in my class, served me the tea herself.

The hostel students were held in awe in the college. Everyone was frightened of us. The hostel inmates were known to be goons, never hesitating to answer back when teachers spoke to them. To tell you the truth, we students came from deeply rural backgrounds; we were poor. But what made us so defiant? It used to puzzle me.

What made us so insolent?

Our childhood had been crushed in many senses. Living outside the village limits, in a house too cramped even for two meals a day. In school, too, always a designated corner to sit in. A constant wariness towards the villagers ... there was no way we could walk with our heads held high. Caste rules were strictly implemented. Even an animal could rush through the village at full gallop. But us? We walked along the very edge of the road, avoiding casting our shadows on anyone. In this atmosphere of dread, we never knew when our childhood ended.

But now we were young men. We had come to the city from remote villages all over the state. Having survived school, and then the college hostel, we had grown stronger, more resilient. Storms that would shake our skies were brewing in these hostels.

A room. In that room, our trunks. Our childhood hidden like cockroaches in those trunks. I am sitting on a trunk. Someone yells, 'Hey, don't sit on that trunk!' I shift, leaning my butt against it. A song in praise of Bhimrao Ambedkar rises to my lips. I start singing aloud. The whole room joins me in a partner-chorus. Someone starts a musical accompaniment on the tabla; another plays a lively beat on the trunk. Our song begins to reverberate within the hostel walls.

Then, standing at the window, Keshav sees a girl passing by. He whistles sharply, and the joy of the song is destroyed.

We all rush to the window. We push and shove to look at the girl. She is an *Id-ka-chand*, a glowing digit of the moon, or like the full moon on *Kojagiri Purnima*. Our eyes rest on her, on her whole body, like aimed pistols. At that moment if she had but smiled, our gaze would have turned into flowers. If she had scorned us, the whole window would have been enraged. But she did nothing. She just flowed out of our sight like a gentle stream. We gaze after her until she is out of sight.

Our crushed childhood thus flourishes again. Our hands shiver. Our heads turn delirious. Our bodies stiffen. We are not human. Anything but human. Animals, boulders, compost and suchlike. Storms crash one after another against our bodies. Lightning bolts of arrogance strike us. We step across the threshold of death and begin life anew. We have left fear behind, like shoes removed outside the door of life.

Once the boys in our hostel had harassed Professor Khanolkar's daughter. Sir usually wishes to retain the favour of the hostel students. His decency must make him rather nervous of the hostel inmates. It must have been this decency and fear that made him invite me again and again to his house. I, too, kept going to his house. I borrowed books from him to read.

As I speak, I have reached Professor Khanolkar's resting-place. The memories of my life flit around his sitting room like so many bats. One darts into his prayer room. One into his kitchen. One flaps around his wife. How fresh and glowing she looked even at that age, Sir's wife who had crossed fifty. Sir's daughter brought out the tea. Her long, loose hair seems to fall over my body like the soft wings of foreign birds.

On these visits to his house, I narrated my life to Khanolkar Sir. Sir took note of my burning voice with discernment. Sir would encourage me and say, 'No one values the experiences of us white-collared people any more. There was a time when people would jump on fiction. Nowadays they want reality. A lot of value is attached to Dalit memoirs. You don't need to be a writer to write Dalit literature. Just write down your life experiences as they happened. People will enjoy it. If your book becomes well known, you will win big awards and fame, earn a lot of money. You've got the guts for it.' Sir was shaping me, and I was allowing myself to be shaped.

On Sir's recommendation, two of my short stories were published in the Sunday edition of *Dainik Kesari*. I started writing. I began to take part in various short story writing contests. I began to send my stories to dailies and magazines. Invariably, the stories would be returned with thanks. I would rage at how high-caste editors refused to publish stories by Dalits.

Sir would patiently listen to me. He would read what I wrote. Make suggestions. That is why I would visit him so very often. Sir's wife would send me out to buy vegetables. Sir would send me to the post office to drop off his mail. His daughter Aparna would send me to the laundry. I would happily do all his household chores for him. The only thought in my mind was that one day my book would be published through Sir's contacts. I had already decided—I would dedicate my first book to Khanolkar Sir.

Sir listened.

I talked.

I peeled my life before him like a fallen fruit.

'Sir, I am the son of a prostitute. She sold her body to pay for my education. We were happy when customers came to her, for that night we would have food to eat. Sir, why do only Dalit women become prostitutes?'

I would falter, overcome with emotion. Sir would gently say, 'Speak, feel free.' And I would control my feelings. My eyes, filling with tears, would once again clear.

'Sir, a man's penis is of itself a great sin. But a woman's vagina is a great virtue. Sir, I am using obscene language in your house. Forgive me. But where I live, such words are used by everyone. Just as a mendicant priest knows the Satyanarayana puja by heart, so do we know such words by heart. What can anyone do about it?'

As he listened, Sir would call out to his wife like an intoned *omkar*, 'Bring two cups of tea—do you hear?'

I would be filled with gratitude. Once I went back to my hostel room, there would be no evening meal. This tea was my only mainstay. Sir would say, 'Come over from time to time. I like it. You speak so well. It is no problem for us. After four or five in the evening is a convenient time. I never go out then.' Sir's voice sounded solitary, like the inner sanctum of a temple. He looked so serene and self-possessed. Suddenly, his false teeth became loose and fell out. 'Oh no, my teeth have fallen out,' he said sadly. He picked up the denture and put it into his pocket. Without teeth, Sir's face looked very old. I took leave of him.

Khanolkar Sir was due to retire the next month. Sir was a good human being. And a good teacher as well.

I was closer to the hostel now.

My roommates had gone for the last show. They would return late. I reached College Road. Students of the Night College were wandering about on the road. One girl was leaning against a lamp-post, snuggled up close to a boy and in intimate conversation with him. I grew enflamed. I should give that fellow one hard kick and chat with that girl myself! But I couldn't. Because I was poor, no girl liked me. I had an enormous hatred of my poverty. I felt like burning up my hut. I felt greatly ashamed of my parents. I felt like pulling off my clothes, tearing them and throwing them away. I had acquired my parents' looks, their culture and their poverty by right of inheritance.

I reached my room. That night my roommates and I sat up and chatted.

'The film was a good one. You should have come,' said Keshav. 'Sir is going to retire next month. We ought to give him some kind of present,' I said. 'Let's give Sir an image of Babasaheb Ambedkar,' Rahul promptly suggested.

'After we give him an image of Babasaheb, he must put it up in his house or it will be an insult to Babasaheb. It would be better to give him something else,' said Keshav in tones of compromise. There was much argument over this. Rahul stuck to his opinion; finally we all agreed to give Sir an image of Babasaheb Ambedkar, and went off to sleep.

Sir retired.

We ceremonially presented a statuette of Babasaheb to him.

Who knows what Sir did with the statuette? It was not to be seen in his house. We went once or twice thereafter to meet him. Sir was affectionate and cordial with us. He gave us tea. But Babasaheb's statuette was nowhere to be seen. A thousand foul curses rose to my lips, but I smiled and kept silent. Resolving never again to climb the steps of his house, we left Sir's house.

No matter how progressive a high-caste man may be, in his house he still swears by caste. The teeth he displays are different from the ones he eats with. These poisonous teeth must be uprooted. Their bite is poisonous—it can destroy an entire generation.

Days passed. One after another.

It was my last year in college. Next year I would have to leave the hostel. I trembled at the mere thought. I didn't want anything else in this world. Not even a mother or a sweetheart. I only wanted my room in the hostel. And my roommates. I couldn't forget the hostel.

I remember the Rector. I remember the Rector's daughter, leaving the hostel like a princess in her jeans. How often I had sat at this window, gazing at her. How could I leave behind all these memories? The crisp new posters of our favourite actresses on the walls of our room. The words 'Jai Bhim' written on cupboards, windows, the door and the walls. This room was a part of me. Lust and thought, these were my two organs of reproduction.

I took up Sir's novel to read again. Sir had given it to me, the leader of the hostel students, as a present at our first meeting. I had often read this novel. With what ease he wrote of young people's feelings of love. He used to say, 'I want to write a novel about Dalit life.' I even wrote a review of one of Sir's books. Sir had it published. He always said, 'Today's young generation likes my writing. That's all I need.'

Recently, I had read a few accounts of Sir's public speeches and some of his articles in the newspapers. Sir had reminisced about me to one or two people. 'That boy used to come often to our house. We never regarded him as inferior.'

Aparna had changed her college, and I no longer met her.

One morning my roommate Keshav said to me, 'Khanolkar Sir's new book is being released this evening. He has written a novel on Dalit life.'

I had not met Sir or gone to his house in a long time. I must go to the release function.

My roommate and I presented ourselves at the function. Many girls and boys from the college had come. The novel had been published before we heard about it. Professor Deshpande was speaking about Khanolkar Sir's new novel. The speech was in full flow. 'Khanolkar's new novel is an excellent example of Dalit literature. The idea that only Dalits can write Dalit literature—this work of art disproves that,' Professor Deshpande was saying with great enthusiasm.

'*"Sir, I am the son of a prostitute. She sold her body to pay for my education. We were happy when customers came to her, for that night we would have food to eat. Sir, why do only Dalit women become prostitutes?"* One is totally shaken when reading this passage—not even a Dalit could write so realistically.'

I had suddenly grown numb. The sentences in Sir's novel were all mine. I had given Sir my story to read. He had liked it. 'We'll publish this somewhere good,' he had said. 'We can give it for the next Diwali annual. Leave it with me. I'll send it to the editor.' And I had said yes. But my story was never published. Sir had adapted my story into a novel. Only the names of the characters had been changed.

Sir rose to speak. Several people passed notes to him. I passed one, too: 'What made you think of the story in this novel?' Sir skimmed through everyone's notes and began to speak. 'My father was a very progressive man. Although he was devout, he was not a puritan. In those days there was a Harijan woman who came to our house to do the washing. Later, when I became a professor, I got to know many Dalit students. My emotional universe expanded. I was able to write all this because of the progressive environment at home.' The journalists were writing it all down. The photographers were taking photographs. I thought that Sir would refer to me in his talk. But he never mentioned me, not once.

The programme ended. I met Sir. I congratulated him. He enquired after me earnestly. 'I want a copy of your book, Sir,' I urged him. 'I want to write about it.'

'Come home tomorrow. Pick up a copy. You haven't come to see me for a long time,' he said, warmly pressing my hand. The crowd of admirers around Sir had begun to grow. I stepped out through the crowd.

Copies of the book were being sold at a reduced price at the launch venue. A crowd had gathered round the stall. I went there with my roommate. We had no money. I warned Keshav, 'No matter what happens, we are going to steal this book.' Keshav quietly picked up a copy, stuffed it into his waistband and gave me a pinch. Mission successful.

We quickly stepped outside and slipped into an Udipi café. We had two half-cups of tea. I gave Keshav a full cup. As I leafed through the book, my eyes began to burn. My temples began to heat up. 'Keshav, this is my story. Khanolkar has stolen my story and written a novel out of it.' It was the first time I had taken Khanolkar's name without adding Sir.

'He stole your story; you steal his daughter!' Keshav rumbled with laughter. I did not laugh. Keshav lit a cigarette. 'That's why I said, what can this Brahmin write about Dalit life? The bastard stole and became a great writer. It is my firm opinion that every writer is a thief. He steals other people's experiences and writes about them.' And Keshav blew some artistic rings of cigarette smoke into the air.

'Hey, put your philosophy aside. What do I do now?'

'Read through this book tonight. We'll decide in the morning,' was Keshav's reply as he put out the cigarette and got up. We went back to the hostel. Night had fallen. The whole hostel was immersed in studies or in singing games. Light emanated from each window, like a lamp quietly burning in a temple. All the windows were glowing peacefully. Some boys were sitting and reading on the hostel terrace. Keshav's guest had arrived. He worked in a mill, and used to stay in our room for free. In return we would see movies at his expense, drink cups of tea. The guest had brought some *vada-pav* for us. I was pleased.

It was four in the morning. Only the last few pages of the novel remained. '*Sir, a man's penis is of itself a great sin. But a woman's vagina is a great virtue. Sir, I am using obscene language in your house. Forgive me. Just as a mendicant priest knows the Satyanarayana puja by heart, so do we know such words by heart. That's the way in our slum. What can anyone do about it?*' I was growing more and more uneasy.

This was not a novel—it was my life. Each and every word I had uttered was in it. How had the bastard remembered all this? Perhaps he had a pocket tape-recorder. I had been a fool. When I went to the house of this modern, urban man, before gawking at his wife and daughter, I should have first looked for a tape-recorder. I finished the novel. A fever had risen in my body. I covered my face with the book and fell asleep.

I dreamt.

I have drunk a lot. I am supremely drunk and I have slipped into Khanolkar Sir's house. I am shouting, 'Aparna is mine! You are a thief!' Sir and his wife are extremely agitated. Aparna is standing there panic-stricken. I make a strenuous effort. I don't want to speak, I want to scream: 'This novel is mine! You are a thief!' But no matter how hard I try, I just cannot. Suddenly I find my voice. 'Aparna is mi-i-ine!' I scream. Sir grabs my hand and starts dragging me out of the house.

My dream broke abruptly—Keshav had woken me up by pulling my hand.

A little later the same morning, we reached Khanolkar's house. There were three of us: Keshav, his guest and I. Aparna opened the door. Seeing us there so early in the morning, her expression altered. 'We want to meet Sir,' I said.

Aparna remained standing in the doorway and said, 'Sir went to Dharwad at dawn. There was a phone call at night. My uncle has had a heart attack.'

'Open the door at least,' Keshav said boldly.

'Sir is not here,' Aparna repeated. We entered the sitting room.

Perhaps Sir's wife had seen us coming and told Aparna to close the door.

'Keshav, follow me.' Keshav and I raced to the bedroom. Madam came in after us, shouting, 'Hey, what are you doing?' But we heard nothing and pushed into the bedroom.

Sir was lying on the bed, reading accounts of the book release function in the newspaper. Seeing us, he smiled and sat up. We felt very awkward. He said, 'Sit down. There are no touch taboos in our house. Sit.' We remained standing.

'Let's go to the sitting room. We have a guest with us.' Sir agreed. We went to the sitting room. Aparna was embarrassed. 'Papa had a BP problem last night. He became unconscious. The doctor has advised him total rest. Don't let him talk too much.'

I was beside myself and couldn't wait to vomit out the anger in my heart. 'Dr. Khanolkar, you have written this novel on the basis of my story. I am the main character in it. All the sentences in it are those that came from my mouth.'

Sir remained silent and serene. But Aparna was shaking with rage. 'Papa is one of Maharashtra's great writers. He has served the Marathi language all his life. He has received many awards and honours. And you accuse *him* of stealing? Our mistake was to let you into our house. Your place is outside, by the steps. Do you understand me?'

I was infuriated. 'Sir has stolen my story. How else could he write about our lives?'

'Anyone can use the power of their imagination to describe Dalits. It isn't so difficult for a gifted writer,' Sir responded in a calm and grave tone.

'*Gifted?*' Keshav laughed sarcastically. His guest remained sitting peacefully. But I had lost my balance.

'This novel is not a work of imagination. This novel is real life—my life. You spoke kindly to me, fed me cups of tea and drew many things out of me. You made a novel out of my life story. The main character in your novel is me. *Me!*'

As I talked on furiously, the phone rang. There was a tense silence in the room. Aparna picked up the phone. It was a call from the editor of a daily. Sir took the phone from her and began to speak as if nothing had happened. 'You know, this very first day a procession of Dalits has come to my house. This shows the success of my writing. They are young Dalit men from the hostel. They say the novel doesn't seem to be a work of imagination. In fact, one of them says he himself is the protagonist of the story. For a reader to think this way is the true strength of an artistic work. These people have taken up a stance and they are still sitting here. Send a photographer and a representative over. It will make a good news item. And if you have the time, come personally. You can also have your lunch here. It's been a long time since you came. Yes. Yes.' And he put the phone down.

'Let's go,' I said.

'Wait. Have some tea. What's the hurry?'

'The press photographer will come. He will take photographs of you, us. The news item will come on tomorrow's front page. The sales of your book will double. No. Come, friends, this man's tea is too expensive for us.'

We all rise to leave. Sir again urges us to stay. We walk out of the house. Sir comes with us to the door.

'Keep writing like this. Soon there will be statues raised in your honour,' Keshav says bitterly as he leaves. Sir stands in the doorway with palms joined, still as a statue. Madam is trying to pull him into the house, and Aparna stands waiting to close the door.

As we are leaving, the photographer arrives. Keshav bursts out laughing. But I walk back numbed, as if I am returning from a cremation ground.

2

A Life Lived

Dalit literature was a much discussed topic. Dalit autobiographies were beginning to acquire considerable fame. An autobiography would be published, and overnight its author would become an important man. He would receive an award. Programmes would start being organised to felicitate him. Articles eulogising him would constantly be published. He would be appointed on government committees. Then, his clothes would change. His language would change. His lifestyle would change. He would change.

A fledgling Dalit writer like myself, being witness to all of this, would also yearn to flower. I, too, must write. I must become famous. I, too, must win an award. I used to devour Dalit literature obsessively. It was a movement, a struggle. Dalit literature had shaken and shocked established literature. The very genetic basis of Dalit literature was quite different. Whoever wrote became a writer. His experiences were such as had never before been expressed in literature. His crude, graceless experiences were such as to plumb the depths of the reader's heart. The harsh, real-life experiences in the books of Dalit writers caused the reader to introspect.

This abundant discussion of Dalit literature made power surge through my body. My experiences were quite distinct from those of others. I, too, had gone through a lot. Seen a lot. No one could have endured as much as I had. If I wrote an autobiography it would definitely become famous. It would stand out in sharp contrast to all others. I would become the stormy new name in Dalit literature. I just had to write it. I read up all the autobiographies by Dalit writers. What I had suffered had more substance and power than what they had.

But who would publish my book? I had no contacts. I should try sending letters to some established Dalit writers, I thought. I got their addresses and wrote each of them a letter. I praised each of them. I wrote admiringly about their work. I ended each letter by saying, 'I, too, am writing my autobiography. Your guidance would be valuable.'

After a week I started getting responses from some Dalit writers. Each of them encouraged me to write my autobiography. I read their letters again and again. I wrote back to them. I was obsessed with the mania of becoming a writer. I started writing daily. I had to write my autobiography as soon as possible. No one else's autobiography must be published before mine. I must be acknowledged as the first writer of my caste. If I delayed, someone else would write it first. He would be talked about and I would fall behind.

Among the Scheduled Castes, my caste is distinct. The features of my caste are unique. The sorrows and sufferings of my caste have not as yet been expressed in Dalit literature. Only those of the Mahar caste have been articulated. There are so many castes among the Dalits. The benefits of education have not yet reached them. They have not yet been able to take advantage of the various concessions made available to them. Because of Babasaheb Ambedkar, the Mahar people rapidly got educated. They became united. That caste has an organisation. That is why they were able to avail themselves of the concessions. But there are many other Dalit castes which are still groping in the dark. They have now realised the importance of Babasaheb's thought. His thought is all-conquering. His thought is about liberation for all of us. The recognition of this truth is spreading.

All the Dalit castes were beginning to unite. I, too, must get down into that struggle. Dalit literature is a revolutionary movement. That movement must succeed. The sorrows of my caste must be expressed in Dalit literature. And autobiography is an intimate literary form in which to convey grief.

I completed my autobiography. I met the writers with my manuscript. I read out some scenes from it to them. They all listened with affection and empathy. They were stunned. They said, 'You have written very well. Your autobiography will become famous.' I was happy. Now I would get awards. I would make trips abroad. I began to float like a kite in the air. Now I would truly become a writer. My book would be famous. I was possessed by that idea.

I called on Professor Balasaheb Kamble. He, too, was delighted. He thumped my back. I showed him my manuscript. He took the manuscript and leafed through it. I was given tea. As I gulped mouthfuls of it, Professor Kamble started to speak. 'No one publishes such a long autobiography. It'll have to be chopped down. Let's remove the monotonous repetitions. An autobiography must be readable. The price of paper has gone up. If a book is too long, its price will also be high. Then readers won't buy it. I'll read your manuscript. Leave it with me. Come back next Sunday.' I agreed. I left my manuscript with Professor Kamble and took my leave of him.

He would read the manuscript. He would give me valuable advice. But the manuscript would not go missing, would it? I grew uneasy at the thought, but I kept a strong control over my mind. Because I desperately wanted his advice. Professor Kamble was going to find a publisher for me. He had contacts with publishers. I began to count the days like rosary beads, impatient for Sunday to come.

Sunday came.

I reached Professor Kamble's house. I pressed the doorbell. The door was opened. I asked for Professor Kamble. I was told, 'Sir works till late in the night. He is asleep now. Come in the afternoon.' I was dejected. Now what was I to do till afternoon? By then Professor Kamble's door had closed once more.

I went again in the afternoon. The door was opened. I entered the house. I sat down in the sitting room like an intruder. Some Sunday editions of newspapers were lying on the table. I leafed through the newspapers. There was a review of Professor Kamble's book in one. I started reading the review. In the meantime the Professor had woken up. I could hear the sound of his coughing. Tea was sent in to his room. I, too, was served tea in the sitting room. I could hear the Professor moving about. But he had not yet emerged. He had been informed of my arrival.

I made a note in my diary. I would get an award. This was the kind of bungalow I would build. When a fledgling writer came to me for advice, I would cough like Professor Kamble. I would hum a tune. My wife would say to the novice, 'Come back later. Sir is busy. Etc.' Professor Kamble came in while I was still enjoying this daydream. I brought out a smile when I saw him. He sat down in his chair. Before I could enquire about the manuscript, he said, 'I have read your manuscript. It is good. It can be published. But you must make some additions to it. Without that it will not become famous.' I sat listening obediently like a student. Professor Kamble continued, 'You will have to write some more. If you have finished recording your own experiences, then think of others. You may have written about what happened to you, but remember some more. Take out your notes. This is not sufficient. There is no law that all experiences in an autobiography should be your own. Put in some imagined ones. Write about what happened to your friends and to other people as if they had happened to you. That will add to the number of experiences. There is no police enquiry about whether they are true or false. You must gather experiences from everywhere like a bee gathering honey. Then there will be a honeycomb of experiences. If the experiences are yours alone, it will be a nest. But what we want is a nest of stinging horse flies. You must add to this.'

I thought Professor Kamble's advice was invaluable. I had not met a guru like this before. I was delighted. 'Sir, I will write as you ask. There are many experiences like that. I am going to dedicate my autobiography to you. My book will be released by your hands. You are my godfather.'

Professor Kamble calmly said, 'At least write it first.' He sounded so experienced. Perhaps when he was a novice he, too, had gone through such apprenticeship. I realised my own naivete and fell silent. 'Write it out once more as I have told you. Then we will read it. After that we can decide which publisher to give it to.'

'Sir, will I get a Sahitya Akademi Award?'

'Hey, don't start dreaming of awards before you've even written it. Your autobiography is good. It will get an award. Just write it out properly first.'

'Sir, your words have greatly encouraged me.'

'Look here, the title of your autobiography is very good. Don't tell it to anybody, or someone will steal it.'

I grew sober. I was reminded of Professor Khanolkar.

Professor Kamble got angry when he heard Khanolkar's name. 'We should never go to high-caste writers. We should go to Dalit writers. We should take their advice, get them to write introductions. We should dedicate our books to them. Does a high-caste writer ever ask for an introduction from a Dalit writer? Does he ever dedicate his book to a Dalit writer? Then why should we?' I liked Professor Kamble's thinking.

I came back to my room. I leafed through my manuscript. Professor Kamble had read through my manuscript with devoted attention. He had made notes on every page. He had written suggestions. I felt respect for Professor Kamble. On the very first page of my autobiography, I wrote of another person's experience as my own. Now my autobiography would be much better in the truest sense.

I felt I should not take advice from Professor Kamble alone. I must meet one or two other knowledgeable people. That would make my book even better.

I went to Advocate Bandsode's house. He had done a Ph.D. on Dalit literature. I gave him my manuscript to read. I told him about Professor Kamble's advice. Advocate Bandsode grew angry. He poured a torrent of abuse over me. 'Professor Kamble is a Hindutvavadi! He appears on common platforms with Hindutvavadis. He has no right even to utter Babasaheb's name! We must unmask all these Hindutvavadis. They are the hidden enemies of our movement.' Advocate Bandsode's eyes had reddened with anger.

My manuscript had been lying at Advocate Bandsode's for a long time. I wasn't able to meet him. Finally I went to the court. I met him. He had not yet read my manuscript. I went with him to his house. I asked him to return the manuscript. He got angry. 'I have a lot of manuscripts lying here with me. I don't have time. I'll read them when it's convenient. Take your manuscript and go.' I quietly took the manuscript and left his home-cum-office.

I had mentioned my going to Advocate Bandsode's house to Professor Kamble. He had been furious with me.

After many days I received a letter from Professor Kale. He was the editor of a monthly journal. I used to write to him. He would enquire about my writing from time to time. I once went to meet him. He was very happy and read my manuscript with great interest. Advocate Bandsode's name arose in the course of our discussion. Professor Kale was infuriated. 'Advocate Bandsode is a Marxist. Babasaheb opposed Marxism. That was why he accepted Buddhism. We must remain at a distance from these Communists.' I was rattled. Professor Kale called himself an Ambedkarite. I listened to him quietly. He said, 'We have a magazine. We will serialise your autobiography in it. Every

Dalit writer's first book has been published in our magazine. When we have our own magazine, why should we send your writing anywhere else?' I started doing the numbers in my mind. My autobiography would appear in the magazine part by part for a whole year. Then it would be published as a book. That would take a long time. Suppose someone else's book appeared before that? I got a hold over myself. Saying that I would revise the autobiography and send it for publication to his magazine part by part, I said goodbye to Professor Kale and left his house.

Rather than publishing the autobiography in the Dalit magazine, why shouldn't I publish it in some good daily newspaper? Dailies sold in large numbers. I would reach a much larger number of readers. I made a decision and sent one part of the autobiography to the daily *Kesari*. Now Professor Kamble, Advocate Bandsode and Professor Kale would only be able to read my autobiography in the newspaper. I could do without their advice; my writing had staying power.

It was evening. I went to the public library. I would meet friends there and have cups of tea. There would be a discussion. At the door of the library I met Aparna Khanolkar. Out of the blue. She was smiling. A smile gathered on my face like dew. She came closer. 'Hey, your autobiography has come out really well! I liked it a lot.' I was nonplussed. How did Aparna read my autobiography? I couldn't understand it. She herself gave the explanation. 'Since Sir retired, he looks after the Sunday edition of the *Kesari*. The writings that come to the newspaper are sent home for him to read. At present, Sir is busy translating an English novel. So I read what comes from the newspaper. The first section of your autobiography has been included for this Sunday. Why don't you bring me your photo? So it can be printed along with it.' Suddenly, Aparna seemed very important to me.

My autobiography was published in the Sunday paper. People I met praised it highly. It felt very good. If there was so much discussion on it when just one part of it had been published, I would definitely become famous when the whole book was published. I had to give my whole manuscript to Professor Khanolkar. It would be published in instalments in the newspaper. I took my manuscript and reached Professor Khanolkar's house. Sir was seated in comfort. Professor Kamble, Professor Kale and Advocate Bandsode were seated like novices in front of him. Some sort of discussion was going on between them. I went in. They all congratulated me. They praised my writing. Their eyes were all fixed on the manuscript in my hands. I sat like a man indifferent to the outcome of my labours.

After a while Professor Kamble, Professor Kale and Advocate Bandsode left.

I got up and went and sat near Khanolkar Sir. I gave him my manuscript. He looked through it. Suddenly, with an air of having remembered something, he looked sharply at me and said, 'It was good that you came. I had a phone call from Kulkarni this morning. He has read what you have written in the newspaper. He said he felt like crying when he read about your experiences. He will be coming here just now. Let us give him the manuscript. He brings out books quite well.'

I was thrilled.

'So will you write an introduction, Sir?' I asked.

'Certainly. I would like to. At present I am translating an English novel. I don't have time to read the manuscript. Write a synopsis of your autobiography in three hundred words. Note down some points. Bring me whatever has been published about Dalit literature. It will be useful while writing the introduction.' I immediately accepted whatever Sir suggested. He was pleased. He then told me, 'Professor Kamble is doing a Ph.D. under my guidance. Professor Kale, too, wants to do a Ph.D. with me. No Dalit guide is available. I have no time for this. I am retired. My own work is lying unfinished. Long ago I had written an article on Dalit literature. It was much talked about. But no Dalit writer ever mentions me.' Sir's voice had grown heavy and sad.

I felt like a criminal.

3

Enlightenment

Professor Khanolkar had given me an appointment for four o'clock. I was a student of his. My collection of verse, *Surya*, had just been published last month. I wanted to present Khanolkar Sir with a copy of *Surya*.

I pressed the bell at his door and heard its ding-dong resound through the house. When I heard that sound gently announcing my arrival I felt an affection for that doorbell. After some time I heard footsteps. The door was opened. This must be Sir's wife.

'I am Amar Bansode. Is Sir at home?'

'Yes, he's here. Come in.'

I entered Sir's sitting room.

Sir's bungalow was spacious. The atmosphere of the sitting room was luxurious. The library was abundantly stocked. An unrealistic oil painting of Jnaneshwar hung on the wall. A handsome wall clock. Vases of flowers all around. Lush green velvet curtains hung heavily at the windows. On the left side of the sitting room, a TV. Next to it, a phone. Beyond, a tall image of the Nataraja. Neatly arranged cushions and seat-cushions.

Sir arrived. I rose and greeted him with a namaste.

Sir seated himself grandly on his seat like a member of a princely family.

I gave Sir a copy of my poetry collection. Sir took the book from me, smiling.

'The book is very well produced. I will read it and write about it. And Amar, you must write a great deal. Read a lot. Don't get carried away by fame. You people have endured so much. You must speak out fiercely against inequality. But your literature must not contain hate and vengefulness. What will we achieve by bloodshed? The first Marathi Dalit writer was Jnaneshwar. The bitterly orthodox harassed him greatly,' Sir was saying. I was murmuring agreement.

Just then Sir's daughter Aparna arrived. Sir introduced me to her.

'This is Amar Bansode. He is a Dalit poet. At present he is working as a clerk in a Pune bank. He was at our college four years ago. This is my daughter Aparna. She is in the second year of her M.B.B.S.'

Suparna looked as beautiful as an exquisite book. In the breeze from the fan, her hair swayed like the plumes of rice plants. Aparna went back inside, but her momentary presence lingered in my being like a perfume. I took leave of Sir.

I once met Khanolkar Sir at a function. He had come with his wife and Aparna. The guests at the function were all his friends. Khanolkar Sir was a colossus in Marathi literature. I went up to Sir. He welcomed me with a smile. There was a subdued smile on Aparna's face, too. Sir introduced me to the guests. 'This is Amar Bansode. He is a Dalit poet.' After the programme we all drank tea.

I went home. On the table was the book I had given Sir as a gift. I could not understand. How did that book get here? I leafed through it. Lines had been drawn in many places; asterisks marked obscene words. I asked my mother, 'Who brought this book?' Mother told me the name of Bhosale Guruji's son.

I went to Bhosale Guruji's house. Guruji was sitting reading the *Bhagavad Gita*. I had no acquaintance with him.

His son had gone out to get some medicine. I waited there to meet him.

After a while Bhosale Guruji's son arrived. I asked him about my book. He said he, too, had been given the book, by a friend. His friend, Sadaphule, had a job in the railways. He had looked through my book on a journey, which was why he had sent it to me through Bhosale Guruji's son. On reading my book he had learned of my caste. His small son had read some obscene words in the book, and asked him the meanings. There had even been a quarrel at home about it. 'How did you let this book fall into the boy's hands?' he had scolded his wife.

Once, on a journey, Sadaphule and I had become great friends. That is how I had given him my address. I, too, had his. I set out for his house.

Although Sadaphule worked for the railways, he greatly enjoyed literature. He had read a great number of books while doing night duty. It was on account of his tremendous craze for reading that I had sought out and made his acquaintance. He had read *Upara*, *Balute* and *Taral Antaral*.

I reached Sadaphule's house. A Satyanarayana puja had been organised at his house. I, too, put an offering of twenty-five paise before the shrine, had a darshan of the deity and took some prasad. Sadaphule asked about the occasion for my visit. I raised the subject of my book. He said he had found it at a waste-paper depot.

I could not understand at all. How had the book I had given Khanolkar Sir as a gift reached Shahid Waste-paper Depot? I went to the owner of the depot. The waste-paper seller had given the book to Sadaphule to read. The book had come to the depot brand new. Sadaphule was diligent in his reading. He used to regularly buy good books from this depot. The owner had given him my book free. In return, Sadaphule had treated him to tea.

I sat down beside the waste-paper seller. I bought him tea. I told him I was Sadaphule's friend. We chatted a little.

The *Bhagavad Gita* and works of Tukaram, Kusumagraj and Mardhekar were lying among the waste paper. Diwali issues, magazines, study guides and fat books in English were arranged among the paper. Shakespeare was being sold here by weight. My book weighed only ninety grammes. It could be posted anywhere in India with a fifteen-paise stamp.

The Shahid Waste-paper Depot owner gave me the name of Vinod Shah. Vinod Shah was a novice poet of the *Satyakatha* stream. His poetry collection had received an award that year. He was to be found at the Sahitya Sangh at this time. Vinod Shah also wrote book reviews in dailies from time to time. It was at Khanolkar Sir's house that I had got to know him.

Vinod Shah had been extremely pleased with my poems. He would even quote lines from my poetry while speaking. He would discuss each word. He would ask me the meanings of words that he had not understood. I found those romantic comments of his about my poems quite unforgettable. Vinod Shah was like brown sugar, a real *gard*. His ornamental expressions, his attractive gestures, his brimming eyes, the rings of smoke that rose from time to time from his cigarette, his habit of breaking off momentarily while speaking ... It was on account of all these that I had forgotten my irritation.

Vinod Shah had liked my poems. Why then would he throw my poetry in the rubbish?

'Give me an extra copy if you have one. I don't have a copy of your book. I'll write about it. I'll pay for it. Your poems are a wrestler's training ground for enlightenment,' he said. 'If you do not have an extra copy, give it later. In fact, I have already read it.' Interrupting him as he was speaking, I took the book out of my *shabnam* and gave it to Vinod Shah.

'I found this at the waste-paper depot.'

Vinod Shah's face turned white as a winding-sheet.

'There are some obscene words in it and the speech is very rough. Everyone at home reads. If they come across this book, they will be needlessly angry.' Vinod Shah was embarrassed.

'There is a conspiracy to curb new ideas by calling Dalit literature obscene. Licentiousness is on the rampage in Marathi literature. That is tolerated. You read it with relish. Why don't you say outright that what you don't like is the subversiveness in Dalit writing?'

Vinod Shah said much to try and mollify me. He apologised to me.

I set out for Professor Madhusudhan Joshi's house; he was the one who had given my collection of poems to Shah.

Saraswati Colony. Anandavan Bungalow. Khanolkar Sir's bungalow is at the end of this very row. I rang the doorbell. As no one opened the door I rapped on it. Disconnecting the doorbell, everyone in the household had sat down in front of the TV. Professor Joshi was doing a Ph.D. under Professor Khanolkar's guidance. Professor Joshi opened the door with an irritated air. His wife and children were engrossed in watching TV. I had disturbed his mood.

'What work have you cooked up for me?' he asked.

'Just this: where did you get this book that you gave to Vinod Shah?'

'From Khanolkar Sir. He doesn't read poetry, you know. So he told me to take it away.'

'I ask because I am the poet who wrote these poems.'

'Oh, ho! Yes, I met you once at Sir's house. Sorry, I forgot. Come in, come in. Have some tea before you go.'

'No, I don't have time. I'll come some other time.' And I turned away sharply from his door.

I rang the doorbell. The music of the chimes fell on my body like a crumbling cliff.

Suparna opened the door.

I went inside. Khanolkar Sir was watching TV. He got up and came towards me. Sir's imposing drawing room. His impressive personality. His high forehead. His thinning hair. The grim expression on his face. His eyes like the scorching heat of the afternoon sky in summer. Sir took his seat.

'What brings you here?'

'I'm leaving tomorrow. I thought I'd say goodbye.'

'When do you return?'

'I haven't yet decided.'

'All right.'

'Sir, have you read my book?'

'I'll read it this week. I have a lot of work these days. I do want to read your book.'

'But I found the book in a waste-paper shop.'

'How is that possible?'

I took the book out of my shoulder bag and placed it before him. Sir could not comprehend any of it. He grew visibly uneasy. I, however, was noting every gesture and expression of his like a book of records. White patches had begun to throng Sir's face.

Just then Sir's wife came in. She saw my book, and got furious. She hadn't yet seen me.

'Who has brought this book here again? Suppose it falls into Aparna's hands? What stars has Ravi caused to shoot by reading it? How filthily these people write! Who is going to read books like this?'

I was beginning to be enlightened!

4

Sudha Dear

The bell rang. Kulkarni Madam set out from the staff room. I took my notes from the cupboard and left for the twelfth standard classroom. There were students hanging around on the verandah. The sound of their banter, their laughter, their taunts fell on my ears. Other lecturers were also going to their respective classrooms. Some were exchanging classes. The girls in their groups were going into class. I was proceeding towards my class, casting my glance from side to side. Suddenly a few boys from the hostel came up to me and said, 'Jai Bhim!' 'Meet me in the break,' I said, and walked into the class.

The students stood up; they sat down.

I smiled at them like a TV announcer.

There was a rustle in the classroom; then silence.

I put the book on the table and wiped the blackboard with the duster. I looked at the class. The students' rows were as arranged. Their seats were as assigned. I walked through the rows of desks. On the left were the boys from the hostel, with their faded, and sometimes gaudy, clothes, their familiar smiles. In the middle rows were the boys from the city, well-dressed and well-built—the ones who spent two years in just one class. And beyond were the girls' rows.

I went to the front past the rows of girls. The scent of flowers strung in their hair and the fragrance of perfume stimulated my nostrils. Their wet hair, wet kumkum, their whispers and furtive gazes mocked me. On the last row sat the flirtatious girls. To show the boys around, to sit for hours in cafes, to catch a new victim every day, this was their hobby. They just came to college to pass the time before they got married. Gathering friends, having parties, arranging pleasure trips, finding greater enjoyment outside the class than inside it; for the girls, this was their education.

A few Dalit girls occupied the middle benches. Their appearance and bearing truthfully revealed their caste. Even in their poverty they had made an effort to remain neat and tidy. On the bench before them were some girls who had careers. On the front bench sat Kavita Gadre.

Kavita was the inspiration for my teaching. If she were absent, I would lose the desire to teach. When she was present, the period would liven up greatly. Her rapt way of listening; her way of matching glance for glance; her shy smile: all this intoxicated me while I taught. I would hardly be aware of when the bell rang. I would wish that I spent every period teaching this class. Kavita never missed my class.

Behind Kavita sat Sudha Thatte. I would look at Kavita, but Sudha would think I was looking at her. She sat there, a snare of glances cast before her.

It was my job to teach. I was still young. I had just completed my M.A. before coming to teach in this college. My age stimulated me, but I was still a teacher. All around me there blazed a forest of many-coloured flowers. Girls so beautiful it was hard to decide which one to look at. Their affectionate company, their calling out 'Sir, Sir' to draw me closer would create many a storm in my mind. Girls making way for me with respectful smiles; girls shyly standing in my way; girls approaching me quite unnecessarily with difficulties to solve;

bold girls saying, 'Sir, please advise us'; forward girls asking, 'When are you giving us notes to study from?' The lecturer's girls; the girls' lecturer.

Professor Avinash Swami's girlfriend regularly comes to the staff room. Who knows whether or not she sits in the classroom. Professor Swami was adept at netting girls. It was his amusement to take a third-year girl to the library and sit there chatting with her. Even in his old age this creature wore brightly coloured bushshirts and makeup to make an exhibition of his youth. I remember his girlfriend, the class representative of the third year, Sudha Thatte.

Professor Swami and Sudha, to tell the truth, were of an age suitable to be father and daughter. Seeing them I was reminded of the marriages of old men and young girls in earlier days. Two days ago, I had seen Professor Swami and Sudha crying, both with reddened eyes. Now he was the Head of my department; I could not say anything. I came away at once, but with a firm resolve—one day I, too, would sit there with some girl. Should I ask Kavita Gadre?

Did these girls come here to study or to weep?

I was reminded of the Ladies' Corner. That corner decorated so fashionably, it riveted the gaze of many. No matter how strongly one resisted the urge to look, one's glance invariably raced back to it. You could not tie back your gaze. The Ladies' Corner meant half-closed, kajal-rimmed eyes. How many butterflies there were in this Ladies' Corner! And how many buds were blossoming for these butterflies!

Two girls who had been loitering in the college canteen appeared and asked, 'May we come in, Sir?' Their voices echoed shrilly in the classroom like a whistle. I said 'Yes.' There was much fidgeting and murmuring in class. The two girls took a seat on the last bench.

Who knew which boys' pockets they had ploughed? And those boys—poor sacrificial animals!

I began to teach.

'Page 145, poem 20.

'"My Words."

'By Sharankumar Limbale.'

The Dalit girls were all smiles; the high-caste girls' brows were wrinkled.

My beloved words,
Become the chant of my heart,
Become the inscription of my tears,
Become the sculptors of my liberation.

As if delirious, I started reading out those lines. My tongue, which daily spoke intoxicatedly of leaves and flowers, began to crack like a whip today. My lips began to snap. The veins on my forehead stood out. My voice acquired an edge. My eyes began to vomit fire. My words shot out like cannon balls. I forgot I was in a classroom. I spoke exuberantly, passionately. The class fell silent.

'Because of Dr. Babasaheb Ambedkar's revolutionary struggle, a huge awareness has been created in Indian society. Especially Dalit society, which has lived meekly in silent servitude for thousands of years, has now begun to speak up and write. Their hopes and dreams and ambitions are now being expressed in Dalit literature.' My voice was rising. As if the skies had darkened with clouds, as if a stormy wind had arisen, as if lightning were crackling. I could no longer see Kavita Gadre. I went on teaching about pain like a madman. The bell rang.

My face was beaded with sweat.

I had no class in the next period. I cast a last look at the students. One of them was asking another about my caste.

Something collapsed within me.

It is because I was a Dalit that I taught with such abandon. My becoming so emotional was not appreciated by some of the high-caste students. I could hear some of their remarks as I set out for the staff room through the crowd of students. A few Dalit boys told me they had enjoyed the lesson, but I was too dispirited.

If Kulkarni Madam had taught this lesson, these students would not have been so affected by it.

We were not teaching in the next period, so Professor Kamble and I set off to have tea. The college canteen was full of students. We seated ourselves on chairs in one corner. My face had fallen. Professor Kamble put on an air of seniority and started giving me advice. As I was his junior, I also paid for the tea.

'Who knows when they are going to fill the new vacancy? Unless we get a new person the workload is not going to get any lighter.'

'Do you know who's going to come?'

'No.'

'Oh, she is Swami Sir's girlfriend. Sir wants his girlfriend near him. I knew when she came in for the interview that she was the one they would take.'

'Then why go through this farce of interviews?'

'It's a formality. Mrs. Rane was Professor Swami's student. They got on very well together. She still meets Sir every Sunday. She's doing her M.Phil. with him.'

My head spun. My mouth felt dry. My vision was blurred. Kavita Gadre came near, but I avoided looking at her and left the canteen. When I entered the staff room a peon came with a message from Professor Swami.

'Swami Sir has called you.'

'Where?'

'To the library.'

Swami Sir was a real headache. I taught much better than he did, so the students were happy with me. Swami Sir had got his job through influence. He owned a grocer's shop. He had nothing to do with literature or culture. Rather than enquiring about new books, he always talked about market prices, construction and bank loans. He could not tolerate my popularity with the students. Apart from that, I had also seen him and Sudha Thatte talking to each other a couple of times. He was in any case furious about that. Besides, I was here in a reserved job. Next year my term would be over. How to get me out: that was the one idea constantly churning in his head. Kulkarni Madam, too, was working in what was supposed to be a reserved post. Because there was no suitable candidate, she had occupied that post for the past four years. But when a candidate like myself had been found, to try and remove him on false grounds! To humiliate him! I felt myself sinking into despair.

Even a *talati*'s job would be better than a college lecturer's.

I met Professor Swami in the library. Sudha Thatte was sitting in front of him as usual.

'You taught a poem by Sharankumar Limbale to twelfth standard students. One that was likely to inflame their caste sentiments. You do not know how to teach. There are complaints from the students. When you teach, you should forget your caste.'

'I haven't taught them anything wrong.'

'In the class there are students from all castes. You will not teach Dalit literature henceforth. Kulkarni Madam will teach it. You cover other portions.'

'Why shouldn't I teach it? This is an injustice to me. Kulkarni Madam doesn't teach Dalit stories and poems at all. "I'm not in the mood to teach today. Put this lesson among the optional ones. There's nothing in it worth teaching. Read through it yourselves." This is what she keeps telling the students. I have studied Dalit literature. That is why I enjoy teaching it.'

'Let's meet later. We'll talk to the principal about it.'

'All right.'

That is how Professor Avinash Swami insulted me.

Then he turned to Sudha with a sneering smile and said, 'Today's poetry is so complex and difficult to understand. Just like today's girls.'

'Sir, I'll be off now.'

'Sudha dear, do wait. We'll leave together.'

Those two words, 'Sudha dear'—they did so inflame my youth.

5

Dalit Brahmin

Lately, scooters belonging to a few of my high-caste friends had begun to stop outside my house. 'Have to do something.' So we would tell jokes and stories to kill time. The handcart-puller who lived near me would park his handcart at a distance to leave space for my friends' scooters. When my high-caste friends came to my house, it would inconvenience the gamblers who played in the maidan. My friends came and went as they liked. The noise of their scooters and their horns filled the neighbourhood. Now I, too, often came home and went out on my friends' scooters. My clout was growing in the area. Because I had four high-caste friends, people in the hutment colony would bow and say 'Jai Bhim' to me. Old and young would address me respectfully as 'Bhaiyya'. Some people would come to me with work relating to the Sanjay Gandhi Niradhar Yojana, some with matters concerning a bank loan. It was I who would have to settle quarrels between wives and husbands.

My friend Joshi (affectionately Josha to me) had come over once. At that time, the colony women were at it again over the question of drawing water. They were throwing torrents of vile abuse at each other. Hearing those obscene, vulgar oaths, Josha was appalled. He was terrified seeing those bawdy gestures.

Josha said, 'Hey, get out of this neighbourhood. There are really dirty people here. It's a question of your children's upbringing. You don't want such bad influences on them. Your children are very nice. How can you live in such filthy surroundings? You are a writer now. Some respectable people will come to visit you occasionally. You must live in a good house. Now your status has risen. How can you possibly live here?'

I could agree with what Josha was saying. A thin white coating was beginning to cover me. My wife's face, however, was growing pale.

I don't understand how these indestructible ways of life, sunk so deeply into me, can ever be destroyed. But what Josha says is true. I must leave this neighbourhood. Otherwise, what would become of the future of my children?

We must change our dwelling.
We must change our language.
We must change our culture.
We must leave this neighbourhood.
We must leave the company of these people.
These people's culture is dirty.
They will never improve.
I become a row of storks.

I would leave this neighbourhood. I would go live among the high-caste people. There, I had to speak and behave like them. I had to give up my dirty language. I had to behave like one of the middle class. To mingle one by one with the 'white' people was the true revolution for Dalits. To become a Dalit Brahmin was the true enlightenment, the true transformation. Learn to behave like Brahmins. Learn to speak like Brahmins. I was happy to become a Brahmin. Now I, too, must wear a sacred thread.

I changed my house. I became a resident in a 'white' neighbourhood. I remember the farewell my old hutment colony gave me. Like the story of the stork.

There was once a lake, just like our neighbourhood.
In the lake there were fish, just like our people.
There was once a white stork, just like a wily Brahmin.
The stork used to tell the fish a story.
He would talk about transformation and revolution.
Poor fish! They believed every word he said.
One day the stork arrived, making a commotion.
The lake rose to listen, overflowing with emotion.
The stork began to speak:
Friends, this lake is going to dry up. Every day the water level is falling. And if this stays the same, you will all be annihilated. So you will have to do something. Fast. If you make me your leader, I will take you to another lake. Where there will be equality, freedom and brotherhood.

The fish cheered for the stork. The stork agreed to be their leader. Every day he would take a fish in his beak and make a great leap into the sky. The fish thought they would go to a new lake. The stork was very crafty. He would swallow up the fish. Every day the struggle enabled him to eke out his sustenance with ease. The fish, too, were delighted. They had found a leader.

I was a fish. I had got out of one lake only to head for another.

I, my wife and children, grandfather and grandmother climbed into a cart and set out. The cart was stuffed with our belongings. We barely had space to sit. The cart was going through the main road of the city. I was acutely embarrassed. I got down from the cart and started walking. We would reach the new colony in a little while.

There was our house. And our white-complexioned high-caste neighbours.

Our belongings were far too few. Just a cartful. It should have been a truck filled with furniture. Cupboard, refrigerator, TV, gas cylinder, fan, table, chairs, sofa set, cots, mattresses and so on. We had none of these. We had to raise our standard of living. We would have to compete with the culture of the new colony. We would have to forget the friendships we had made in the hutments. Just the other day I had met Dinesh Kamble. I'd given him tea and sent him on his way. He looked such a pure Mahar. For some their name, for some their appearance was the stamp of their caste. My features, in fact, don't quite look like a Dalit's. My language and pronunciation aren't pure.

My wife had started wearing a gown. Two days later, we were going to perform a Satyanarayana puja. Not for our own sake—we didn't believe in such things—but for the colony. We would make an exhibition of our middle-classness. I, too, could behave like a caste Hindu. All Dalits must become like caste Hindus. Now that would have sounded more befitting coming from Dr. Ambedkar's mouth, wouldn't it?

Dinesh Kamble visited me. He brought me the newsletter of the march. Now the only obligation that remained was for me to read newsletters, or at the most to tear off receipts for a few rupees. I had begun to count it an auspicious blessing that I was a part of the struggle on the strength of feeding a few cups of tea to the activists. If someone visited me, I would lose my head and talk about revolution: 'We must do something.' I would be inflamed, I would burn as I spoke of revolution. My eyes would ignite. The audience would be greatly moved. I would declare: 'We must change the system.' I had borrowed this style from the high-caste people.

Dinesh Kamble asked me, 'Are you coming to the march tomorrow?' I answered, 'How can I? Even if I am not directly involved in the struggle, I do write about it. It is a form of obligation with me. The struggle is not one-sided. The activists have to fight. We can only supply them with a provision of thoughts.'

Dinesh Kamble smiled mischievously. 'The rust of the colony is already creeping up your body. You are finished. You have become a Dalit Brahmin.'

I flared up. He was irritated because he could not stay in the colony himself. Useless fellow!

Dinesh Kamble left.

But he had wounded the stork in me.

In the same way as some people say 'We are freedom fighters', we, too, say 'We have come through the struggle.' Struggle, society, revolution, activists: those were the boundaries of our words. March, agitation, satyagraha, camp, people's problems and gatherings: I had been raised on these from embryo days.

Many people preferred me as an orator. I was soft-spoken. I had balanced views. Other Dalit writers spoke one-sidedly. They abused Hindu gods and goddesses. But people were content with what I said. So I went there. I earned a small sum. My name was printed in a few newspapers, because of which I was invited to give talks in other places. I got chicken. I got beer. I enjoyed the hospitality of resthouses. I made a few acquaintances.

All this was thanks to the struggle. I was surviving on the tremendous experience of the activists. I had conversations with activists. I wrote. My books were published. They were discussed. Interviews with me appeared in dailies and journals. I was invited to give speeches. I moved through assemblies, conferences and bungalows. I was about to inaugurate a programme as chief guest with the same hands that had dragged dead animals, swept the ground with a broom. The times were changing. Classes were changing.

Staying in resthouses in several cities had become a habit with me. Every suit was as familiar to me as a mistress. Drinking beer and gossiping had become a custom. People's questions were also the same. So were my answers. Only the cities were different. The audiences were different. Each year I decided on a topic, and circulated it everywhere. People came in crowds to listen to me. The organisers made arrangements for news items and photographs to appear. They would send me news clippings. Everything was going smoothly for me.

'How did you accept today's invitation?'

'Why?'

'These people are from the RSS.'

'What is the harm in speaking out your thoughts from any platform? If you are honest with your opinions, that's enough.'

'These people will swallow you whole and digest you. All your fire will be doused. These days you talk in a very subdued fashion as it is.'

'Previously I used to speak for one particular class. Now people of many classes come to listen to me. They like me.'

Dinesh had again reminded me of my limits. I grew disturbed. It was true. The struggle had become a source of livelihood for me.

I phoned the organisers and informed them I had arrived. After a while a car came for me and took me to a luxurious bungalow. That entire lifestyle was alien to me.

These days my language was improving. My accent was becoming pure Brahmin. My attire, too, was becoming sober. Now that was a transformation!

'How was your journey?'

'You must be tired?'

'Would you like to have a bath?'

How smothered I felt by all these loving blandishments! I passed my time in the lap of royal luxury. Eating, drinking, chatting, enthusiasm and delight. The owner of the bungalow was a connoisseur. There was music. Art. Entertainment. There was a large and eminent gathering of people there. The owner's elder daughter, Mugdha, was exquisite to behold. Her beauty seemed touched by the divine. To look at her was to forget death, such was her charm. Daya Pawar, Narayan Surve, Lakshman Mane and P. I. Sonkamble stayed in this house whenever they came to this city. Amrita Pritam, P. L. Deshpande, Ranjit Desai all purified the house with their presence. And today my footsteps, too, have decorated its threshold.

I was photographed along with the family. I, too, was now being album-bound. The only sorrow was that Mugdha was standing far away from me.

Dinesh Kamble said, 'He is a fanatic Hindutvawadi of this region. Last year when five huts belonging to Dalits were burnt, it was his people who burnt them.'

'We don't need to go back into history. People change. I believe in a change of heart. I believe in transformation. The person at whose house I shall be staying today gave me a warm invitation. If he were casteist, he would have put me up at a lodge.'

'I know. You are a Dalit writer. You are going to stay as the guest of a rich man of this locality, and tonight you are going to talk about the sorrows of Dalits at a magnificent auditorium dressed in a suit. You will take a fee. This is an anomaly. What connection do you have here with us, with ordinary people? You are holding one big *mela* here.'

'Look, I do have some limits. Each individual has his or her designated role in the struggle. The activists must carry out their activism. The artists must present the case for the downtrodden through their words and works on the cultural front. I work at my own level. I'm not writing against the struggle, am I?'

'You have made the struggle your source of funds and you are living off it. Do you understand? The activists are going to jail. You, on the other hand, are accepting welcomes in assemblies and conferences. What kind of duty is this?'

'I am not an activist. It would be better not to have unrealistic expectations of me.'

Dinesh Kamble saw the struggle in everything. He thought every caste Hindu was a Hindutvawadi. This was not right. I had made a mistake. I should not have brought him here with me.

The talk went off well. Afterwards, one of the organisers came up to me and said, 'Our Chairman doesn't go to any programmes. But today he was present at yours—and to the very end. Knowledgeable and eminent people were there. Today you have conquered the people. They had the satisfaction of having heard something good after many days. A few days ago, the speaker who came—no point in naming him—had drunk so much that, let alone speak, he could not even eat properly. He gave us a lot of trouble. But we liked you. When a man goes out of town, he drinks. We have no objection to that. After all, we drink, too. But one should drink after the programme is over.'

I was to go to the chairman's house for tea. The principal, the secretary, the chairman, the heads of department, the organiser of the programme, the professors, the old Rama temple in the town, this upstart theatre, that famous local mill. Visits to many people and places. How nice all these people were. No discrimination, no bias anywhere. Just genuine affection, friendship and warmth in everything they did. It was for nothing that Dinesh wrote against them. Spoke against them. They must have a dialogue so that all misunderstandings could be cleared. How distressing it would be to say goodbye to them now.

'Sir, there is no discrimination at our house. Till just the other day there was a Dalit student staying with us. It was he who made my tea for me.'

I felt gratified. The maidservant picked up the cups and saucers and went away.

After a while I took a friendly leave from that house. Then Dinesh opened his mouth.

'Do you know—all the utensils that you used were kept separate. All the cloths you used have been taken and given to the laundry.'

After the maidservant picked up the vessels, how disturbed everyone had been. What Dinesh said was true. In that house, every article meant for my use had been decided in advance. The shawl. The cup. The cot. The thali. The chair.

'You as a Dalit writer stay at his house, and *his* progressiveness and generosity shine forth for the world to see. Do you understand? He would not serve even a charity meal to a Dalit from this town.'

Dinesh's words were piercing me like arrows. I had become numb like a lump of clay. I had understood the limits of that house. The limits of its humanity, and my own.

6

Son-in-Law of the Government

Just this morning a new clerk joined us. His surname was Waghmare. The names Kamble and Kulkarni have become veritable seals of their particular castes. What caste did Waghmare belong to? It was impossible to tell. It would be good if he was a Dalit. It would strengthen our numbers in the office. The surname Waghmare exists among Dalits.

That afternoon I took Waghmare to tea. We talked of this and that. But I could not discern his caste from his speech, his appearance or his behaviour. While talking to Waghmare I had hurled abuse at caste Hindus.

After two months I came to know that Waghmare was a Brahmin.

Every Thursday there would be a Lakshmi puja in our office. I didn't like that. I raised an objection to the puja. They were all high caste. Everyone stood in opposition to me. I did not pay my contribution for the puja. The next day I brought a photograph of Dr. Ambedkar to office and wanted to put it up. Everyone opposed me. Deshpande said, 'Ambedkar is not a national leader. You can't put up his photograph.'

The blood rushed to my head. There were four of us Dalits. All four became one.

'You do a puja to Lakshmi. You've put up the picture of Lakshmi. Was she a national leader?' I said in desperation. I was trembling with rage.

Josha said, 'Hey, Lakshmi is a goddess.'

'I don't believe in gods.'

'Who's asking you to? Don't believe in them.'

'But I won't allow this Lakshmi puja of yours to go on in the office. You sit here doing puja while you are on duty. Why? Do your puja at home!'

'How does it harm you?'

'Fine. Tomorrow I shall invite a Buddhist *bhikshu* and arrange for a prayer.'

'What are you saying?'

'Yes! Stop this puja. Or I'll call the boys from the Panthers and create a commotion.'

'We, too, can bring the boys from the Shiv Sena.'

'Bring them! Bring them!'

'Are we here to work or to quarrel?'

'No, to perform Lakshmi pujas!'

My traitorous tones. The tension in the office was palpable. Spectators had gathered outside as well. In the end, when it was decided to halt the puja, I brought the photograph of Dr. Ambedkar back to my house.

Deshpande lived next door to me. News of our opposing the Lakshmi puja spread like an epidemic. Two camps formed in the office. We were adjudged to be the 'Jai Bhimwalas.' Controversy overflowed in every matter. Sneering smiles followed us everywhere, as did the playing of pranks. We, too, responded in our own manner. The educated barbs became unbearable. I would feel torn. Uneasy. Kamble put a voice to the fear, '*Sala*, no matter what we do, they're going to win. Our confidential reports are in the hands of Deshpande, isn't it?'

The very next day Deshpande gave Kamble a late mark. Now we, too, were inflamed. We responded in our own manner. Recently we put a stop to the Ganesh festival that had been celebrated for years in our office.

Dinesh Kamble was transferred.

A fighter from among us had gone.

But we did not lose heart.

'Even if they break up our unity, we must not be afraid. We must continue our struggle. Babasaheb's blood runs in our veins.' Kamble's parting words to us at his farewell had become ingrained in us. Like an embryo they grew in our minds.

After a few days, a worker named Irwadkar joined the office. He was a Chambar by caste.

Irwadkar did not socialise much with us. He was sometimes with us and sometimes with the other group. Because he was neither here nor there, we, too, were reserved in our behaviour towards him. We would, however, hurl oaths at Chambars occasionally.

Deshpande was becoming very refractory. We kept receiving memos over trivial things. Or talkings-to. Stopping the Ganesh festival was like pouring oil on the flames.

Nothing would work unless we intimidated Deshpande.

I went to Bhimnagar. I met the activists of the Panthers.

There is injustice against us in the office, I said.

We are ill treated because we are Dalits.

Come and intimidate them a little.

They won't come to their senses unless you do.

Deshpande must be transferred.

We are happy to bear the expenses.

Deshpande is a coward.

Etc. Etc.

We gave a party so that the activists would intimidate Deshpande.

The activists were smart. They would say they were coming, and then not come. They would take us for a ride. They would all say yes until they had had their tea. Then they would evade us. On one hand we had Deshpande's daily harassment to bear with. On the other our movement was of no help to us. They only came to collect our subscriptions. But our complaint was not a personal one. We wanted to put up Dr. Ambedkar's photograph in the office. We wanted to stop the Lakshmi puja. That is what we were fighting for, weren't we?

Why wasn't anyone taking this seriously?

I was tired of explaining everything repeatedly to the activists from A to Z. We had needlessly fought with Deshpande. How would it have harmed us if the Lakshmi puja had continued? Now it would be best to apologise to Deshpande and close the matter.

Dinesh Kamble came to the office.

I hadn't met him since we had last quarreled. But the fight in the office had reached Kamble's ears. His arrival instantly changed the office atmosphere. There were a dozen activists with Kamble. Deshpande had a group of five.

I prompted Kamble to speak aloud. 'It is only because we have both society and the struggle at our back that they speak so humbly to us. Otherwise they would have eaten us alive,' I said to him in front of everyone.

'You only remember the struggle when there is an injustice,' Kamble responded with a smile. His words hurt. He said goodbye to the activists and left.

'It's going to be hard to work in this office now,' said Josha.

Everyone understood.

I swallowed the barbs of both Josha and Kamble, and got back to my desk.

There was a note lying on my table. On it someone had written with the left hand:

SON-IN-LAW OF THE GOVERNMENT.

7

'Ganpati Bappa Morya!'

I remember when I was of primary-school age, they used to instal an idol of Ganpati in our school. We would conduct the installation of the god with great joy. We would dance; we would throw *gulal* powder. The puja would be celebrated with music and song. The days went by in great pomp. The immersion, too, took place amid show and spectacle.

Nowadays, while I remember those times, my daughter plucks out the stray white hairs from my head. My wife says, 'Let it be; your whole head has gone white. You can't hide old age by uprooting white hair.' But my daughter with great devotion keeps hunting for white hairs and plucking them. That removing my white hair gives her a reason to be close to me makes me very happy.

Besides, outside the house, there is Ganpati, sitting in the square.

Whether it is Ganpati or Devi, Rama, Krishna or Mahadev, these Hindu gods all carry weapons in their hands; they all appear aggressive. I am afraid of the weapons they carry. Even Ganpati has a weapon in his hand. He is the Remover of Obstacles, but with his coming, obstacles also arise. My daughter, the plucker of my white hairs, says, 'Papa, Ganpati's body is that of a man, but his face is an elephant's. What do his father and mother look like?' I pale at her question. 'Child, don't ask such things. They hurt people's religious feelings. Hurting religious feelings doesn't harm religion, but it does harm national property. There is arson; cities go up in flames. Tilak started the Shivaji birth festival and the Ganpati festival to awaken national feelings. But today in these festivals, only religious feelings are aroused.' My daughter pulls out a black hair instead of a white one. My wife shouts, 'Now stop plucking that hair! The bald spot has already spread far enough.'

A Satyanarayana puja is in progress in front of the idol of the deity. We can hear the loud chanting of the puja. From a distance, the mulla's *azaan* rushes into our ears, just as loud. There is a rap on the door. I open the door; a group of eight to ten young men is standing there to ask for a contribution to the Ganpati puja. If we don't give it, these young men would tease or harass my daughter. I would rather give them the contribution along with everyone else. But twenty-one rupees from the monthly budget would be too little. We will have to give up eating meat this week to pay the contribution for Ganpati.

The Ganpati festival and Mohurram have come together this year. Police patrols are alert so that an epidemic of tensions should not break out in the city. A peace committee has been set up. Positive opinions are being spread so that brotherly feeling and harmony are maintained. The route for the Ganpati immersion procession has also been chalked out in another, safer direction. The police have drawn up that route. They are sitting by the side of Ganpati. Whether it is Ganpati or Shivaji's festival, while welcoming them we feel fear rather than joy. Now for ten days loud recorded music will be played; the *lezhim* dance will be danced; there will be an uproar until late at night; there will be pandemonium accompanied by dust coming through the windows and doors and piling up throughout the house.

Who is to tell these people to reduce the noise? Who would wish to drag a quarrel onto oneself? I will have to cover my ears and endure this nuisance for ten days. If I say anything, they will say that I am an enemy of the Hindu religion, that I am an atheist. In the end, I do have to live in this neighbourhood. Because I go along, because I compromise, my relations are good with everyone. This is my business; I don't do it out of love. But Dinesh Kamble does not approve of it. He keeps picking on me.

'Hindutvawadis are growing more numerous in the Ambedkarite struggle,' he says. 'Ambedkar and Hedgewar are compared. Our Dalit writers frequent the platforms of Hindutvawadis. They have no respect for their caste.' This criticism by Dinesh Kamble does not seem valid. It just fans the flames. In this land of Hindustan Hindus are in the majority. Hindus have a history of thousands of years. We can't do battle with them. We must understand Hindu psychology. If through living together, I start expounding thoughts of revenge, I begin to be criticized. These days Samir Joshi comes to my house. I go to his. We eat and drink together. Will we acknowledge this change? Dinesh does not like my friendship with Samir.

We live in a neighbourhood of caste Hindus. There are Brahmin tenants all around us. Discussions about the BJP go on at their houses. At ours, the discussions are about Ambedkar. Even so, we live next door to each other. My wife goes to *haldi-kunku* events with theirs. It's not that she is not an Ambedkarite. I, too, go for *tirtha prasad*. We cannot live isolated from this Hindu environment. New culture comes about through struggle and crisis. Now we gave a contribution for Ganpati; we are obliged to. Dinesh Kamble didn't give one, but his entire household has moved out of town for these ten days. He can't stay on in this atmosphere at all. If anything happens tomorrow, they will burn Dinesh Kamble's house, and in such times, no one can hold back anyone. The police take on the role of spectators. During the Ganpati festival or

Shivajayanti, Dinesh goes out of town. He doesn't like to see rampaging Hindus. He is afraid of their violence. He incessantly hurls curses at Hindu gods and goddesses, but the result is that rather than any transformation's taking place, the enmity is preserved. Because of my prudence, I manage to enjoy these festivals. Sometimes I get to hear bloodthirsty comments. My mood changes; I feel sad. But I must stiffen my mind.

I see all of Samir Joshi's doings. He looks after my house. Caste never comes in our way. Last week Samir Joshi and I went to drink beer. We drank a lot. We left the bar late at night. On the way some thugs obstructed us. They demanded money. There was a scuffle, during which Samir's hand was grievously injured with a knife. The thugs ran away, but there was a very bad outcome to this incident.

'Hey, by becoming obsessed with Mahars you, too, have become one! For centuries, there has been enmity between Brahmins and Mahars. Perhaps Limbale himself must have hatched this plot. The thugs didn't attack him with a knife; how is it they only attacked you? Hey, you are a Brahmin. That's probably why they decided to remove you, a thorn, from their way!' That is the kind of discussion that went on in Samir Joshi's family. This is a common experience. Everyone sees my caste in instances of bad behaviour. I, too, get annoyed, I get furious, but I can hardly change my caste, can I?

Dinesh sees my caste, too, despite being of my own caste. He picks on me, saying I am a Hindutvawadi. Because Samir Joshi spends time with me, the entire Brahmin colony calls him a 'Jai Bhimwala'. I, however, live like a *sthitapradnya*, detached. Give a contribution to Ganpati; give one to Ambedkar; but don't fight. The Dalit activists don't approve of this. I only write; I don't go into society or live in it; I write books on Ambedkar and earn both fame and money; I am a traitor: that's how Dinesh's tongue keeps wagging. I can't keep everyone happy. Even though Samir Joshi is a Brahmin, he is my friend. I like him. I break my friendships with all Mahars and start living in the Bamanwada as a Dalit Brahmin, like a meek snail.

There was a Hindu-Muslim riot. Some young Muslim men gheraoed me. I was flustered. I freed myself, saying, 'I'm not a Hindu, I am a Buddhist.' In the next square a swarm of Hindus caught hold of me. I freed myself, saying, 'I'm not a Muslim, I am a Buddhist.' When there are Hindu-Muslim riots, Yakub says the same things to free himself. It's good that Dinesh leaves the city.

Ganpati Bappa Morya,
Come much earlier next year.
But the next time you come,
Leave behind the weapons in your hands.

How many times have the boys in the lane thrown stones at my house! Many times I even saw them from the window, but who was I to fight them? I live in the Bamanwada. There is inconvenience for those who live in the hutment colony. They are subject to bad influences. So I live in the Bamanwada. If now and then a caste Hindu boy throws a stone, I accept it. One must pay at least this price, mustn't one? Without it how will I get a good neighbourhood, a good house and good neighbours?

Even if some incident brings tears to my eyes, I have to pretend something went into my eye and hide them. But how hot-tempered Yakub and Dinesh are! Let all this suit them. I will seek out Josha's company and start behaving as if *van nahi tar gunn tari lagla*; so what if I have lost my forest, I still have my good qualities. I was a tiger before, but now I am just a sheep. Last year, because a little of Ganpati's gulal powder had fallen on his shoulder, Yakub had sent four youths sprawling. Dinesh refused to give a contribution. When the youths got furious, he pulled out a dagger and attacked them. How would such a thing be possible for me?

My daughter came to me crying. I could understand nothing. Some workers of the Ganpati mandal had harassed her. I was writing a story. My daughter was crying. I said, 'Let it be. Whom shall we confront? The whole colony is theirs. If we say anything, we'll have to leave this house. You behave cautiously.' But my wife could not endure this. My son came in just then. He had championed his sister and started a quarrel. He had beaten up a few people; then they had all united and beaten him up. His scalp was wounded. Later, some boys came to the house, created a rumpus and left. These were the days of the Ganpati festival. For no reason the atmosphere had suddenly turned volatile. So I grew calm. But my children were far from calm. 'Let us go back to the Maharwada. We don't want this daily torment.'

'Whatever part of India you live in you will be tormented for being a Dalit. So are you going to leave the country?' My question was appropriate, but it did not meet with agreement. 'Let us go among our own people; they will help us. Such a Ramayana took place today, but nobody came from Joshi Uncle's house. If Dinesh Uncle had been here, he would not have sat silent. We need people of our own blood.' My son is a diehard casteist. Circumstances have made him embrace casteism. I was silent.

Samir Joshi came. We told him everything. Tears welled up in his eyes. He swore at everyone. I was very happy. Josha was enraged at the injustice. Hearing his words, I, too, grew inflamed. I said, 'Josha, let's go to those boys. Let's have a meeting. You tell them what you said just now. Speak just as blazingly to them. It will have an effect.'

Josha's face fell. He bowed his head and said, 'I am not a spirited person. I cannot fight. I won't come. You must look after yourselves. Behave like tigers. Do not be afraid. Such tendencies must be crushed. But don't draw me into this. I know my limitations. I cannot orate. *You* are the tigers—go.'

I was disheartened hearing Samir Joshi's words. If I had given my love to a Mahar, he would have offered his life for me. I had made the wrong choice. Samir Joshi left.

I rose, saying, 'I will fight them like a tiger. I will not endure injustice. I will smash them all.' Outside, there were raucous shouts of *Ganpati Bappa Morya!* The sounds of *tipri* and *lezhim* pierced the ears. My blood was seething. My endurance had reached its limit. I was on fire. 'Oh, the Brahmins have always done the work of inflaming others. Joshi has set you alight. Don't behave so crazily.' My wife was holding me back.

I couldn't understand. In times of need, we remember each other's caste and do things that raise that caste. Isn't that so? Samir Joshi coming to visit on Ambedkar Jayanti. My wife going to haldi-kunku ceremonies with Mrs. Joshi. Joshi's children coming and eating mutton at our house. My son going to the temple with Joshi's daughter. And this atmosphere can be destroyed in just a second! This Joshi, who could give a speech on the morning of Ambedkar Jayanti and recite a puja in the evening, now appeared to be a hypocrite to me. Usually Joshi was just my intimate friend. Life should always be smooth; there should never be occasion to put people to the test. Then everyone would appear to be a saint.

A few stones fall on the house. My head flares up. Joshi is reciting prayers in front of the image of Ganpati. I go straight to the puja mandap. I take control of the mike. I shout. All the boys from the lane gather. A riot begins. Everyone starts insulting me. Samir Joshi, however, stands by watching in silence. At the time of Draupadi's disrobing, perhaps Bhishma and Drona must have observed a silence just like this. More than the abuse of those hundred people, I am upset by Joshi's silence. That is his limit.

Dinesh Kamble comes. He pulls out his dagger and stands there. Everyone runs away. I clasp Dinesh's legs and say, 'Dinesh, stay in my house! Till the Ganpati immersion is over, you must live with me!'

8

Madhavi

Fire that burns away the darkness. Fire stretching out, rising up. The naked dance of the mob. I with my heart in my mouth. People running helter-skelter. A scream that freezes the night. The covering darkness was alight. All my sheltering shadows were being destroyed. The mob was shouting. The dreadful sound of physical belabouring was audible from somewhere. Screams echoed wildly. This moaning must be from Shalan.

Shalan's hut was burning like a funeral pyre. In the light of the fire, horrible faces could be seen running here and there. A terrifying silence held the whole forest. After a while there was an explosion. My house had been flattened to the ground. My mother wasn't in it, was she? Tears came to my eyes and disappeared in the darkness.

When we built the house, Dharmanna had stood as an obstacle.

'Live in a hut. Why do you have to build a house? Have you got too much money? There should be only one pucca house built in the village, the Patil's.'

I set out, hunting in the dark for the trumpeting of the sacrifice. I spilled tears like dew drops at every step. The scream that choked the throat, the helpless cry that rose to it were cut off by someone. I was without a voice; how could I scream? Even at such a time of devastation, Madhavi's laughter was like a ripened field.

I chose another life, one other than my own, just for Madhavi. A life in which dwelt our beautiful dreams. Our inerasable memories. Our meetings were bonds several lifetimes old. Our meetings should never end, I felt. We would talk and we would talk. There was no end to our conversations.

'Hey, how much we talked!'

'I didn't understand a thing!'

In every empty space of my life, memories of Madhavi were stuck on like tulsi leaves. How adorned sat my vacant mind, waiting for her footsteps. But won't there be a single footstep for me?

Things of the mind soak into the mind. I should praise her hair today, I thought. It makes better sense for such emotions to remain unexpressed. Sometimes I thought, today I should not speak at all. But Madhavi started speaking to me of her own accord. And my silence ended. And sometimes, how beautiful silence can be. Like a huge statue at Ajanta.

'Don't you like the cinema?'

'I would like to go with you to the cinema.'

I called out Madhavi's name, and a row of innumerable lights illuminated the darkness. My lips trembled like henna leaves. Give me the shelter of your gaze. Adorn me with your breath. Madhavi was intertwined with every moment. That day she pinched me. I, too, pinched her, and a welt came up on her hand. Madhavi used to show me that welt, pleased. As the welts flared up, a fragrance would spread in my mind. The pinches would turn to flowers.

'Madhavi, I want to pinch you very, very hard.'

Now when had I begun to guard my nails? Madhavi was a beautiful dream in my life, one which was being destroyed today. The night was dead silent. Through the dark, I could hear the fierce groaning of the old man, Genu. The mob had beaten him up badly. He was talking to me in a voice soaked in blood.

'You shouldn't have got mixed up with the Patil's daughter. Hey, you'd already made enemies of the whole village by building that house. We've been flattened in the dust because of that.'

Hearing Genu's words, I felt as if someone was laying an explosive mine inside me. I said nothing. I just swallowed the darkness. My wounds began to awaken one by one. The wound from Madhavi's pinch was still fresh.

Madhavi and I studied together. We were both students of art. She would draw flowers; I drew thorns. I once drew a picture of her. After she had coloured it, I drew moustaches on it and called it a picture of me.

'You behave like a little boy.'

'And you speak like an old woman.'

I loved the colour schemes that Madhavi used. She would pour her heart into her brushes. She would become possessed. She would become the picture. I would become the god Krishna in her picture. She liked the sky; I liked the earth. Tomorrow I would paint a picture of my ruined village and show it to her. Madhavi was the cause of my sorrow. She was the cause of my joy. Madhavi was not a soaking-wet figure of a woman; she was a peacock feather marking the chapters of my life. In the desert of my past, she was an oasis.

Shalan was Madhavi's friend; she, too, was in our class. The amount of love I felt for Madhavi, Shalan felt, too. The three of us once acted together in a play. And right there, sparks had begun to emanate from us. Those sparks had led to the blaze, and the old man Genu's hut had been burnt in that blaze. Tomorrow our tears would become a news item, there would be a police *panchanama*, and the rioters would come round with relief funds.

The night was ablaze. Shalan stood in front of me like darkness. The village hooligans had tortured her. Fire danced on her lips. A helpless lamentation in her eyes. How dreadful her face looked, swollen with rebellion. We wandered through the entire neighbourhood. Collecting agonies. Through forests of tears, the cries of wild beasts pierced the soul.

'Shalan, where are our people?'

'They must have fled by whatever road they could find.'

'This village is no longer ours.'

The wall of my house caved in. It made a big sound as it collapsed. The night was crushed under the wall. In my mind somewhere far away a house was destroyed. I needed someone to lay mines in my eyes. In the expanse of my sight Madhavi's *mehenḍi*-filled footsteps were ready and waiting. But the crowd had caged her in a mansion of stone. And even in that tight surveillance, thoughts of me must be giving her strength.

'Just for a moment, you look so handsome.'

'That's how a lightning bolt looks.'

Madhavi's enchanted laughter...She met me in that desolate darkness, and on account of her company the darkness was laden with moonlight. Her lips like crescent moons...the fragrance of her body like musk... how flocks of the birds of memory crowded my mind. In the heavy rain, the pairs of soaked birds were folded into each other like closed leaves. The sprays of rain filled my mind.

The old man Genu's mortal cry fell on my ears. Blood-bespattered Genu was soon to become the property of the earth. The darkness in the old man's eyes was truly ghastly. Shalan's sole support was now level with the dust. I shuddered at Shalan's scream. Her cry pierced the surroundings. The night insects were screeching. The hut was still burning. From the temple of Rama in the village, I could hear the sound of bhajans.

The next day dawned.

The police came. Also people came carrying food and clothes. We were sitting out in the open. Some people voiced their sorrow. Some expressed their opposition. The children were happy—they had got their fill of food and enough clothes to cover them. The old man Genu's funeral procession was about to leave. The cremation ground was arrayed on Shalan's face. The pyres were burning in her eyes. She looked very calm, sensible.

I remembered Madhavi. She would not be tortured. I became restless. I became angry at the fact that we were outcastes. Madhavi, I thought, your world is different. We belong to the burning huts. Outside the village, our endless agonies and rebellions have been ruthlessly denied. Our breath has gone through the agony of fire. A crushed sound comes out of our many calls for help. Madhavi, we, too, are living people.

Madhavi, the many gifts you gave me were burnt to ashes last night. Like Sati. Memories don't burn; they live on. You are not here now, but my memories of you do not allow me to feel the lack of you. Sometimes memories are greater than real living people. Madhavi, do you remember me?

'What are you thinking about?'

'Nothing.'

'Let's get ready to go to the burial ground. We must put the old man under the earth. How long are we going to wait like this?'

'At least let the people come.'

'They've all run away, afraid for their lives; how will they come?'

'Shalan, I am sinking.'

'Hold my hand. You'll get strength from the sky.'

I resolutely remained standing. My lips were burning to do battle.

I went close to old man Genu's corpse. I observed the violence that had been done to his body. In his wounds I saw myself. I saw Madhavi adorned like a bride, seated in the palanquin of my wounded heart. Strains of the wedding *shehnai* started to bloom.

The sound of the funeral drum could be heard. Now the old man Genu's final journey was about to begin. We were going to bury our wounds in the burial ground. How many sorrows, fallen victim to injustice, we had buried in the bosom of the earth! Our burial ground was the living record of our orphaned sorrows.

'Genu, come back and be born again in our hutments. Become a sun to us. We are all waiting for you.'

'Genya, you died, you escaped this torture. Go be born as a dog, but don't be born from a Mahar's womb.'

A bellowing cry had burst from my mother. Many storms were coming to ruin on Shalan's face. I took Shalan's hand in mine. Her touch felt like a horrendous riot. The police and the press were now in preparation to leave. The surroundings of the burial ground had encircled me. I was annihilating my sorrows. The voices buried in the earth were germinating in my mind. Green leaves were sprouting in suppressed throats. Blossoms were breaking out on the tears. Through a dreadful scream Shalan was standing before me. The reason for all this was the love between Madhavi and me. A mansion made of shadows spread across the village. And Madhavi, living like a rumour in that mansion. It was not possible to extend one's vision to that place, but I heard the sound of her breathing. The echoes spread across the body were from her touch.

'Shalan, we must say some final words to Madhavi. It's important that we should meet her.'

On Shalan's face one could clearly see the corpse of the old man Genu. It was on account of me that she had been tortured, that her father had been murdered. She was Madhavi's friend. She was witness to our love. She said nothing. By now all the questions and answers had taken place. The panchanama was over. Shalan's hut had been burnt down. The village leaders had built a new home for her, knocking a few tin sheets together. It was stronger than a hut. Little children were playing around it. Realising that the government was helping people, those who had left their house and goods and run away had now begun to return. Cooking fires were being lit in the colony.

Day dawned. Like explosive ammunition. Madhavi was taken away to Delhi. She was married off there.

'Are you crying?'

'No...I am not.'

'Your eyes look like it.'

I couldn't think what answer to give Shalan. I floated a little lighted lamp in the flow of tears in Madhavi's name. It would float to the sacred confluence of rivers. I looked at Shalan; she looked even more beautiful than Madhavi.

'Shalan, Genu should come back as our child, shouldn't he?'

Her sound of assent filled my entire body. A breeze was flowing from the colony. Some new houses were being built there. Small children were playing.

My mother came from the village. She said, 'All the people who attacked us have been held not guilty and freed. There will be a victory procession for them soon.'

The colony was terrified once more.

9

Sujata

My whole life had been imprinted with memories of Sujata. I hid my own whole existence in thoughts of her. When I held her flowerlike cheeks in my palms, it was as if rain fell heavily throughout my body. I saw a wringing wet mind. My eyes brimmed over with emotion. Those tears fell from the eyes and entered my whole body. Her footsteps began to take root in my every vein. Sujata, a fully formed flower.

Our hutments were in front of the bungalow named Parijat. On one side were shabby huts; on the other there was a self-contained colony. It was from here that men went to maintain the colony, to be labourers and coolies, and that women went to wash the pots and clothes. My sister was a maidservant at Sujata's house. Then she got married. She went off to her husband's house. Even there she went to wash clothes and pots and pans. From time to time my mother went to Sujata's house.

When I was small, I would go with my sister to Sujata's house. My sister would scour the pots. I would help her. When my sister fell ill, my mother would go to wash the vessels. Sometimes I would go. 'Sister's ill; won't come today,' I would say. At that time, Sujata, too, was small. Once we two got into a fight.

Now she was a grownup. I was, too. The times had grown as well. The eye of society, too, had grown very large. Sujata appeared in the window of the bungalow like a crescent moon. My gaze was constantly planted in the direction of her window. She appeared in the window, and the whole bungalow came to life. That window began to mass like a cloud over my sight. There were moments when I came very close to her. Close to her soul. But the very next moment I was pushed far from her, rejected. I couldn't give a name to this relationship. Sujata was an emotion which rode me day and night. I lived in the shade of memories of her. She smiled. My body began to melt, like spreading moonlight.

The sharp exhalation that escaped through a tight embrace became a source of happiness that loosened in the mind like the knot of a blouse. Her glances told the history of my eyes. I planted my eyes in her gaze, making my eye a rising moon. Just like her laughing face. Her innumerable breaths knitted around my lips. The two of us in each other like the two panes of a closed window.

How intelligent a window was! How full of life. When the window opened, the mind's darkness found something like the brightness of the moon. The window was the warmth of life. It was the unease of loneliness. The closed window drove me mad. The area of the window is very large, as huge as the Almighty's soul. How often I have imagined climbing these walls! Leaning in and looking through the window.

The window, an entity consisting of many memories. Sujata taking her broken-down scooter and leaving. I heard her calling out my name. I helped her. This help sowed palmfuls of flowers between us. She was setting out for the temple, and I for the central square. When she appeared at her window, I would be standing before my hut. Our huts didn't have windows. We all had been served notices asking us to move our huts. If here was a place where people feared to come, then there a hut fell and construction took place.

We took out processions in protest. Then roads were built, electricity came, and we acquired taps. Little by little, one by one, bungalows came to adhere to them. A colony was formed. The city came spreading out to this place, like flooding water. Now they would once again snatch us up and throw us out of the city. The stomachs which had taken root here would be uprooted; a plough would rake through our minds.

With the help of the police, municipal workers began to intrude into the huts. The police picked up one or two people and beat them up brutally. A little while before, the people in the hutments had been involved in stone-throwing. Meera's hut had been smashed down. Meera's tears were crushed like flowers under the boots of the police. The huts were choked with emotion at Meera's screams. People were being destroyed. The world of our households, built gathering piece by piece, was being torn apart in every direction. A garden was going to be planted here. The hutments here would move outside the city. The people from the bungalows in the colony would enjoy the garden. Where there had been huts, fountains would play. What kind of flowering tree would they plant instead of my hut? The flowers on it would gaze unblinkingly at Sujata's window, with the hot coals of the hutments draped on them, petal by petal.

'This area was reserved for a garden.'

'It is not good to have a slum in the middle of the city.'

'The city must become more beautiful.'

'I'd become fed up of listening to their daily quarrels. That place was a den of thieves and rioters.'

'If the hutments are shifted, where will we get maid-servants?'

By evening half the houses had been removed. The hutments wore a paralysed look. That day there were no songs. The cooking-fires were not lit, nor was there the daily mess. The next day the whole place would be clear. There would be no trace left of any single cooking-fire.

When Sujata comes to the window, what will she see? The sorrow of the empty soil will be transformed by her gaze. She will fix her gaze on the place where the hut used to be. The flowers will put an end to their lives.

Grasping the darkness in its fist, the settlement came together. The broken men grew united in their unease. The huts began to speak:

'We must resist this. We must take out processions. We must fill the jails. But we must not leave this place. We've been living here for many years. We have rights over this land. It does not matter if we are killed; we will fight.'

'Hey, we don't have leaders; they're all eunuchs.' The darkness all around was catching fire. The wailing of the darkness in the flames had begun to sound out. The darkness had broken out into dawn's red tinge. That window in the darkness, glowing with gentle light. So much of a stranger to me, in all respects, it still felt as if it was my own. The windows closed one after another, like leaves of the touch-me-not creeper. That window was the eye of my beloved. Sujata, I have arrayed your bed with a thousand memories.

The municipality truck and municipal workers landed up with a thud. In a little while the police van arrived. Tension spread all around. Mehboob's hut was shifted. Chand Bibi began to wail. She had given birth to a child just a week before. She was turned out along with the baby. Mehboob was somehow tying up his tattered household into bundles.

Soon a crowd gathered. It turned violent. In the face of the crowd's fury, the police became defenceless. The police van was set on fire. Stones and bricks fell in piles on the street. A storm of stone-throwing broke on an approaching city bus. The bungalow colony on the other side, however, was totally busy watching the Doordarshan channel on TV.

The window of the bungalow named Parijat was continuously open. The sky clouded over. But there was neither sun nor moon. Keeping the crowd in sight, I was looking at the window. Why didn't Sujata come to the window today? What stone-throwing this was that I had done on my own soul! How disturbed I was at her not coming to the window. Every moment was double-edged. She would definitely come. One would have to wait a little longer. Every moment oozed out drop by drop, till my mind was empty. Where was she? Why didn't she come to the window? How could I make my torments reach her? The torments of the bud turning into a flower, of her voice becoming a tune, of my eye when her beauty held its festival... My mind, however, was like her empty window.

Reinforcements came for the police. A lathi-charge began. Tear-gas canisters began to explode. Heads were broken. The police pushed into hut after hut. Taking their lives in their hands, men turned their backs on the police. They, on their part, were arresting everyone they could lay their hands on. Some of these were women. The police had crammed Mehboob, Chand Bibi and her baby into the police van. They had no home. They had no ration card. They did not know the name of their country. Their name was not in the electoral roll. What they needed was some work for their hands, some bread for their bellies, and a home to rest their backs.

All those people came together, forgetting their caste and their creed. Now they were behaving like human beings. My mother went into police custody a long time ago. I was in the custody of the window. That was since Sujata had stood in the window to dry her newly washed hair. My hair was like the mob. The police ran helter-skelter all over my brain. Tension spread through my eyes. In a little while this settlement would be a deserted ruin. Human beings once lived in this settlement. Anyone who said it was demolished would be thought mad. If I lingered here tomorrow at the same time, the police would catch me and take me away as a thief. Our rights over this place had come to an end. We had been given an alternative place outside the city.

There would be no window there. When windows started appearing in the bungalows there, when TV antennae began to chirp, then once again they would find us an alternative place to stay.

Those windows began to appear to me like villains' eyes.

10

Niloo

My body, laden with pain, had begun to melt. My body turned into just two flowing tears. The sound of my footsteps had begun to sob like the siren of a fire engine. I was slowly walking in the direction of the hutments. Bhimnagar was within calling distance. I was Bhimrao and I lived in that Bhimnagar. Everyone called me Bhimya. Some people however called me Bhimrao. But Niloo called me Bhim. She did not know the darkness I belonged to.

'Hey, don't go by this road. It's where dirty people live.'

Niloo said goodbye to me.

A great churning was taking place in me. My thoughts were setting fires all over my body like a rioting mob. My eyes were burning like cars set ablaze in the riots. Any moment now my eyes would turn into ashes. My sight would burn away. Would my tears burn? When would all the tears I had swallowed in my life be totally destroyed? I strangled those tears.

Niloo was a civilised pain.

Niloo and I met on the playing field, as sportspeople. We played many games. We lost; we won. We wore injuries from sports all over our bodies like ornaments. Sometimes we became the game, sometimes the sports ground, sometimes the sport. Water sports; miniature cookery; sandcastles;

names carved in the sand; setting afloat in the river either my little boat or her small lamp. I used to become her shadow; she became mine. We used to swing in the fresh air, under the stars. That was how those days were.

Her intense blue gaze used to fill my sight. My entire body would melt away. Her gaze and my gaze were like the darkness of the sea. I saw the henna on her hands; I smelt it. I came into form. My breaths came alive. I opened the doors of my future fate. The sound of the wedding shehnai resounded throughout my mind. Her vows were exuberantly acquiring for me the form of nectar.

Niloo must by now have reached home.

When I went to set foot in my neighbourhood, it was as if my feet had rusted. She thought of this place as one for dirty people. I was disgusted at my neighbourhood. Avoiding the other huts, I reached my own. Just as my hut was, so was my mother. And, as she was, so was the hut. I, however, had been dug out by the roots, deeply.

Niloo was a cultural division.

Niloo was a cultural border.

Niloo lived in Saraswati Colony. There flowers ruled. Every instant there had come alive because of Niloo's breaths and exhalations. What must Niloo be doing at home there? Would she have memories of me? Maybe she was absorbed in watching TV on Doordarshan. I, however, was in the kingdom of memories. Without the mind, those memories were orphaned. One memory came like a tidal wave. Other, smaller waves arose. She arrived like a butterfly. Her touch was like drops of dew over my entire body.

My mother approached. Niloo went away.

'Have your food, Bhima.' Mother's voice.

'Dirty people live in that place.' Niloo's voice.

'*Buddham sharanam gachhami.*' The voice of the hutments.

My voice cut off in my very throat. I was voiceless. In my voice was Niloo's dress. Niloo had never enquired about my home territory. My mother went to Saraswati Colony to sweep it. Why would Niloo scan my mother's face?

The night within us had lightened. The sun within us had risen. According to our custom, we came together. She in my view, I in hers.

'You look like the Queen of the Forest in this saree.'

'Thank you for the compliment.'

'Your hairstyle yesterday was lovely.'

'Enough compliments.'

Then a meaningful silence. How eloquent that silence was! Even to fail for her would be a joy. She was not herself; nor was I myself. We were ourselves; our joy was each other's. I wanted to speak a great deal to Niloo, but couldn't think what to say to her.

Would Niloo be my wife?

Niloo and I.

From that side came my friends.

From them came 'Jai Bhim'. From me, too, 'Jai Bhim'.

Niloo in Saraswati Nagar. And I in Bhimnagar.

You there. I here. Beyond the two poles. Human beings beyond humans.

'I'm off.'

'I feel sad.'

She left even while I was feeling that she shouldn't. I said a disagreeable goodbye. The farewell was cruel. For a moment I felt like holding her and detaining her. But my courage slackened and fell flat on its face. She went far, far away—in body. She left memories behind her. I became all about memories. Memories blossomed throughout my mind. And the road beneath my feet came to an end. The dogs kept barking. Groups of women kept quarrelling.

Prayers went on in the *vihara*. I came back to my hut. My mother had gone out to do her sweeping. She came back late. Dead tired. The next day a minister was to visit, so she had to sweep out all the lanes and alleys. She started cursing the minister, 'May he fall dead!' and gestured to one side as if putting away a broom.

Niloo had found me out, along with my caste.

How would she behave with me the next day? I had concealed my caste when courting her. I had seen her house and her mother and father as well. But I had kept the place where I lived unseen. I had behaved like a secret lover. What was I to tell her the next day about this vicious circle?

'Niloo, I am in love with you.'

My youth was beyond the pale. My touch was forbidden, untouchable.

Niloo was probably listening to ghazals!

'Niloo, give me back my dreams.'

What a huge falling of leaves of the day and night! It was the day of Niloo's wedding procession. Bursting joy throughout the procession. My mother was walking in the procession carrying a gas lamp on her head. A stormy wind was coming. The procession was moving and swaying along. Niloo, the ornamented bride. With her was her husband. I was at a distance near the pan box, waiting to gaze my fill at Niloo. Like the others. The crowd swelled and overwhelmed me. I felt stifled. The excited crowd slid forward like a cloud. My view was trampled on. What was lacking in me? I was a man, too. But my wretchedness was my caste.

Niloo, how can I forget you? Your vows. Your falling into my mind. How you blossomed in my embrace. How my life broke into flower in your company. We rained in the moonlight. We shattered the sea. We danced in the sky. We played among the flowers. I searched my body for your breath. Someone was burying landmines and destroying all the gardens.

'Niloo, will the flowers be destroyed?'

Niloo was adorned with flowers. The wedding procession was slowly spreading out to cover the whole square. Should I shout out to the crowd that I have rights over Niloo, or should I offer myself a messy consolation? Niloo, be happy. Forget about me. She was rich. She was from a high-class family. I should not have fallen in love with her. I had made a mistake.

A stormy wind arose. The wedding procession moved. It swayed. The tattered leaves in my mind tore away and fell. Rama arrived. He said Jai Bhim to me. He was playing the shehnai in this wedding procession. There was a commotion. The crowd ran helter-skelter. I was thinking, I should abduct Niloo. People's shouts grew louder. Somebody was on fire. I pushed into the crowd. My mother was on fire—her gas lamp had exploded. From head to belly she was ablaze. The fire had totally encompassed her. She was screaming. She was running, taking with her the fire that covered her whole body. She collapsed to the ground. I looked at her. I let out a groan. A few people came. They lifted my mother. We set out for the government hospital.

'How gruesome Mother looked.'

The doctor announced that Mother had died.

Now money would be needed for her last rites.

I was burning within like a funeral pyre. Rama was standing by my side, holding his shehnai. The shehnai had been silenced by a surge of emotion. Now, little by little, friends and relatives would assemble with tears in their eyes. Bhimnagar would be awaiting the body with groans in its throat.

Niloo's wedding procession is sliding past the government hospital. Another Dalit woman was walking with a gas lamp on her head in Mother's place.

Both the wedding procession and the funeral procession were moving away, as if my life itself was departing.

11

Sunita

At the height of noon, when the sun was blazing down, the villagers attacked our house.

Our household was well-to-do, well-fed and happy. Our elder brother had a job in the district office. Two of us ran an eatery near the bus-stand. Our father was a member of the Gram Panchayat. The others in the village could not bear to see our family's self-sufficiency. Our family used to take part in the quarrels in the village. Because of the eatery business, we had money to play with. We also paid attention to village politics. People didn't like that. At that time we were in a campaign to make our father the elected sarpanch. Because of that we had fallen out with the Lingayat community. The whole village was shying away from us.

Sunita, the daughter of the Deputy Sarpanch, was a fellow-student of mine. Since we were studying together, we had an easy relationship. We used to roam around at any hour. We saw films together. As we were studying at the District headquarters, no one in the village had come to know of this matter. But just last week, someone from the village had seen Sunita and me walking together, and the news had spread like the wind through the whole village.

Sunita's father brought her home and belaboured her and sternly forbade her to set foot outside their house. 'You're ruining our good name. You are walking around with a low-caste boy. Have we sent you there to study or to flirt? How will we show our face in society?'

Sunita bore her father's torture. She endured his blows. She was in love with me. My caste was irrelevant to her. The two of us quietly ran away together. And her father's temper was set ablaze. He was maddened with thoughts of revenge. Finally he caught Sunita and took her home.

I came to the village. I went to Sunita's home. I slipped into the house. 'I'm going to take Sunita and go away. She is mine,' I quarrelled. On account of all this, the atmosphere in the village grew very tense. 'Today one of our girls has lost caste, and if we keep quiet, then in the future they will deprive all our girls of their caste in front of our very eyes. We must teach them a lesson today.' The villagers called an assembly and took a decision.

All the men of the village—even very little boys—had taken weapons in their hands: stones, sticks, axes, spades and sickles, and were now approaching our houses. We felt the foreboding of a riot. We saw a mob of a couple of hundred coming towards us. Shouting at full volume, the mob started pounding on the doors. Some of them climbed up on the roof. They prised off pieces of the tin roofing and started throwing stones into the house. The people in the house hid, sheltering among the sacks of *jowar* to avoid being hit by the stones. The people on the roof now threw inside lighted brands of wood with rags soaked in kerosene, so clothes caught fire. Smoke began to spread. The flames grew. We started getting smothered. We opened the back door and began to run to save our lives. The mob had surrounded the house on all four sides. They caught us one by one and began to kill us.

My elder brother was lying dead on the ground in a pool of blood. Next to him they had gripped my father tight. Giving him a blow on his neck with an axe, they took his life, too. Then they turned to my second brother. He began to tremble violently with fear. Seeing that these monsters were about to take his life, my mother, who had lost her voice with sheer fright, let out a great scream. Crying and screaming, she went before that mob. 'Don't kill my son, please don't!' As she said this, she went on her knees before them, spreading the *pallu* of her saree in front of them and touching their feet in supplication. But they just landed blows on her back with the handles of their axes and picked her up and flung her aside.

They surrounded my second brother, too, and fell upon him. One of them broke his leg with a sickle used for cutting sugarcane. Another attacked him on the head with an iron rod, and my second brother, groaning, writhing, fell to the ground in a pool of blood. After he died, the mob turned to my third brother who had been hiding behind the sacks of jowar. My mother rose again and went sobbing in front of the mob. She was crying loudly. She was falling at their feet and imploring them. But those people pushed her aside once again. They fell upon my third brother, too.

Just then, someone shouted from the back. I turned and looked behind. My fifth brother had left the house and started running on the road. About fifty people were running after him with axes, harrows, machetes and sickles. While he was running a few people came and obstructed him from the front. Then everyone surrounded him. For a few moments I could not see him in the crowd. All I could hear was screams. The mob was yelling loudly. Drops of blood had spattered onto their clothing. They were incensed. I could not bear to see their wild dance. After some time, when the shouting mob moved aside, my brother was lying soaked in blood. At another side, the people had also murdered my fourth brother. In front of my very eyes, my own brothers had been cut to pieces. And I could do nothing. I was sitting crouched there. When Mulla Chacha from next door intervened, those raging people attacked him, too, and killed him. My mother was lying unconscious.

The mob now smashed the house with iron rods. They destroyed the furniture and goods in it. They broke the telephone wires so that the police should not be informed. They did not allow the trucks and buses that went along the road to stop at the village. They threw stones at the vehicles. I was quite terrified. I couldn't think what to do. Close by I could see my brothers lying dead. I could see the completely demolished house. I had no idea what would happen next. My mother, looking at me, said, 'Don't give up. Take some paper and register FIRs everywhere. And call my brother.' Listening to my mother had turned my heart to stone. She was moaning. My sister was offering her comfort.

Before we could say two words, the news had spread like the wind. Many country people had run there. The police had started to make their rounds. The DSP was saying, 'This massacre has occurred because of a love affair. No one should give it the character of a caste battle.' The Dalit activists were saying, 'This massacre has taken place because of caste prejudice tendencies. If it had occurred because of a love affair then only the young man who was the lover would have been murdered. The entire family would not have been killed. If this were on account of a love affair, one family would have killed another family. The entire village would not have turned into murderers. "Today one girl from the village has lost her caste. Tomorrow the village itself will lose caste." It was such feelings that were behind this butchery.' I felt terror at the atmosphere. The villagers had held a meeting. They had picked up the gauntlet of killing the remaining Dalits in the village. The whole Dalit settlement looked like a cremation ground. No one was saying a word. They had swallowed their gazes out of fear. The activists were saying, 'The police should take charge of the complainants. They should give them protection. Otherwise they will be killed. Witnesses will be eliminated.'

The police scattered the onlookers who had gathered. The corpses lay in the open. One individual was standing near me. A journalist asked him, 'What will happen now?' He gave an extremely neutral answer, 'What will happen? They will sell a couple of acres of land and fight the case, and get off blameless. In such cases, the result is always acquittal. What difference does it make to sell off a few acres out of several? Then they will remove the remaining thorns in their flesh. Their reach is right up to the Ministers.' I was terrified, as if I was listening to a verdict from the judiciary.

The police came. They went.

Whenever I went with my story to seek justice from Dalit organisations, their first question was, 'Is there a branch of our organisation in your village? If there is a branch, we will come and take your case in hand.' I would go to everyone with my request. I would meet people. Some people even collected funds for us. But not one paisa of that ever reached us.

People from the countryside would come, bring us clothes and food grains. Politicians would come and make speeches. Journalists would come; they would interview us. There was much media play. Photographs and posters of leaders were printed. News items were printed about everyone who came. What next?

A Maruti car came, flying a blue flag. In it were Dalit leaders. We gave them detailed information. They consoled us. They drew me close. They had many photographs taken. Many photos of me appeared. They made speeches:

'Mother, do not worry. Your sons have become martyrs.' My mother meekly wiped her eyes and brought a smile to her lips. The Ministers gave her a gift.

That day I met Sunita in the bus. I summoned up courage and said to her, 'This massacre took place on account of you.' She said, 'I had no connection with it.' I asked her, 'But weren't you in love with me?' She replied, 'That was my mistake.' She disengaged from the conversation and went ahead. I was numbed. I found Sunita even crueller than the murderers.

My journey had begun. There were blue flags in my hand. I had to put them on my house and open a *shakha*. Of the blue flag. Of the fight to remove injustice.

12

Rajani

I was standing at the gate of the University. Rajani came by here every day at this time. But there was no trace of her today. I had to leave this city an hour from now. I had packed my luggage. I had got a reserved window seat. I would have to spend a week away from Rajani, but it was important to go. I had to give a story for the Diwali number of a magazine. Rajani's office must not have closed yet. Or else, could she have got stuck with a colleague? She should have been here by now.

Waiting is like an ebbing and flowing tide in the mind.

Since I had won a Central Government scholarship, I had become the most famous scholar in my department. My well-researched articles had become well-known in newspapers and magazines. Rather than my intelligence, Rajani died for my good nature. We had blossomed for each other from the stems of our minds.

The time of my departure drew near. And she had not yet come.

The road by which she was to come filled my sight. Sometimes I felt an uncontrollable rage at the road. And sometimes I wanted to kiss it as if it were Rajani's hand. Sometimes the road would fill my eyes; sometimes it would remain empty in my sight. Rajani would not be there. Rajani, I am so entangled with you; I'll collapse without you. I have put down very deep roots in the thought of you.

I had to leave a message for Rajani and depart.

I was going to be able to reach my father by the next day. Then my grandfather, and after him my great-grandfather, who was as yet far from this mess. I wanted to write an article on my interviews with them.

I got down from the bus.

Vinay had come to receive me. Vinay was my younger brother who was studying to be an engineer. My elder sister Shashi was a college teacher. Her marriage was fixed for the next month. Her future husband was a lecturer in the same college as her, and a Maratha by caste. It would be a registered marriage. Our father was a cash officer in a bank. Our mother was a housewife.

'CHALO MUMBAI—BIG PANTHERS' MARCH FOR THE CHANGE OF NAME'. Walls all around bore this painted slogan. The atmosphere of our University was heating up, too. Vinay said he planned to go on the march.

We reached our bungalow. We got down.

Our mother and father came to the door. My mother was fairer than my father. She was a Brahmin by caste; my father in his former state was a Mahar; now he was a Buddhist. In front of the house there was a statue of Buddha. I thought of it as a poster attached to his untouchable caste. Mother and father belonged to two different cultures. We children were fair like mother, and sturdy like our father. We used to visit mother's relations. There we had to move in a different atmosphere. We also visited father's family; there we moved in a different universe.

Activists from the Dalit Panthers had come to the house. They wanted a donation from Papa for the march. The activists' features resembled those of my father. But Vinay, Shashi, my mother and I were very different from this crowd. I could well understand their discussions, their questions.

My mother made tea for everybody. In her parents' house, these activists would not even gain admission.

'Our Vinay is going to come on your march,' Papa said, putting special stress on the words 'our' and 'your'. One of those activists was fanning the flames against Brahmins. I didn't think anything of it. But I took a surreptitious look at my mother. Her face was unclouded. She must have got used to all this. Papa was pacifying all of them. 'Babasaheb Ambedkar was not opposed to Brahmins, only to Brahminism.' For the past several years, he had known this one sentence of Babasaheb's by heart.

The people from Panthers departed.

The bearer Kamble came to pick up the cups and saucers. My mother was explaining the tasks to him. Kamble's face. Papa's face. The Panthers activists' face. Mine. Circumstances had given all of us different faces. I bore the burden of my face; my mother bore hers.

I remembered Rajani's face. Vigour awoke in my mind once more. I went to the appointed meeting place to meet her. I took her hand in mine, like a spray of roses. I caught in my lips the dimple on her cheek. I remembered the pinches I gave her, and those she gave me. Remembering her, I counted the marks of pinches on my hands. The memories became uncontrollable. I filled my eyes with the photographs in my diary. I kissed the photos. Rajani was in every atom of my being.

Vinay was discussing the name-change proposal with Papa.

Vinay and I reached our grandparents' home.

We were coming to this village for the first time. Our only connection with it was minimal. Because of his job and his marriage, Papa had been stolen away from this village. Sometimes Grandpa used to come, just to look us up. He would stay for the odd day. He would look at us with diffident eyes. He used to behave deferentially even with his own son. I used to feel sorry for him. There was a great difference between his speech and demeanour and those of my father. Sometimes I thought he could not be Papa's father. My mother's father, however, was plump as a rabbit. He was perennially moving around humming *slokas*. Even at our house he would be dressed for ritual purity. Whenever he came, I felt happy. One felt good to talk even to a stranger who was handsome in feature and complexion; an ugly man, even if a relative, was unwelcome.

My mother's father was called Ram. My father's father was named Dhondya, meaning block of stone. What a distance between these two names!

Papa's original name was Dagdya, or boulder. Later on, he changed it and took the name Kamalkishore. Papa must have felt embarrassed at his original name. Even higher caste people felt embarrassed at Ambedkar's name; that's why they were opposed to the name-change proposal. If Marathwada University was given the name of Dr. Babasaheb Ambedkar, then their degree certificates would bear the name of a Mahar. These high-caste people did not find that acceptable. No one addressed our grandfather with respect. Even small, snot-covered children knew him as 'Dhondya Mahar'.

This upset me greatly.

Seeing our comfortable lifestyle, people treated us with great warmth. When they learnt we had come to visit someone, they would show us to the Mahar area from a distance. At my grandfather's house, just as they had a photograph of Dr. Ambedkar, so, too, would they have the holy alms-basket of goddess Ambabai. 'We worship Babasaheb, but we also pray to the goddess,' they agreed. 'We need both gods,' they said. Vinay used to corner them suddenly.

After a while we went out and visited the field. Papa had helped them buy this field. After a while Papa's younger brother came. He farmed the field. Although he was younger than my father, he looked older than him. His name was Kachrya or Rubbish. We were to go with this uncle to our great-grandfather the next day. His name was Maryappa. Our great-grandmother's name was Satvai. I remembered the names on my mother's side. Sumati, Kusum, Anagha, Anjali, Vandana, Jayu, etc.

I remembered Rajani. When coming here, I had not met Rajani.

We reached my great-grandfather's village. Great-grandfather Maryappa came along placing his staff on the ground. Ahead of him came a few Mahars who were entitled to *balute*—a share in the harvest—carrying a dead animal. I felt disgust. There were dogs barking at them. Our uncle spoke to our grandfather about us. Grandfather looked up at us and muttered something. Uncle must have understood. He was to have the dead animal skinned and bring a *shakuti* prepared from it. We reached our great-grandfather's hut. Our great-grandmother was sitting in the doorway. Uncle spoke to her about us. She just kept looking at us.

'This isn't true. These people aren't ours. They're Banias or Brahmins. They're not ours. Why are you telling lies?'

Our roots had been uprooted from here long since.

That day it was decided that we would visit my mother's family. There was a Satyanarayana puja at their house. That evening Papa would come there direct from his office. Shashi would come, too. My mother's other relatives would gather there. Everyone would have a chance to meet and chat. Usually it was not possible for us to get together. Having some programme or the other gave people an excuse to be together, so I had no objection to the Satyanarayana puja. Formerly Papa had had no faith in such things, but recently he had begun to believe in them.

That evening a discussion arose on Shashi's marriage. My mother opposed it. 'We have endured a great deal through our inter-caste marriage. Don't you fall into that fire!'

I remembered Rajani. I remembered her caste.

The Satyanarayana puja ended. Dinner was over, too. Everyone was enjoying a good gossip. Suddenly the voices acquired an edge. Someone was arguing with Vinay over the name-change issue. Papa, too, was taking Vinay's side. The atmosphere was heating up. 'You find the name of the maker of the Constitution impure? Would you have objected to Sanjay Gandhi's name?' Papa said.

'You people have been pampered too much,' said Mama, my mother's uncle, pouring oil on the flame.

Papa abruptly left. Vinay was shouting. Mama came forward, his body shaking with rage. 'Vinya, this Mahar-mang language does not befit you.'

'I am a Mahar...a Mahar.'

'According to our Dharmashastras, a Mahar cannot enter our house. He cannot talk so arrogantly.'

'I'll burn your Dharmashastras!'

Even as we watched, Vinay had played havoc with the Satyanarayana puja. I restrained Vinay. The entire household was roused to side with Mama. He was shouting.

'They aren't ours, either! They will always behave like this!'

'This caste will never improve itself.'

Shouting out loud, Vinay left the house. I followed. Shashi and my mother remained sitting there.

Rajani and I. Glasses of beer for company. A dim light spread around. The young man at the next table was casting stolen glances at us. We were sinking into each other. Rajani's body seemed honeyed.

'I've had enough.'

Rajani slid her glass in front of me.

'I have something important to discuss with you.'

'Speak.'

'About our relationship.'

'What's left to discuss?'

'About marriage. I—'

'Sorry.'

'Why?'

'We can be good friends.'

'But why?'

'You know my father is an orthodox Hindu.'

'My mother is of your own caste.'

'But your father?'

'I don't understand anything.'

'I can't do anything about that.'

'All right. Let's leave.'

The glass of beer. The half-burnt cigarette. The decorated tables. The dim atmosphere. The people enjoying eating and drinking. The waiter, Rajani and I. We stepped out.

'Is that your final word?' I asked her.

'Why talk of the same subject again and again?'

'You won't marry me?'

'It's impossible.'

'Friendship?'

'That's there, anyway.'

'Let's end this subject right here.'

'You're just passing the time.'

'Friendship's not a way of passing the time.'

'You've been playing with me.'

'Don't put words into my mouth.'

'Rajani, I love you; I won't be able to forget you.'

'I have been in love, too, but I can't say the same thing.'

'Why?'

'Sorry. Good night.'

The two of us grew more and more distant in body. What can I write about the mind?

13

Soni

The streetlights were lit in a row. Like a necklace around the throat of the city. The streetlights in front cast a splash of moonlight on the courtyard of Soni's house. Night meant day to Soni. The secrets of her life were hidden in the darkness of night. Every night Soni helplessly became barenaked in order to meet a new life. As moment by moment light faded from the earth, even so a dreadful darkness suffused Soni. Soni herself was an ancient night. In this darkness, innumerable lamps blinked out and many storms were destroyed. Becoming an enticing night, Soni goes to confront the thoroughfares of the city.

Today Soni was hardly adorned with youth. Her body was like an enchanting white heap of thousands of parijatak flowers, and beneath those flowers, her emotions were like a rotting unclaimed corpse. She stopped at Mehboob's paan shop. She bought a masala paan. Mehboob tried to provoke her. Her whole body shaking like a vine tossed by storm and wind, Soni laughed uproariously. She bought a gajra from Nadira. She tucked the gajra into her childishly playing plait.

She was wearing an eye-catching garish pink saree with a matching pink blouse. Her free behaviour was stopping the traffic of people walking past. Seeing her, gazes were stopped dead, then turned around to look at her. Some conservative gazes became frightened. Soni's gaze however was expert. She returned every look, glance for glance. She had left the fear in her gaze like a patrolman on all the squares in the streets.

Soni was a man, all man. What did she have, other than a woman's body, to be called a woman?

I knew Soni very closely. Her house, her mother, her caste, her husband. Why only that. She had two beauty spots on her chest. Her thigh bore two scars branded by her husband. I knew how much she earned daily and how much she lost. You could ask me, how did you know all this?

I would say, 'That's my private business.' About Soni, however, I spoke to everybody. Empathy seeped from every word I said about her. Why should she have been my private business?

When Soni's mother Girija first came to live in our neighbourhood, Soni was still wearing the skirt and blouse of a little girl. Girija had no further children after Soni. Girija's husband, saying he wanted a son, took another wife and threw Girija out of his house. Girija felt that Soni was a stone weight on her chest. Soni had achieved beauty great enough to satisfy the sight.

Soni was married when she was very young. Soni's husband was Babu. Babu's first wife, tired of his torture, had committed suicide. Babu used to torture her daily because the agreed dowry had not been paid. Babu's wife died singed from head to foot, but never talked about her torture. Where did the woman get such tremendous powers of endurance? Babu's second wife left him and ran away. She had been married off to Babu by force. She had been in love with someone else. Soni was Babu's third wife. Babu was very much older than her, and Soni was an innocent girl. Where was Girija to find a good husband for her daughter? She did not have two paisas to rub together. If her daughter were not married, there would be scandal. A woman was not a vessel to keep in the house; she was the possession of another house. She must go where there was fodder for her. What could a destitute mother do other than to hand her daughter over to some slaughterer?

Soni's husband Babu was a drunkard. The very first night he raped Soni several times. Soni was a helpless wound. Every night would make her stand while pain was rained upon her, and her young body was drenched with tears. The pungent smell of liquor from Babu's mouth, his old body, his powerful hands, his obscene curses—and Soni. It was her fate to be his prey every time.

One day Soni ran away from her husband. He kept another woman and started living with her. I felt amazement at these women. How could even a man like Babu get women one after another? Were they not realistic? Or had they never given thought to themselves? Once, Babu got drunk and came into our neighbourhood. He caught hold of Soni and was dragging her away. Girija was shouting and crying. A few of us got together and beat up Babu. From that day he never came in Soni's way, but Soni always mentioned Babu as her husband's name. Soni came to her mother and became her support in old age. Girija's age was playing upon Soni's body like a lizard. Little by little, Soni began to be given as an offering to the darkness. She was being sacrificed to the hunger of her house.

Now Soni was a prostitute walking the streets. She kept wandering through Hutatma Baug, Navi Peth, Bhagwat Theatre, the bus stop, the vegetable market, the railway station, with anklets of hunger tied around her ankles, hunting for clients. She met, talked with and laughed with many people. When she acquired someone as a customer and went to Manoj Lodge, I would be standing in the square like a tonga. She would go to the second floor. Her usual room was in the corner. She would go into the room, with her customer behind her. But the darkness in the room would corrode me with unease.

Soni, the paan-seller Mehboob, the gajra-seller Nadira, Sakharam the manager of the lodge, I, my tonga, and the many people who passed by on the street, corroding. Soni was standing near the bus stop. Two young college boys had gone to her. Just then, the police van appeared. Soni deftly disappeared into the lane. That was the only lane in the city that sheltered her like a mother. The lane led straight to Appa's *adda*. Soni had paid fines in the court a couple of times. She would say, 'I paid one client's fee to the court. Well, I didn't pay it to the police.' If Soni did not return home early, then Girija would set out to hunt for her. The old woman Girija would walk like Gandhi-ji, tapping her cane down again and again. 'Soni, Soni,' she would call. And her voice, breathless in the traffic on the road, would become indistinct.

Soni would come home early. For Soni who would bring home earnings, Girija would have water heating on the stove. When Soni came home, she would scrub her and rub her and bathe her. The two of them would add up the account of how much money she had got. Sometimes Soni would tell stories of some naïve customer who had come to her and sometimes she would throw out curses at a customer who had given her trouble. Girija, however, on hearing of her pain, would become subject to the darkness.

The night ended; the day dawned. The day ended; the night dawned. Soni set out to earn money. Girija would fuss. 'Soni, bring home whatever you earn. Don't make it too late. If you don't get anything, we'll sleep hungry.' Soni would bend her head in assent and leave. If she met any known old customers in the street, she would argue a paan out of them and eat it. She would make a joke of it. When Soni ate a paan, it would add a lot of colour to her face. Like a *gulmohur*. When I looked at her reddened lips I thought of rose petals, and like an unseasonably blossoming flower, I was maddened.

It was only morning when Girija came to our house. She came to our house when she was in need, but my mother would get irritated. She was not comfortable with our having any connection with the house of a prostitute. She had thrown

Girija out of the house a number of times. Girija was poor. What pride or ego does a poor person have? I didn't go to Soni's house. Soni had once quarrelled fiercely with my mother. She didn't come to our house now either.

Girija was standing in the doorway. My mother was telling me, 'Go to the tonga-walla.' I used to have to get up early and take the tonga on hire. Otherwise someone else would hire the tonga and my day would be wasted. Now that I felt I must go with Girija, the tonga had gone to someone else. I went along the road to Soni. I felt that Girija's time was very valuable. We reached the hut.

Soni was pregnant. She was going to become a mother. In her home, the number of mouths to be fed would keep increasing. Soni wanted to have an abortion and then have an operation to prevent further pregnancies. That would not only stop children, she would also get some money for having a contraceptive operation. She had to buy herself a good saree. If she wore good clothes, she would get good customers. But how would she get an abortion?

Soni put tea on the stove. The tea was boiling, and so were we. The next day, Soni and I set out on the road to the Civil Hospital. Soni wore a *mangalsutra* round her neck. Her forehead wore a large *kumkum*, and she had me. As her husband. The two of us were going along the road as husband and wife. I was feeling immeasurably tickled. I would gaze at Soni. I thought Soni was beautiful. But how awkward it was to accept the idea of Soni as a wife! My mother, my relatives, the neighbourhood. When Soni and I went along together, many people looked at us. The occasional old client of Soni's came and met us, urged us to eat paan. Soni said, 'I'm married now. This is my husband.' I gave a strained smile. Each client would become a satirist and say, 'Brother-in-law, take care of our Soni,' and leave. My rage boiled over. Soni just laughed.

After two days Soni and I left for the neighbourhood. She had had her abortion. She had had a lot of trouble. I even had to donate blood. It was at my suggestion that she had postponed having the family planning operation. In just two days a deathly look had come over her face. Soni's body had become weak. Neither of us had any money. We had to walk to the neighbourhood. Then there was the question of livelihood. After walking for a long time, we sat down at a bridge for rest. Soni took my support.

The road was busy as usual. Vehicles were running at their own speeds. Before and behind us stood huge multi-storeyed buildings. Less than two years before, this land had been empty. Now new construction was taking place. What had that to do with us? I took Soni's hand in mine. She had a little fever. A policeman known to Soni was walking in front of us. She went up to him and took a little money from him. We each drank half a cup of tea. The people in the teashop were watching us guardedly. We hired a tonga and set out for the neighbourhood.

I came home. The house was locked. My mother had fought with Girija and left the city forever. She had gone back to our village. She did not want to live with me. She had gone away saying that I should look after just Girija and Soni, and live at their house. I couldn't understand my mother's behaviour. She had always been inflamed by jealousy of Girija. She said there had been a relationship between her and my father.

After my father died, my mother's jealousy had surged. Girija was a woman seared by circumstance. She used to address my father as Dada. It was my father who had arranged Soni's marriage. My father used to call Soni 'Daughter-in-law', but my mother was not happy with this. They often quarrelled about this. My father would beat my mother, and I would come in between. After my father, my mother was my only protection. When I heard that she had gone away, tears sprang to my eyes. My throat felt choked. I opened the lock with a nail. I looked at my father's and mother's photographs with eyes filled with tears. My mother may well have gone away, but she had cooked a meal for me before going.

I was holding back my tears. Just then, Hanmya, Mhadya and Bhimya stood in the doorway. They had come to ask for a subscription. They had collected a little money. As usual they had bought some liquor out of the subscription money. When I said I had no money, Bhimya said, 'If you won't give money for your mother-in-law's funeral, then who will? Eh, Hanmya?' Suddenly everything became clear, and I set out for Soni's house. I could hear Soni's moans from a distance. With every step I took I was sinking. I entered Soni's house. Soni let out a loud groan. There were ants on Girija's body. I tidied up the body. Hanmya, Bhimya and Mhadya had come prepared. Several of us gathered. We took the body out of the house. The whole neighbourhood had assembled, and Girija's funeral procession swept over my body and went its way tapping a staff like Mahatma Gandhi.

Night, with its criminal footsteps, was gradually capturing the city. I walked towards Soni's house, like spreading darkness. Soni was beginning to come forward to meet the city. I started following Soni. Soni in front, I behind. A customer met her in the square. Fire surged into my feet and, forgetting all else, I went and met her, too. I stopped her. She stood still. The customer was enraged with me. Soni got angry. I slapped the customer in the face. We had a fight. The customer went off. Soni was watching me. I was watching her.

'Soni—come on.'

'Where?'

'Wherever I say.'

'This is the time for clients.'

'Consider me a client.'

'But you are my husband in the morning.'

'Now I am your husband all the time.'

Just then someone's grasp tightened round my neck. I turned around to look. Our hands were not bound together by bonds of matrimony but by handcuffs, and the police van was moving fast, taking us away to Jail Road. I was dumbstruck. Soni was used to such things. She was sitting there unafraid. I was saying, 'Soni is my wife,' but the police, thinking I was her customer, were beating me, and my weeping was splattered on the wall of the jail like pangs of grief.

14

Ratna

It was a monsoon day. The sky and the river were swollen. The black soil had found a green adornment. Our village was at the foot of a hill, and outside the village was our Mahar settlement. Leaking huts. Paths made marshy by mud. Dungheaps swollen with water. Darkness would come to our house dancing to the rhythm of frogs croaking.

Ratna and I had grown from childhood to adulthood in one place. Her house and mine touched each other. When we were children we used to play husband and wife. But now we were grownups. The eyes of the neighbourhood were riveted on us. Our love had become a subject of discussion. Our people had found a good topic to pass the time.

Ratna's father was in the army. My father had been carried away in the river when I was a child. Our village was by the side of the river. In the monsoon, when the river was in full flood, it was my father's job to do things like ferrying people from this side to the other, and from that side to this. He used to earn several annas per head.

Sometimes the river would swell with so much water. The water was full of force. People on this side of the river would remain on this side; those on the other side would remain there. It was a roadblock for the village. Once the water receded a little, people from our Maharwada would go into the water. They would start ferrying people through the water. But you cannot play around with water. Crossing a river in flood with green chillies or green pumpkins is a dangerous thing. But my father laid a bet and jumped into the water with green chillies and a green pumpkin. My father, by the way, was a proficient swimmer. He was someone who played unconcernedly with the water, even when the river was flowing with both banks absolutely full. But that day he was swept away in waist-deep water. People on both banks set up a bellow. But my father drowned. On the fourth day, my father's body was found at Kurnoor. It was stuck in a thornbush by the river. My uncle went and had a look. My father's funeral took place right there. As an unclaimed body. I never saw my father. Whenever the river floods, when both banks are full and start to overflow, then the memory of my father gives me great unease.

Every year someone would be swept away like this in the river. Unknown bodies also came by from upstream. It was my father's job to lift out the corpses that came by in the river. Sometimes it was a young woman, sometimes a young man. And sometimes an old man caught in the flood. When a corpse was seen, our village Patil would say, 'Let it go ahead; push it on. Who wants to sit doing a *panchanama*? The unnecessary headache of the police.' We would push the floating corpse on its way. The same thing would happen at the next village. The police, for fear of having to conduct an enquiry, would ignore it. Why, just the other day the river was in flood. Two coconuts came floating down. I was about to jump into the river to fish out the two coconuts. Ratna was in the river. She stopped me, saying, 'What? Planning to follow your father, are you?' The tears in her eyes looked like the river. Ratna herself was like a flooding river. I turned back.

An incident from last year. There had been torrential rains. The water level had reached the main entrance of the village. Once Ratna had slipped and fallen into the river. I was on the bank. I took a leap into the river and pulled her out. Ratna was saved, and became mine. But there was a blood feud between my family and hers. My great-grandfather had run away with some woman of their family. Since then we had been at daggers drawn with each other.

Ratna's life was grafted onto mine. She used to say, 'If I get married, it will only be to you. Otherwise I'll jump into the flooded river and take my life.' My mother said, 'This won't be possible.' My mother was very humble. She was frightened even of the village schoolteacher. And Ratna's father was in the army.

Ratna came into my life like a flood. Her eyes were like fresh water. Her lips were like wet earth. Her teeth were like round drops of dew. Her nature was like foaming, rushing water. Those incomplete meetings with her, taking place under watchful eyes, like a shrinking river.

Ratna would move through the settlement like a forest breeze, piercing more than one pair of eyes. Her beauty itself was inflammatory. It had become difficult for her even to step out of her house. Her sister would be with her all the time. My behaviour and Ratna's was creating a darkness in the settlement. I would go to the river and talk to the water. I felt that Ratna should rise out of the water like the river goddess Ganga. But nothing of the sort happened.

A flood of tears would rise to my eyes. I would remain standing like a Shiva temple destroyed by the flood. The water would flow away. I would think it would have been good if Ratna and I had been carried away. Ratna was mine. I would watch the river with tear-filled eyes. Ratna would come to the water. She would fill the pot on her head, while I would collect the water that had touched her feet in the cupped palms of my hands. I would touch it to my eyes. I would touch my lips with it.

Ratna would go away. I remained as I was on the bank. A pool would fill my eyes. I never tired of gazing at the river flowing away into the distance, or at Ratna moving away from in front of my eyes. Ratna would return. Her buxom face had been sculpted onto each wave of this water. She would return in order to see me. She would give me a lot of memories and depart to flow away with the river.

Evening on the riverbank. A line of storks assembling at the river's edge. Cattle returning home. A pleasurable darkness filled the cowherd's throat. Exhausted men returning home from the fields and forests. The bell that could be heard accompanying the reading of the *pothi* in the Mahadev temple. One cooking-fire, one lamp being lighted after another. Darkness lay on the water like the skin floating on milk. Stars were blooming one after another on the water. The stirred-up waves filled the banks. Mai, who had gone to weed Devappa's field, crossed the river for the cool breeze blowing in the darkness. The tremor of her footsteps could be sensed through the voices of the night-insects. The warmth of her breath could be understood through the fully lit moon. She was sinking through my mind like the gurgling water. Someone's steps that had been taken through the water. The sound of a pot filling with water. And at such a time Ratna clung to me even more.

'How many more days must we meet stealthily like this?'

'Suppose someone sees us.'

'Let's run away.'

'Otherwise I'll kill myself.'

'Gana is giving me a lot of trouble.'

'Do something.'

'Talk.'

I could understand the passion and urgency in her speech. In that coal-black darkness, I had her touch as a witness, and the voice of the flowing river. Suddenly, I heard the voice of Ratna's mother that sounded as if a bird had fluttered by. And as if the moon should slip out from behind a cloud, Ratna went away. Her mother would give her trouble.

The moon was rising slowly. Stars were crowding the skies. The water looked silvery. The rushes were silvery, too. The sand was adorned with a silver glaze. A lapwing was crying out in the grove of wild dates. Now one must return home. Or else my mother would come shouting to the river.

Taking some shells and conches in my hand, I set off for home.

I could hear the sound of Ratna crying. The night was tearing apart in my heart. I was uneasy throughout my house. My mother, too, had become gloomy. After a while Gana left the house. He had arrived there from Ratna's house. Seeing him, my mother was startled. He had scolded her.

Gana was the village's number one goon. The whole village was terrified of him. He was obsessed with Ratna. He had caught hold of Ratna's hand. These days Gana often remained sitting in Ratna's house. Nothing Ratna's mother could say got anywhere with Gana. He gave her a lot of trouble. It wasn't easy to suffer Gana's enmity. I would need to pull out the thorn Gana right away, or else take Ratna and run away. Otherwise I would have to forget about Ratna. I didn't know what to do.

Meetings with Ratna would leave burning coals on my heart. Sometimes it would be torture from her mother; sometimes Gana's misbehaviour; sometimes the memories of Ratna's threats to commit suicide and sometimes my mother's unbearable misunderstanding would constantly make me disconsolate. One should now just vanish from the village. Without that, Gana would not allow us to live in peace.

It had been two days, and the flooded river had not yet subsided. They had let the water of the Katgaon Lake into the river; the heavy rains had created a great danger for the lake. So they had allowed that water to drain out. The river was in full bloom. The river was running in full spate. That day Ratna and I were going to say farewell to this river forever.

Darkness had gathered on the ground. With tear-filled eyes I said goodbye to my home. Mother was cooking. Ratna was not to be seen. She must have reached the riverbank long before. Breaking through the bushes, I, too, was almost there.

The coal-black flowing waters. A meeting of night and mud. The night was blossoming. I impatiently reached the appointed place. For a moment I could understand nothing. Gana had caught Ratna. She was resisting him. Gana was beating up Ratna with kicks and blows. The water in my eyes ignited. The blackness in the womb of earth made a huge noise. I fell upon Gana like a flood. I sent him sprawling on the ground with all my might. I clamped a foot on his throat. Gana's body was flailing around. The night was shaking and my foot on his throat was growing stronger. My foot had acquired the strength of a tidal wave. Ratna was standing still as night. Gana's struggle ended. I took hold of both his legs and threw him into the flood. Now his corpse would float downstream. Somewhere or the other, a panchanama would be held over him as an unclaimed body.

A barbarous darkness had merged into the flow.

The flow of the river had gained speed. The water was boiling up.

I pulled Ratna close. I gathered her into an embrace. I saw Ratna's mother on the riverbank. Behind her came my mother. I couldn't understand anything. Ratna's mother came near. 'This girl was born for you. Live happily together. I tortured you both out of fear of Gana.'

The roar of the water was clearly audible.

As we were returning by the side of the river, I remembered Gana's corpse once more. Where would he have floated by now?

15

Womb of Darkness

Bali was chopping wood. The blows of the axe were landing hard. Pieces of wood were flying. The knot of wood was just not splitting. Bali was gathering all his strength to move the axe. Half the wood had been chopped. Half of it remained.

Bali had been taking the sun on his body since the morning. He had to finish chopping the Patil's wood in two days, and on the third day, he had to go to the Sarpanch's house to chop wood there. Chopping wood in the village was his livelihood. Everyone in the village knew him as the woodcutter.

The sound of chopping had disturbed the peace of the colony. The rapid strokes of the axe were splitting the wood. The pieces were flying and landing at a distance. The axe embedded in the wood was difficult to pull out. Bali would jerk the axe that was in the wood. He was bathed in sweat. The veins stood out on his body. He was breathless. Because of the light gusts of breeze his body, soaked in sweat, felt a chill. Bali wiped the sweat off his forehead, and adding lime to tobacco in his palm, started to rub the mixture together.

The sound of anklets came to his ears. His mind leapt alert. His gaze became distracted. He remembered the story that Krishna Gawandi, the mason, had told him.

Krishna Gawandi had come to the Mahar settlement to drink liquor. He had become very drunk. He couldn't walk. It was very dark and a heavy rain had begun to fall. Krishna Gawandi could not think what to do. The dogs in the settlement were barking at him. At such a moment Bali had been a support to Krishna Gawandi. He had picked him up and carried him to his home.

Krishna Gawandi was from another village. He had come there with his father to build the Patil's mansion. The construction had been going on for two years.

Bali could not forget Krishna Gawandi's words. Even today those words burnt him like acid. 'I built the Patil's mansion myself. Do you know? By day I would build, and at night the construction would sink into the ground of its own accord. The walls of the mansion just wouldn't rise. No matter what the effort, the construction just wouldn't move along. We were tired out. The Patil brought in a *mantrik*. Do you know what the mantrik said? That the building of the mansion would never be complete. If we wanted to complete it, we would have to perform a *shanti* ceremony. Without that ceremony, the building would never rise. Do you know what that means, to perform a shanti?' Krishna Gawandi was speaking. 'What did the mantrik say? That a pregnant Mahar woman would have to be buried alive in the foundation of the building. Do you know whom they buried? Your mother. She was pregnant. It was after you were born.

'Your mother was returning from the forest after her work. She had a load of hay on her head. The Patil's men met her on the road. They lifted her and took her to the Patil's fields. That night they buried her alive in the foundations of the building. The mantrik was shuddering in a trance, muttering mantras, and your mother's body was trembling in mortal fear. "I have a child in my belly; let go of me!" she was shouting, she was screaming. From that day, I began to drink.

'The Patil gave the mantrik five fistfuls of cash. He had a rumour spread in the village that your mother had run away to Mumbai. Later the Patil gave your father a piece of land as a gift. At the time you must have been three or four years old.' Krishna Gawandi was speaking, terrified.

At the sound of the anklets, Bali was in a state like that of calm water that had been stirred and in which mud had risen. Bali was disturbed. His mental state was as if all the dry leaves and foliage on the ground had flown up in a storm and then come down whirling. Varsha was Narayanrao Patil's only daughter. His elder son was Anantrao, the Vice Chairman of the Panchayat. He was active in the politics of the taluka. He lived at the seat of the taluka headquarters. Every week he would come once or twice to the village. Just the past year Varsha had got married. Just the other day there had been the fifth month ceremony to celebrate her pregnancy. In just one year, Varsha's appearance had changed. Just as the sky would fill with clouds, her body had filled out and rounded.

Her delicate feet adorned with henna, her rounded and high buttocks, her pregnancy hidden by the folds of her saree, like a moon barely visible through clouds. Bali's gaze fumbled around the area of Varsha's abdomen. He puffed up. On seeing the pregnant Varsha, he was reminded of his mother. Bali picked up his axe. Like a man possessed he started splitting logs, falling on the wood like an enemy.

He should kidnap the Patil's girl. He should bury her alive in the ground and build a hut over her. Bali's strength was splitting like the wood. Axe-blow after axe-blow was smashing into it. Bali neatly arranged the wood he had chopped. He slung his axe on his shoulder and stood by the steps near the door of the sitting room. 'Ma'am, I'm leaving. Give me something.' Bali's voice slipped into the mansion like a cat. A chip of wood had flown down and struck Bali's big toe, which was now covered in blood. The blood had clotted. Bali dug into the mud with the handle of his axe. He stirred the mud and applied it to his wound. After some time Lakshmi the Patil's wife came out.

'Have you finished chopping it all?'

'No, ji. I'll come again tomorrow.'

'Tomorrow we have guests coming. Don't come tomorrow. I'll send word to you again.'

'Ji.'

Bali put forward a fold of his dhoti. Lakshmi the Patil's wife poured some jowar grain into it. She gave him some bhakri wrapped in newspaper. Bali's face brightened with contentment. Limping away, he left the mansion.

Bali reached home. His father was sitting smoking a beedi. Bali went close to his father and sat down in front of him. Chokha Mahar looked carefully at his son.

'What did the Patil's wife give you?'

'I have something to ask you.'

'What, son?'

'About my mother.'

'Meaning?—'

'Is it true that the Patil buried my mother in the mansion?'

'It is true.'

'Then why didn't you tell me?'

'What was the use of telling you? Were you going to bring her back to life?'

'How did you find out?'

'Hey, the entire village found out about it at that time. But who was going to oppose the Patil? The Patil gave me a piece of land and shut my mouth. What was I going to do on my own? And what can you do? The Patil who built the mansion is long dead. His child Narayanrao is close to death. In a year or two he will be in God's house. Why should we go up against him?'

Chokha Mahar was quietly puffing at his beedi. Bali had become very disturbed.

All the stars had come out in the sky. A breeze was blowing. Bali had set out like a storm in the moonlight. The machete in his hand glittered in the silver light. He was going towards the two fields given by the Patil. The thought that he should not do anything opposed to the Patil was constantly gnawing at him. The field had a waving crop in it. Bali reached the field. He put forward his machete. He began to cut the bright green standing crop in the field. The farms all around had become terrified. By dawn, Bali had cut away the entire crop.

Bali had completed his task and come to the dharmasala. Putting the machete by his pillow, he lay down to sleep. He did fall asleep. In the afternoon, someone awakened him. 'Bali, all the crop in your fields has been cut down!' He snapped at the informant and quietly went back to sleep.

In his sleep he had a dream. Bali's mother was arranging the cut crop in heaps. After arranging the heaps she was setting fire to them. The Patil's mansion was burning down to ashes in that fire. Bali woke up. The sun was descending in the sky. He arose and went to his own house. Chokha Mahar was sitting leaning against the wall of the house. Dogs were lying in front of him. Hens were feeding at one side. Bali came there. He splashed water on his face. He looked at his father. He felt pity for him. What could his father have done against the Patil? The Patil would just have removed the thorn that was his father. He himself would have been cast out into the world. But his father had raised him, from boy to manhood. He went and sat down by his father.

That day there was no work. Bali just sat at home. The time was afternoon. On days when there was no work, he grew bored. He set out for the village. He began to roam around the village in the hope that someone would offer him work. One or two women came in his way in the street. Bali stood aside and made space for them to pass. He came close to the village panchayat office. A large crowd had gathered there.

The Panchayat was sitting in the office. The leaders of the village were there. The members of the Panchayat were seated on cushioned seats. Near the steps were seated Lakhu Mahar and Yema Mahar. Narayanrao Patil used to attend the panchayats of all castes, but today he had not come. He had become old. His health, too, was not good. People used to go to the mansion to meet him.

Bali had become numb. He looked towards the mansion. It had been built so large that you could see it from wherever you were. His mother's screams were making him ill. He was beside himself. 'I won't be able to move even a stone of this mansion,' he would tire himself out thinking. He would remember the pregnant Varsha. Her dazzlingly fair and attractive appearance began to torture him. He had to go to the mansion to chop wood. Varsha must come into the courtyard of the mansion, and he must chop her just as he chopped wood. Her child must be killed by beating it on a stone, let happen what would. Bali was being hollowed out by vengeance. As if he had been taken over by termites.

Varsha's fifth month celebration of pregnancy took place. The whole mansion was decorated with electric lights. A feast had been held for the whole village. Bali had been called to the mansion. As he climbed the steps of the mansion, Bali was tortured by thoughts of his mother. He went into the mansion. Narayanrao Patil was sitting on a swing. The mansion was filled with guests and visitors. Bali went and stood like a beggar near the steps of the sitting room. His eyes began to search for Varsha, circling the mansion like those of a predatory animal. Varsha could not be seen anywhere. A house servant came out of the mansion. He had brought some of the sweet food made for Varsha's fifth month ceremony wrapped in a leaf-plate. Bali took it. He saluted the Patil and left the mansion. As Bali stepped out of the mansion, he felt as if he was wearing fetters weighing a ton on his feet.

This sweet food was in fact his mother's funeral feast. This was his rite to remove the bitterness of her death. He was blazing like a roaring fire.

Bali was climbing down from the mansion step by step, and his eyelids were heavy with tears. He thought he should destroy the walls of this mansion, and wake up his mother lying quietly asleep in them; he should call out to his mother; he should embrace her: all this was the play of his imagination.

Varsha might not have been counting the days of her pregnancy, but Bali counted each one of them. As the day of her delivery drew near, he was gradually going crazy. He was weighed down by the thought that he had to take his revenge while she was still pregnant. The ninth month would soon be over. Then after just a bare nine days, she would safely give birth. Once more a surge of happiness would come to the mansion. But that day of happiness would not dawn. This mansion would be bathed in blood. Day and night, Bali dreamt dreams of revenge.

The nine months ended.

Bali set his axe on his shoulder and set out towards the mansion.

It was the day after the night of no moon. The moon had not yet risen. There was a smaller gathering of stars. The breeze was flowing gently. The village was peacefully asleep. A storm was brewing in Bali's steps. Flashes of lightning had started in his head. His eyes looked terrifying, like a blaze of fire. The darkness seemed eerie. The mansion undulated like a mirage.

With great speed Bali raised the axe from his shoulder and made a run at the entrance threshold of the mansion. With just one run the entrance of the mansion fell into two pieces and the threshold came loose. Bali, now delirious, made run after run at the stately door of that stone mansion and the door was now becoming rickety. The tremendous noise of the axe had frightened the whole mansion. Narayanrao Patil was shouting, 'Who's there? Who's there?' Bali made a final run at the door and it crashed to the floor. It slid down the steps and fell on the ground outside, making a great sound. Immediately after, he heard the sound of a baby crying.

Varsha had given birth.

The moon had risen.

Bali disappeared into the darkness like the wind.

16

The Yeskar's Bhakri

Anasa climbed up on the roof of the hut. She spread the *bhakris* that had come from the village on the rooftop to dry. Anasa's husband Nama Mang was the watchman of the village. He used to patrol the village at night, and in return was fed by the village—that was the custom. Compared to others, Nama got along well. The rest of the Mang settlement used to live days of hunger. Nama used to get a pot full of bhakris as the Yeskar of the village. Who was going to eat so many bhakris? He had to dry the heap of bhakris in order to keep them. Sometimes Anasa used to lend out bhakris to friends and neighbours. Nama used to sell off the heap of bhakris to people in need or trouble. The pieces of bhakri were plentiful. If the bhakris were not dried properly, they would smell. They would gather mould.

When the requested bhakris came daily and Anasa had put them out to dry, Shiva would take a stick in his hand and sit to guard them. Otherwise the crows would pick up the bhakris one by one. A flock of crows flew over the heap of bhakris. So what if they were crows, they had stomachs and hunger, too. After she had finished eating, Anasa would put out the bhakris to dry. When the sun descended in the sky, she would remove the bhakris. The entire household sat down to eat in the courtyard of the house in the evening. Nama's household was comfortable and well fed.

There was a garland of tulsi around Nama's neck. Nama was a devotee of Vithoba. He could not eat meat. Nama was a simple, pious man. He never meddled with or took sides with anyone. He was content with his life and his work. What use had he for others' goods or concerns? A person should become one with his work. There should be no comment from anyone; that was all. The village trusted him; he must be faithful to that. He ate the salt of other people. He should be in the mouths of ten people but not stuck in anyone's teeth. What was he going to take away with him from this life? Only two things should go behind him when he died: the good and the bad. When the Marwari Ranglal died, the whole village wept. When Ambya Mahar died, everyone abused and cursed him. Nama Mang would tell many stories like this to those who would listen. If you gave him a pinch of tobacco, or a piece of supari, or the stub of a beedi, the strap of Nama's mouth would start moving.

When evening came it was time to ask for the bhakris. Taking a basket and his Yeskar's staff, Nama would set out to walk the village. Then his young son, Shiva, would begin to cry. He would stubbornly say, 'I'll come, too.' Then Nama Mang would take Shiva along with him to ask for bhakris. He would go and stand in front of every house. 'Mother, let it come, the Yeskar's bhakri,' he would shout. The dogs of the houses would bark and come to attack him. Nama would fend them off with his staff. A woman would come out of each house with a half or a quarter bhakri. From a height sufficient to avoid any contact, she would throw the piece into Nama's basket. And Nama would turn towards the next house to ask for his Yeskar's bhakri.

He would roam the village asking for the bhakris. Some Dada or Appa in the street would give Nama a beedi and make enquiries about Shiva. When Nama went to the Patil's house to ask for bhakris, he would fold his hands in entreaty and say,

'Jowar, mai-baap, jowar.' He would stand there in supplication. The Patil would say in the arrogance of his pride, 'Namya, you bastard, is this how you guard the village? Last night there was a commotion in the Gujars' lane. Pay some attention! Or doesn't your wife let go of you at night?' And Nama would guffaw with laughter. His laughter was in fact his helplessness of seventy generations. Nama would then say with entitlement, 'Give a little curry, Mistress.' 'Why every day, I say,' the Patil's wife would respond, and give him a few leftovers. Nama would fill his mouth with blessings for her, and come down the steps of the mansion.

When he came back home after roaming the village, Anasa would take over the basket with joy. She would kiss Shiva, who had gone to help his father. 'Take note of all the roads; one day you'll have to go round the village yourself,' Nama would stroke his son's back and say. Anasa would sort out the bhakris that had been brought. She would put aside the choice pieces to eat immediately. Nama would wash his hands and feet. Taking the name of Vithoba, he would sit down to eat.

After one nap, Anasa would wake up Nama. 'Get up; it's time to go.' Nama would get up at once. He would splash water on his face. Taking his sword and a torch with batteries, he would set out to guard the village. The entire village was asleep. Anasa would take her child to her belly and consign herself to sleep. Nama would take the road, saying the name of Vithoba. Nama would announce himself loudly with great yells, square after square, lane by lane. Dogs would start barking. Nama's calls would shake the whole village. If a woman heard Nama roaring, barking, shouting, she would get a fit of trembling. Nama, who appeared a meek bovine in the daytime, would seem like a ghost when he roared at night. Half the night would have passed. The whole village would be asleep. Nama's yells, however, would protect the village. Going lane by lane in the night, Nama would call out anyone's name, shout it out. But no one had the courage to open the door at night and look at him.

If there were thefts or other crimes at night, Nama would be held responsible for them. During the past month there had been a burglary at the Marwadi's. Nama solved the crime in a week. Thieves were frightened of Nama.

In the afternoon, however, Nama would sleep. He always made a mess of his sleep at night in order to guard the village. So he needed to sleep in the daytime. While Nama slept, Anasa would not allow Shiva to play noisily. When Nama slept he would start snoring. When a servant like an elephant begins to snore, there would be a huge noise. Shiva would marvel at his father's snoring. He would pester his mother. 'Mother, why is my father snoring? When will I begin to snore?' He would ask her many such silly questions. Answering and explaining to her son again and again, Anasa was close to tears.

In the afternoons when Nama would sleep, Anasa would sit among the women, chatting about their life experiences. Just then the Patil's Mahar servant, the bastard, came along. The Patil had summoned Nama. Anasa promptly went and woke up her husband. Nama sat up, stretching from side to side. He splashed some water on his face and went off to the Patil's mansion with the man. Anasa went back and sat among the women.

Some people were assembled at the Patil's mansion. There had been an invasion at the Marwari's house the previous night. When Nama heard of the burglary his heart skipped a beat. The Patil sat Nama down in front of him and fired a fusillade of questions. 'You bastard, I told you just a couple of days ago: pay a little attention to the Gujar's house. You eat off the village, but you can't look after it! How did this burglary happen? It must have been with your help! Till today no burglar had set foot in this village. It was you who set them to do this. You must be getting something out of this; that's why you paid no attention to the Gujar's house last night. The burglars stole goods; I know nothing more. I want the stolen goods in front of me within this week. I will not digest a loss.

You are the Mang of this village. How can we have a boundary fence eating up the crop?' The Patil was speaking in a great temper.

Nama Mang was disturbed. He couldn't think straight. He would just have to say 'Yes' to the Patil. How could he say no? But how would he catch the burglar? Whose name should he take? Nama thought he would go mad. He went to one village each day. He would search every last trace of each Maharwada, each Mangwada in those villages. And he would come back with empty hands. Because Nama Mang was going out to other villages, Anasa would go out for the daily collection of bhakri in the village herself. Shiva would be with her. Nama would search a couple of villages and come home. Then he would patrol the village as usual. No glow remained on Nama's face. He could not find the slightest trace of the burglar. In the daytime he would wander the neighbouring villages to find clues; at night he would remain on duty to patrol the village. In eight days, Nama was tired out.

The week ended. Once again, Satva, the house Mahar came to call him. Nama was shaken to the roots. He could not think what to tell the Patil. Tears welled up in Anasa's eyes. Nama Mang went off to the Patil's mansion with Satva Mahar. A number of people had collected at the mansion. The moment they reached there, the Patil started yelling, 'What happened? Did you find it?' Nama sat down with a lowered gaze. 'Speak, you bastard! Tell me what happened.' What could Nama say to the Patil? Several village louts took Nama to the cowshed. Satva Mahar was the first to lay his hands upon Nama. Then the blows began to rain down on him. Nama was bellowing like an animal. People were beating him with iron chains, staves and slippers. Nama was shouting, 'Master, save me! Aagh!'

The Patil roared like a supernatural, 'Bastard, say who did the burglary and save yourself! Say who did it! Point your hand even now. You're not taking his name.' Now that they had the Patil's permission, once again they all fell upon Nama to be loyal to the Patil's salt. Otherwise they would all be in the same plight as Nama.

When night fell, Satva Mahar brought Nama home and left him there. Nama was swollen all over. His mouth was twisted and swollen. His head was wounded. There were bloodied weals all over his arms and legs. Nama was moaning. Seeing him all of a sudden like this, Anasa could not understand what had happened to her husband. Tears rained out of her. Falling on her husband's body, she began to cry. A few sympathetic women gathered. They felt a pang in their hearts.

In the middle of the night Nama woke up. He was finding it difficult to get up. Anasa rose in a hurry. Nama set out from the house. Anasa stood in his way. With tears in his eyes, he said, 'Anasa, let me go. Otherwise I'll be tortured again like this tomorrow. How can I catch the thief? Whose name shall I take? They will belabour him, too, just like me. The village has spoilt my name by accusing me. I just want to go to the settlement. You don't worry. Now go, or Shiva will wake up.' Wiping her tears, Anasa went and sat by Shiva. Nama disappeared into the darkness. A loud and long-lasting uproar from the dogs could be heard. The dogs were taking great bites of the darkness. The night was turning into an enemy. The owls sitting on the bitter lime tree had begun to screech. Anasa grew anxious. The screeching of owls meant that something bad was going to happen. Anasa grew breathless with fear. Just then there was the sound of a horse's hooves, and it came and stopped at the door. It was the Patil's voice. Anasa went forward. He said intimidatingly, 'Where has Nama gone? Who will patrol the village now?' The Patil was in a bad temper. Anasa didn't know what to say. Fearfully, she said,

'He's gone to the settlement.'

'To share out the stolen property?'

'No, Master. He went to see if he could find any trace of the theft.'

'Has the day dawned then? Now who will patrol the village? You survive on the village. How is it you know how to ask for bhakris?'

Anasa recoiled as if she had been slapped on the face. How was she to argue with the Patil? The Mahar was standing there with a stave. Turning his horse, the Patil said, 'If anything further happens in the village, there will be no response worse than mine. Let anyone who wants to guard the village. *You* guard it.' The Patil went off on his horse. Satva Mahar ran after him.

Anasa took the sword in her hand. She took up the torch. She woke up Shiva from his sleep, and she set out to patrol the village. Anasa's shouts rang out over the whole village. Her shouts meant her screams. Anasa was shouting. She was terrified. Anasa was wandering the streets with Shiva. Anasa shouted outside the Patil's mansion. The mansion was torn with her shouts. She cast a beam from the torchlight across the mansion. There was uproar from the dogs. Shiva was heavy with sleep. Anasa was patrolling the village. Today her husband's ardour for the work had surged within her.

When Anasa lay down on her bed in the morning, she had stiffened. To be guarding the village for some half-eaten leftovers? What tyranny was this! Shiva was asleep. Her neighbour Sona came crying to the house. Falling on Anasa's neck, she let out a great sob. Nama Mang had hanged himself.

Lavha Mang had come to ask for the Yeskar's staff. The work of the Yeskar had been given to Lavha Mang. When handing over the staff, a support like a husband, to Lavha Mang, Anasa was reminded of her widowhood. Her eyes brimmed with tears. Shiva was crying because the Yeskar's staff was going to another house. She held Shiva close to her bosom; he felt to her like the Yeskar's staff. Anasa gave way to her sobs.

Because the Yeskar's staff had come into her house, Maina, Lavha Mang's wife, was doing a puja to it.

17

The Saintly Man

For breaking down a tree in the village moneylender's field, a case was filed against our father, and the police caught hold of him and took him away. Later, we found out that our father had been punished. He had been put in jail. That day we cried a lot. Mother borrowed some money and went to visit father. We did not have money for the fare, so we could not go. The police had beaten father badly. There were weals all over his body. Mother told us of the trouble father was undergoing and cried. I wanted to strangle the police, but I was too young to do anything. Mother would take me close to her. She would search my head for lice. There would be boils on my head. Mother made a vow to the goddess Ambabai. There were worms in the boils. This was the anger of the goddess, she said. I would sit close to Mother.

'You will grow up one day. You will be big. You will take revenge for your father.' Mother would say things like this to me as she searched my head for lice. I, too, felt that I should grow up quickly. I should grow a beard and moustache. I once shaved myself with an old razor, just so my beard would grow fast. I used to think that once a man grew a beard and moustache, he was big.

After father went to jail, we suffered a lot. Mother had to run the house on her own. The house had ten mouths to feed. One can't live on dirt. Sometimes we had food, and sometimes we went to sleep hungry. Mother would take us to her bosom and cry. We would feel hungry. There would be nothing at home to eat. We would desperately think of what we could eat. We would cry. So would Mother. Then Mother's crying, more than our hunger, would make us desolate. In order to eat, we had to steal. We were afraid of our thieving, and ashamed, too. But hunger was stronger than fear. When we grew hungry, we could understand nothing.

Take the matter of yesterday. A dog was running with a bhakri in its mouth. I set off after the dog. The dog went out of the village. I was still after it. There was a stone in my hand. I couldn't wait to catch the dog and pull the bhakri out of its mouth. I would throw the stone at it, but the running dog would not stop. At last the dog joined a pack. I had stolen its earnings. I took the bhakri from the dog's mouth. The part which was held in its mouth I left to him. I took the rest of the bhakri to the river and washed it. Then I sat on the sand and ate it.

After eating the bhakri I remembered Mother. I had eaten the bhakri without sharing it with her; I felt very bad about that. But I rationalised to myself. If one ate something that had been in a dog's mouth, one went mad. If anyone was to go mad, let it be me alone. Not Mai. If she were to die, who would look after my brothers and sisters? My father would be freed some day, and come home. The memory of my father made me cry.

Baja-nana had reported that my father cut that tree. Baja-nana was the moneylender's Dalit labourer from the village. Mai always uttered curses against Baja-nana. She would flick her fingers at him or throw dirt at him. 'Bajjya caught my husband and handed him over. His wife will become a widow, too. God above sees everything. We did not destroy anyone's house. We only stole because of hunger,' she would say and cry.

The moneylender was held in awe in our village. Heaps of livestock, a hundred acres of fields, a huge mansion: that was his splendour. When he went by on his horse, the whole village would bow. As for us, if we heard the moneylender's name we would be terrified. I have never as yet seen the moneylender. Mother used to say, 'He is a rakshasa.' Sometimes when the moneylender's men would drag away poor folk, we would be appalled. The moneylender's business was loansharking. Some people would have taken a loan from the moneylender and not repaid the money. Then the moneylender's men would come. They would take hold of the man who owed the debt and drag him away. They would lay kicks and blows on him. There would be a commotion in the lane. As for the man they took away, everyone at his house would weep and wail as if there had been a death in the family. Just seeing that would make us cry, too. It was in the field of such a moneylender that our father had cut down a tree.

Actually, one should steal from a poor man. A poor man does not make a complaint. A man who steals from a rich man is always caught. Who in this world listens to a poor man?

The moneylender's men commit atrocities every day. But who ever goes against them? 'A poor man's daughter-in-law is everybody's wife,' was the custom of this village. Who would question a rich man? He has money. The government, too, is his. I would sometimes think, I should grow up quickly, creep into the mansion and murder the moneylender. A teacher used to go to the moneylender's mansion to give school lessons. I used to think, I must become a teacher. I used to go to school daily; I never missed a day. Letters would come from jail from my father. In them he wrote that I should not miss my school.

For many days now, no cattle had died. Mother had a wish to eat meat shakuti. Our stock of dried meat was finished. It was my habit from childhood to eat bhakris fried in fat. The cat had run away with the pieces soaked in fat. Just the other day Mother had brought some tasty things, which had not been enough for any of us. The people in our house were well-fed people. If it came to his mind, my father would take anyone's buffalo or cow and give it poison and slaughter it. Sometimes he would go to a distant village to see a suitable animal. A few people would go to that village at night. They would catch the animal in the dark and slaughter it in the field. By dawn they would have distributed the portions and be free. As the day dawned mutton would be cooking on everyone's fires. Animals used to be stolen in the dark. Pieces of meat would be drying in everyone's houses.

Mother would say, it's been a long time since we ate shakuti. The animals won't die, nor does the butcher come here. The butcher used to visit our village once every month or two. Nowadays even he didn't come. The village had barred his entry since he did not give the *patti* for the fair.

I thought, I ought to poison the moneylender's buffalo. It was afternoon. After school we went to the river to catch fish. We always kept to our downslope to catch them. As we caught them, we went to the upriver slope. The people of the village filled water at the upriver slope. The downriver slope was where we filled ours. We used to wash buffaloes in the river. Among them was the moneylender's buffalo. In the four or five villages around, he was the only male buffalo. I had scanned him well. If the poison had to be given, it had to be to this male buffalo. We had to kill the buffalo of the man who had sent our father to jail.

The buffalo would last us fifteen days.

We fed the poison to the buffalo and were off. The moneylender's man would come to the Maharwada by evening. Then the village Mahars would go. They would drag the dead buffalo here. Then they would take it and skin it in the field used for ablutions. We would get as much shakuti as we wanted. We would get the skin for a drum. But four people would not be enough to carry the dead animal. It would have to be put into a cart and brought here. We would have to miss school tomorrow.

In the evening Baja-nana came by, his face white. After some time the women and the babies began to cry. The moneylender's male buffalo had died. About ten of the moneylender's men had come with sticks and machetes in their hands. The women and children fled to the forest. Those men were going to houses and dragging out the able-bodied men. They caught hold of about twenty-five men and took them to the village square. Mother was sitting quietly in her hut. I was firm. I evaded mother's eyes and stepped out direct into the square. In front of me was a woman coming with a pot of water on her head. Saying 'Shiva, Shiva,' I made way for her.

People had gathered in the square. There was an uproar. Baja-nana was standing at a distance. The moneylender's men, with whips in their hands, were asking: 'Tell us, who gave the poison to the buffalo?'

In a flash they tied everyone to pillars. The Mahar men were falling at their feet, begging for mercy. But no one was listening to them. They started flogging them all with their whips. They must have flogged my father like this, too. The next day they buried the male buffalo in the moneylender's field. All that beating was given to everybody for nothing at all. Nobody's name came out as a result of it. For a whole month, the village was gloomy about the death of the moneylender's buffalo. The beating with the hunter laid Pandu low on the ground. No one took any care of him. All these people have a butcher's heart. The whole Maharwada was grinding its teeth at Baja-nana. Everyone was angry with him for taking the moneylender's crust, coming here and going and repeating there all the things he had heard. 'If Bajja dies no one will come to his funeral. His corpse will just lie there. No one will touch him. They won't give him a place in the burial-ground. A stink will rise from his body. He is acting against the caste,' Mother used to tell me as she served me food.

One must poison Baja-nana, too. He was a son of a buffalo. Baja-nana was against the caste, but his relative Pandu was with us. He, too, had been beaten when the buffalo died. Even now he was laid low on the ground.

Baja-nana died suddenly. We never understood how he went from being fit to dying. Right till yesterday he was walking around. Then at night he said his stomach was hurting, and by dawn he was dead. In the morning a caste panchayat sat. Baja-nana's Pandu begged pardon for him with folded hands. They agreed to a penalty. Then everyone together gave Baja-nana a funeral. There was one small obstacle. Now where was the moneylender to get an honest Mahar like Baja-nana? What did the moneylender lack? He would bring a Mahar from another village into this one. He would set up a hut for him. Anyone would jump at the chance if called by the moneylender. In fact, it was our family's turn now to act as Mahar for the moneylender. But our father was in jail.

The next day our father came home, freed from jail. He went to the moneylender's house and gave him a salute. The moneylender levied a penalty and freed him from his offence. Thereafter our father registered his presence daily at the moneylender's mansion with scrupulous regularity. Every evening there would be very good things to eat. My mother, too, started going to the moneylender's mansion every day to sweep it. The moneylender was truly a saintly man.

18

War

Because he was wounded in the India-Pak war, Bhagwan was invalided out of military service. He was also given a job in a bank, and a plot of government land. His village's name was Sultanpur. Sultanpur was jealous of Bhagwan's good fortune. He would go daily to Borgaon on a motorcycle. He would do his job. When office got over, he would make for Sultanpur on his motorcycle. The distance from Sultanpur to Borgaon took one and a half hours to cover.

Bhagwan's father's name was Sadashiv. He would do Mahar work for the village deshmukh. While Bhagwan was in the army, his family survived on the deshmukh's leftovers. Bhagwan's sister Bhagirathi worked at the deshmukh's mansion along with her father. She was still to be married. Bhagwan had ended his father's Mahar work. But Bhagirathi would still go to the mansion from time to time and work there. Everyone called her Bhagi.

Bhagwan had got married. His wife Ranjana was from Borgaon. Bhagwan's first child was a son. He had named him Bharat.

There had been changes in Bhimnagar on account of Bhagwan. Children started going regularly to school. Bhagwan used to teach the schoolchildren a drill. When a conversation got going he would tell people interesting things about the war. He would tell Ranjana about his life in the army. He would tell Bharat stories about heroes until he fell asleep. Sometimes he would drink rum. After drinking rum he would sing songs from Hindi films until very late. His military character would show even in small details.

The deshmukh had called Bhagwan over to the mansion. Climbing up the steps of the mansion, Bhagwan remembered his past. In his childhood he would come to the mansion with his mother, clutching her finger. His mother would clean the cowshed. She would sweep the mansion. Bhagwan would remain sitting near the heap of swept up dirt. When his mother heard that Bhagwan had been injured in the war, she lost her life. The memory of his mother brought tears to Bhagwan's eyes.

Bhagwan went to the mansion. The deshmukh was puffing at his hookah. Bhagwan gave him a grand military salute. The deshmukh was provoked. He did not like Bhagwan's martial airs. To tell you the truth, this Mahar brat should have bent down and done a proper obeisance. By stopping his father's Mahar duties Bhagwan had created a great inconvenience. 'Deshmukh, now my father won't do the Mahar work. The government has given me a field. It has given me a job. Now we longer have any need for the Mahar's village jobs. It does not please me that my father should do such low work. I am a soldier.' Bhagwan's answers had hurt the deshmukh. Bhagwan's father used to call the deshmukh 'Master', but Bhagwan had called him 'Deshmukh'. It was an insult to him. The deshmukh controlled himself.

'Bhagwan, it was I who paid the expense of your education. When you went into the army, I paid your train fare. You are young. There is no quarrel between us. I have only one thing to tell you. Don't stop your father's village duties. If Mahars stop doing their work, then who will do it? You must also think of the village.'

'Deshmukh, my father is not the only man in the village. If you pay, anyone will do the work. There is no law that only the Mahars must do it.'

'Boy, don't teach me the law. People should not forget their caste. They should remain on their own step on the ladder. Do you understand?'

'See here, Deshmukh, these are no longer the old days. Mahars have now become soldiers. They have become teachers. They have become lawyers.'

Bhagwan's words had fallen like a bolt of lightning. Deshmukh had been injured.

The deshmukh's dog came from the cowshed and started barking at Bhagwan. The deshmukh stroked his back and said, 'Moti, this is our Mahar. Don't bark at him.' Bhagwan was offended. He took out a cigarette and lit it.

While Bhagwan was smoking his cigarette, the village priest Moropant arrived. He looked at Bhagwan with a curious gaze.

'What, Deshmukh, who's this?'

'Oh, Pantji, keep your distance. You'll get polluted. Did you recognise him? This is our Sadashiv's son. He is a soldier.'

'Yes, I remember. He is the Mahar Sada's son. He's grown up. I see. I see.'

The deshmukh's son Ratan came down the stairs. He was on his way out. The deshmukh halted him. 'Oh, Ratan, the priest is here. Bring some cow's milk for him and ask them to make some tea for Bhagwan.' Saying 'All right,' Ratan went inside.

The priest slyly teased Bhagwan, 'It was your good fortune that you took an enemy bullet. You got farmland; you got a job.' Bhagwan understood the scorn in the priest's words. 'Yes, what you say is right. But not everyone gets the opportunity to fight for the country at the border.' Bhagwan's answer had made the priest speechless. Ratan brought the cup of milk and gave it to the priest, then went off into the village. While going, he cast a sidelong glance at Bhagwan.

Bhagwan lit a second cigarette. He remembered his childhood. He used to come to the mansion with his mother. When her work was over, the deshmukh's wife would give her tea. Bhagwan had a memory of his mother. When the deshmukh's wife brought the tea, Bhagwan's mother would bring a cup and saucer and a water *tambya* from the corner. The deshmukh's wife would serve her water from a little height, and the tea also in the same manner. Bhagwan's mother would feed him a little tea, first blowing on it to cool it.

The deshmukh's wife brought the tea. Bhagwan looked at her. In feature and complexion she had not changed at all. Only her hair had whitened in front. 'Hey, Bhagwan, how big you've grown!' Her voice was full of affection.

'Just pick up that saucer from the corner.'

'I'll drink the tea if you give it in a good saucer. Otherwise I won't.'

'Oh, all right. Use this saucer. It seems you haven't lost the stubbornness you had as a child.'

'Silly woman, he's no longer the former Bhagwan. He's changed a lot.'

'Education and town living spoil a man.'

'You're making baseless accusations. It's because of the military culture that he has changed.'

Bhagwan was drinking his tea, listening to this discussion about himself.

After drinking his tea, Bhagwan took his leave of the deshmukh. The deshmukh's wife brought a *tambya* full of water and poured it from above over the cup and saucer from which he had drunk his tea. The cup and saucer were left lying there.

'The Mahars have become too full of themselves,' said the priest, scornfully expressing his opinion.

'That is true, Pant. Sometimes it seems as if we are living in a foreign country. Our word does not count for anything here. But the minorities are being pampered. Compared to this, the British were better. When we said, don't take the Dalits into the army, their recruitment was stopped. Here it's our government, our elected representatives, and all for the benefit of Mahars and Mangs. The Dalits' brats are becoming officers; ours are unemployed. What kind of justice is this?'

'It is social justice.'

'Social justice is just another form of cultural vendetta.'

'Absolutely right.'

Bhagirathi came in on stealthy feet. From time to time she would come, do a chore and go away.

'Bhagi, just break this cup and saucer.'

'But they are good.'

'Just do as you are told. Go.'

Bhagirathi picked up the cup and saucer from which Bhagwan had drunk and went to the cowshed. The priest also left. The deshmukh lighted his hookah again. The dog was lying there peacefully.

Sadashiv came in with soft steps. He came as a cat would have come in order to drink some milk. Bhagwan might well have ended the jobs of his father and sister, but Sada and Bhagi still came to the mansion. They felt uneasy unless they came there. Sada felt uncomfortable without the curses the deshmukh gave him, and tea from the deshmukh's wife. Once Bhagwan went to Borgaon, Sada would go to the deshmukh's mansion.

'My respects, master.' Sada bowed, and went and sat quietly by the steps like a beggar.

'If you Mahars stop performing your village duties, how will things work? Then you will have to close down the village.'

'But Mahars will be available.'

'Haven't all Mahars made the same decision?'

'I've called a Mahar from Savargaon. He's coming tomorrow. He is my cousin. He is good at his work and he's an honest man. He'll come to work from tomorrow.'

'Someone will do the work. That won't remain undone because someone is missing. That's not the question.'

'The caste panchayat has decided that we must not do demeaning work.'

'A Mahar won't become a Brahmin just by giving up demeaning work. You will still have to live outside the village. Or are you coming to live in the village?'

'No, master.'

'Who can tell? Your son is a soldier. Tomorrow he may even invade our house.'

'No, master. We've eaten the salt of this house.'

'Never mind. Never mind. Just bathe that dog.'

'Yes, master.'

Sada woke up the sleeping dog. He caught hold of its leash and awakened it. At once the dog slipped out of Sada's grasp and moved towards the deshmukh. The deshmukh shooed it away. 'Hey, Sadya, catch hold of the dog! Don't let go of it. Give it a bath. Otherwise it will pollute everybody. Didn't it touch you?'

'Yes, master.'

Sada tried to catch the dog, but it evaded him. Sadya went after the dog. But it gave him a wide berth. Bounding, it went to the deshmukh again. The deshmukh picked up a stick and shooed it away. The dog slid back a few paces and started barking at the deshmukh.

'Now the dogs, too, have started barking back at us.'

'He is just an animal, master. What does he understand of high and low?'

The deshmukh got up from his place. He took down the rifle that hung on the wall of the mansion and fired at the dog. The dog dropped on the ground and started to writhe. At the sound of the rifle, the wild pigeons perched on the walls of the mansion flew away. Sadya was looking in terror at the dog. Bhagi came running. The deshmukh's wife came running, too.

'Sadya, drag that dog away.'

'Yes, master.'

Sadya was stuttering with fear. The dog had died. Sadya looked at the dog with tear-filled eyes. Bhagi helped her father lift the dog. Sadya picked up the dog. He went out of the mansion grounds. The dog's blood lay in the courtyard. Bhagi washed the entire courtyard.

The pigeons came back and perched on the wall of the courtyard. The deshmukh began to read the paper. Bhagi began to work in the courtyard. The deshmukh's wife, however, was sitting in the puja room in front of the images of gods, praying.

The next morning at daybreak, Pandurang Mahar from Savargaon together with Sadashiv reached the deshmukh's mansion.

'Master, your Mahar has come,' Sadashiv called out loudly. At that, a voice came from inside the house: 'Who wants to see a Mahar's face so early in the morning? The day will go badly. Go and sit in the cowshed. When a Brahmin has come and gone, asking for the daily donation, you can come here.'

'Yes, master,' said Pandu and Sadya with one voice before going away to the cowshed.

In a little while, the Brahmin came and went. The deshmukh came and sat outside. He lit his hookah. Pandu and Sadya came forward, cowering. They both saluted him. Sadya introduced Pandu. The deshmukh scanned Pandu. Pandu showed as much helplessness on his face as he could.

'How many children do you have?'

'Just one. He's going to school.'

'Then no. Sadya, bring me another Mahar. I can't afford this one.'

'Master, Pandu-dada is an honest man. Why would I bring you a bad person?'

'Were you any less honest? I don't want a Mahar who is educating his son. This man's son will also go into the army.'

'No, I won't send him to the army.'

'But you will send him to school anyway. Once a person has studied four classes he behaves as if he has forgotten his traditions.'

'I'll stop the boy's school. What's he going to become by studying? A barrister? Give him a job, too.'

'Ha! This is the kind of Mahar I want. After you, your son should continue the Mahar work. Isn't that right?'

'Yes, master.'

'Sadya, where shall we arrange for him to live?'

'He'll stay behind our house. After building a hut.'

'All right. Let him start work from today.'

Pandu was as happy as if heaven had entered his grasp. Pandu had his first vision of the deshmukh couple.

'Sit down, the two of you. Drink some tea and then start your work.'

'Yes, master.'

Pandu and Sadya sat down near the steps. Sadya showed Pandu a niche in the wall.

'Our vessels are there.'

With a slight gesture of his neck, Pandu indicated that he had understood. The deshmukh was smoking his hookah. Sadya and Pandu were gazing fixedly at the deshmukh. The deshmukh spread the news throughout the village that he had a new Mahar.

Pandu built a new hut for himself in Bhimnagar and started his Mahar work for the deshmukh. Bhimnagar became restless. Bhagwan was furious.

'We have all given up Mahar work. You, too, will have to give up demeaning work.'

'I'm doing the deshmukh's work because he's feeding me. Are you going to run my household? I am ready to remove people's shit in order to earn food. I am not stealing from anyone.'

Pandu had the deshmukh's power behind him. That's why Pandu spoke without hesitation.

The news spread in Bhimnagar that Bhagi was pregnant by the deshmukh's son. Pandu had broken this news. Ranjana brought this news to Bhagwan's ears. Bhagwan went crazy with rage. He did not go to the office that day. He was writhing inwardly. Bhagi was sweeping the courtyard. He called her to him and asked her, 'Bhagi, are you pregnant by the deshmukh's son?' Bhagi was embarrassed. Bhagwan's eyes were bloodshot. 'Tell me, Bhagi.' Bhagwan's voice was trembling. Bhagi was frightened. She shook her head to signify 'No'. Bhagwan was enraged. He picked up an axe from the corner. 'Bhagi, tell the truth. Or I'll cut you into seventeen pieces.' Bhagi began to cry. Bhagwan shouted, 'I need an answer!' Sadashiv came forward. Bhagi took shelter behind her father. Ranjana was standing near Bhagwan. The household was terrified.

Sadashiv put Bhagi behind him. 'Yes, Bhagi has gone astray.' Sadashiv was admitting the crime like a convict. 'Bhagi has destroyed my honour,' said Bhagwan and began to cry uncontrollably. Ranjana took the axe out of her husband's hand. 'Go to work. Don't put ashes on your own head. We can abort Bhagi's child. No one knows about it yet.'

Bhagwan took out a bottle of liquor. Ranjana said, 'Don't drink.' Bhagwan swore at her. Sadashiv, numbed, was sitting in the corner. Bhagi was sitting close to her father. Ranjana, looking desolate, was looking at her husband. Bhagwan was surrendering to the liquor. The sun was above their heads. The afternoon was blazing.

Bhagwan rose up like a storm. He took hold of Bhagi's hand. Bhagi began to cry. Sadashiv clasped Bhagwan's legs in supplication. Ranjana came in between. Bhagwan picked up Bhagi as he would pick up a rifle. 'Bhagi, dry your eyes. We have to go to the deshmukh's mansion.'

'Don't go to the village, I beg you. The village has you on its radar.' Ranjana stood in her husband's way, obstructing him. Bhagwan kicked her aside and set out in the direction of the village.

Bhagwan slipped into the grounds of the mansion. Bhagi was frightened. It was afternoon. The deshmukh was resting. With military intensity Bhagwan shouted, 'Hey, Deshmukh, come out!' Bhagwan's voice resonated in the mansion. This was a crack in the traditional stone foundation. The mansion had never heard such a frightening voice. The deshmukh came out. His wife followed him. Bhagwan appeared like a raging fire. 'Deshmukh, my sister is pregnant from your brat of a son.' Bhagwan's voice was thudding like the explosions from a warehouse full of cannonballs. The deshmukh and his wife stood there like prisoners of war. 'Deshmukh, you will accept my sister as your daughter-in-law. Go, Bhagi, go into your house. Deshmukh, if anything happens to my sister, I shall set this mansion on fire. Bhagi went and stood by the deshmukh's wife. The deshmukh's wife drew her close.

Bhagwan went away at speed.

The news that Bhagwan had inserted his sister into the mansion spread through the village in a moment. The whole village went to the deshmukh's mansion. The deshmukh looked like a ravening beast of prey. The crowd had boiled up in the mansion. As if a crowd of ferocious beasts had gathered there. Bhagi had been locked up in the cowshed. A session of the village leaders now started in the mansion.

Moropant enunciated in clear and ringing tones: 'Just because a Mahar woman has become pregnant, can she be acknowledged as a daughter-in-law? It is enough that she has been pushed into someone's house. She is not the first Mahar woman in the village to become pregnant by a young man. We should abort her and give her some money. At the most, she should bring up the child and live outside the village as a kept woman. She can be given her food and drink.'

'The Mahars have become insolent. They must be taught a lesson.' People added voice to voice. The crowd had become wild and uncontrolled. The deshmukh gave a verdict. 'Whatever happens, remove the thorn of Bhagwan. It is he who has spoilt the Mahars. I don't care if I lose half my estate. I'll get it restored through the courts.' Hearing the deshmukh's determination, the crowd became delirious. The leaders came to a decision and arose. The deshmukh's son had a rifle in his hands. Others had staves, axes, swords and knives. The crowd had become violent. Each of them was losing his senses with rage.

Some people dragged Bhagi out of the place where she had been locked up. People jeered at her, saying, 'Make way, the daughter-in-law is here.' The tears had fled from Bhagi's eyes. One person pulled at the end of her saree. A second, a third, a fourth grabbed her clothes. In a moment she had been stripped naked, and a procession with her naked body had set out in front of the mansion.

Bhagi was screaming. The crowd was after her. In broad daylight, Bhagi's naked procession was going towards Bhimnagar through the main street. On the way they came to a Rama temple. The crowd shouted in praise of Rama.

The crowd entered Bhimnagar. They seized Bhagwan's hut. They locked the door. Sadya and Ranjana were crying out. Hooligans had encircled Bhagwan. In a moment they set fire to his hut. The flames rose up to meet the sky, and taking their lives in their hands, the people of the settlement started running in every direction.

Bhagwan's hut had been burnt to ashes. Four or five huts nearby had also been burnt. Bhagwan's wife and father had also been burnt to cinders. Bhagwan was groaning with pain. Bhagi had disappeared.

The leaders of the village had taken out Bhagwan's eyes.

The school had just dispersed. Children from the settlement were running home. They got to the settlement, but there was no one there. They could not understand. Bharat stood next to his father, asking, 'Where has my mother gone? What happened to you?' The children from the settlement came together. They were all gathered in Bhagwan's courtyard. The fire from the burnt hut was smouldering.

Bhagwan heard the children's voices. He forgot his pain. He got to his feet and stood up. In military style, Bhagwan began to give the children drill commands. All the children stood to attention.

Bhagwan's voice penetrated the skies, and the children stood facing the village, in an attitude of war.

19

Caste

I can't tell you now exactly when my friendship with Hanmya began. But Hanmya was my first friend in Solapur, and one to whom I had grown extremely close. We had both come here to college. He lived in the hostel. I had taken a room in the town. I sometimes visited his room, and sometimes he came to mine. He used my notes on occasion as occasionally I did his. We met without fail in the library. We became close friends during the college elections. I was standing for the post of class representative. Hanmya had got me the votes from the hostel; since then we used to get together for tea, for a chat, or to study.

In Hanmya's persona there was an absence of the usual distinctive features, spoken language and complexion which are unique to the Mahars and Mangs. Even so, when he spoke, from time to time there would unconsciously be a Mahar-like drawl. Hanmya was a Mahar; I was a Lingayat, the son of a sarpanch. We had sugarcane fields. I had plenty of money. I would treat Hanmya to food and drink. And have his company on walks. Hanmya had a well-built body, so he felt like a bodyguard to me. He did odd jobs for me, too. I had given him my old pants. Sometimes I would give him a meal. Hanmya was a good sportsman. He also wrote poetry and so on. On account of that, he had made many acquaintances among the students.

Hanmya's sister was getting married. Hanmya had given me a printed invitation. I wanted to see Hanmya's house and village. I went to the wedding. But there was inconvenience for everyone on my account. How would I eat their food? How could I sleep in their house? I was from the Lingayat caste; would rules about touch apply? Suppose this got known at my house? Countless questions like these confronted them. Everyone looked at me with curiosity. They acted respectfully. I, too, was confused. I felt acutely that I was different from them. They cooked separate food for me. They had made separate arrangements for my stay. I felt disgusted by their poverty. I felt suffocated when I drank water from their house. The mouthfuls of food I took refused to go down my throat.

I was living at a Mahar's house, eating Mahar food. The thought scared me. I couldn't wait to leave. I stayed for a day, then came home. Hanmya's father and mother looked like the servants who toiled at my home. Some days passed.

Recently Hanmya's father came over. He came to my room. He was not ready to accept me as his son's friend. He sat near my shoes. He would say, 'Yes, master. Yes, master.' He was not ready to forget his status as a Mahar, and mine as the son of a Patil family. I gave him tea to drink. He refused to drink from the cup and saucer that I used. Finally he drank from it. He washed the cup and saucer. Then he humbly folded his hands before leaving. I was reminded of Laksha Mahar of our village.

Sugar was being processed in the boiling pans in our fields. A letter came from the village, and I felt like going to the village with Hanmya. His acceptance of the invitation arrived. But his caste would get in the way. At home, my father had old customs and old ways of thought. He would first ask Hanmya's name, then his caste. Once he heard that Hanmya was a Mahar, he would throw him out. Also, I would be punished. If we told him that Hanmya was a Lingayat, well, my father had many acquaintances in our caste. If he started asking questions about acquaintances, it would be awkward for Hanmya. So Hanmya and I compromised. We found a solution.

The caste of people who most commonly visited our house was the Dhangar, or the shepherd caste. The Dhangars came to our house, but their visit was not polluting for us. My father was not so strict about other castes, with the exception of Mahars and Mangs. But Hanmya began to cringe at the idea of calling himself a Dhangar. Suppose his true caste came to be known? Suppose he met someone known to him? I kept renewing Hanmya's courage. Hanmya and I went to my village.

Hanmya appeared scared in my house. He was frightened to come into the prayer room. Hanmya and I went out to the fields. We strolled around the village. We went to the temple and took a darshan of the god. My mother was very affectionate towards Hanmya. She gave him a lot to eat and drink. But Hanmya was not relaxed in his conversation. And at night he did not sleep for a long time. He looked very uneasy.

If anyone new came to the house, they would make enquiries of Hanmya. Before he could respond, I would tell them Hanmya's name. I would say his caste was Dhangar. There was a Dhangar man working in one of our fields. He was full of admiration for Hanmya. He had relatives who lived in Hanmya's village. One day he came to our house and started asking Hanmya about his relatives. Hanmya panicked.

I quickly intervened and said, 'Hanmya has been at school in Solapur since childhood. That's why he doesn't know much about the village.' The discussion ended there. Hanmya had escaped one calamity. It was our plan to stay in the village for two or three days. But Hanmya was already growing uneasy. Everyone in the house called Hanmya 'Pujari'. We had told everyone that his name was 'Pujari'.

Once my father came to me. He had brought the usual large lumps of jaggery to sell in Solapur. My father was to stay in my room for two days. The Dhangar worker from our fields was with my father. He had been brought along as the jaggery shaper. Under his hands the jaggery lumps came out just right. He had an urge to meet Hanmya. Hanmya was young, he was a student, and in the future some girl from his family could be offered to Hanmya in marriage. This was his reckoning.

My father, our jaggery maker and I went off to Hanmya's. At first I went off on my own, saying I would check whether Pujari was at home. Hanmya and his roommate were sitting and chatting. I called Hanmya outside and told him that my father had come to meet him. Hanmya looked rather alarmed. I called my father in. Hanmya had gone back into the room and was hurriedly tidying it up.

I circled my gaze around the room.

The photograph of Dr. Babasaheb Ambedkar that Hanmya had hidden was still visible. He had taken down two posters of actresses that had been on the wall. Hanmya's nervousness could be seen on his face. 'Pujari, why are you so nervous?' Hanmya had responded humorously to my father's question. His roommate was perplexed by the whole thing. After a short while, we stepped out. My father was asking Hanmya to come out. But I told him that Hanmya had a tutorial the next day, and Hanmya remained in the room.

Once Hanmya and my father met at the bus station. My father hailed him and called him over. He enquired after him and instructed him, 'Pujari, study hard, mind you.' Hanmya had come to the bus station to see off his own father. Just then his father came up to Hanmya. Hanmya was in a predicament. Hanmya introduced his own father, saying, 'This is a man from our village.' When I next met Hanmya, he told me this anecdote. I laughed a lot, but he was burning inside. He brooded over it. I tried to make him smile, but he became still gloomier.

Where had Hanmya lost his playful dignity?

Hanmya had written a poem. Once when I was casually leafing through his notebook, my eyes fell upon it. I read the poem. I felt bad. I thought, I love this man so much, but he is using caste abuse. He was cursing the Hindu faith. I could not agree with him. I had a discussion with him. Writing a poem like this would not destroy the caste system. On the contrary, literature like this would alienate even those minds that had come close. I was angry at his poem. It was very pungent. But Hanmya seemed so humble, so helpless. Whenever I got angry, he would just laugh out loud. How cool was he? How sly he appeared to be.

Hanmya kept a great distance from the Hanmya in his poem. Like a menstruating woman.

My mother was very ill. She had been admitted to Wadia Hospital. She was growing very weak. My father and I kept sitting next to her. Sometimes she would remember Hanmya. 'Where is Pujari?' I would tell her he had gone to his village. Hanmya had heard that my mother was ill. Because I spoke against Dalit literature, he was slowly decreasing his visits to me. I had noticed that. I sent Hanmya a message: 'My mother constantly brings you to mind. Go and visit her.' Hanmya didn't come that day. My mother, too, did not enquire about Hanmya for two days. She needed a blood transfusion the next day. My father and I had already given her blood. If Hanmya had come, it would have been good. Because of his friendship this problem could have been solved. The other friends who visited me would at most have offered musambis or biscuits.

The next day Hanmya came. He sat for a long time talking to my mother. Hanmya's blood group matched my mother's. I had already told Hanmya about her need for a blood transfusion. My father was happy that Hanmya had come.

Hanmya and I went out to buy medicines for my mother. Hanmya was saying, 'Don't worry about blood. I'll give some. I'll bring along my roommate, too. You look after your mother.'

A little while later Hanmya and I went back with the medicines.

My mother's face looked sunken. I saw tears flowing from her eyes. My father had gone out somewhere. I couldn't make sense of anything. Hanmya went towards my mother. She at once became restless. I was disturbed. My mother said to Hanmya, 'Move away. You'll touch me.' Someone seemed to have informed my mother about Hanmya's caste. Hanmya went away. I waited near my mother.

After some time my father came back. He told me the whole story. In that same hospital there was a Mahar ayah who knew Hanmya. She had asked my mother about him.

That evening, my mother was to be given a blood transfusion.

Hanmya came that evening to give blood. I went to my mother and told her that Hanmya had come. My mother was speaking very calmly, 'You brought that Mahar brat into our house. You have polluted our god and our religion. That is behind the suffering I am undergoing. I have no release from this. I don't care if I die. But that Mahar's blood must not enter my body. Your father took me to bathe in the Ganges, but you want to put Mahar's blood into my body. You are a sinner.' I could understand my mother's feelings. Her eyes were overflowing with tears. I was unable to speak.

A little later, my father returned. His eyes held a burning glare. I was frightened seeing his gaze. I went out. At the gate I met Hanmya.

I told Hanmya, 'The blood wasn't needed. The medicines were enough.' But Hanmya's roommate had already told him that my father had come there, furious. I was at my wit's end.

Both I and my Other Self were crumbling like an ancient fort. I was standing up, enduring, while gradually subsiding flat on the ground. My father passed by close to me, and went off to buy medicine.

Just then the Dhangar sugar-boiler from our village came up. 'What, Pujari, you came today? The mistress has been asking about you daily. Where had you gone?' he asked. Hanmya and I had become like lifeless blocks of stone. Hanmya's roommate was speaking, 'This is not Pujari. He is Hanmya. A Mahar.'

20

The Harijan Master

Kulkarni Guruji had been transferred. There was as yet no clue about a new master. Our studies were going into arrears. The master used to come to our home to teach us. We were the Patil's children, so extra care was extended to us. And we in turn affected a greater style than other children. When Kulkarni Guruji came to our house, he would do a namaste to our father. There would be a small discussion on politics. Sometimes Kulkarni Guruji would narrate a couple of incidents from the *Ramayana* or the *Mahabharata* to our grandfather. Our mother would bring a large cup full of milk for the Guruji. All of us siblings would take out our slates and our books and sit on the sofa. There would be free vegetables and greens from our fields for Kulkarni Guruji.

There would be a bustle of young boy pupils to do the sweeping and cleaning at Kulkarni Guruji's house. And the girl students were eager to do the pots and pans and the washing. Kulkarni Guruji was of aristocratic appearance, handsome and fair. His wife, too, was pretty as a flower. Kulkarni Guruji used to walk all over the village. He had an instinct for politics. He attended engagements, weddings and funerals in all earnestness. When Kulkarni Guruji set out on the street, people would come and touch his feet in respect, because before he came we had no Brahmin in our village. There is a saying, 'In a village where there is no Brahmin, there are no quarrels.' This used to be said about our village, but then Guruji came and the seeds of quarrels were sown. Two factions developed in our village. Kulkarni Guruji's tact was strong. He was skilled at *kabaddi*. Our village school held its classes in the mosque. During the days of Muharram, our school would have holidays. As ours was the Patil's family, our household would be shown all the marks of respect. Whether it was the Urs of the Gaibi, or the procession of the Pir, or Muharram, or the Lakshmi Jatra of the Mahars, or a festival like Dussehra, the honour of the chief ceremony would be ours. I would move around in splendour at these festivals. Clothes of zari on my body, a zari cap on my head. I would have a different presence from most young boys.

It was now the time of Muharram. Symbols of the martyrs would be installed. As usual there would be a school holiday. But Kulkarni Master unexpectedly got angry and was unwilling to give a holiday to the school. 'This is a school. There will be no symbols of the martyrs here.' That was Kulkarni Guruji's claim. 'This is a mosque. There are symbols of the martyrs here every year. We will instal them this year, too.' This was the Muslims' claim. Kulkarni Guruji had indoctrinated his friends among the kabaddi players. Right at the time of Muharram a quarrel broke out: 'Is this a school or a mosque?' The quarrel grew exacerbated and at night ten people had head injuries. People with jobs to go to started setting out with umbrellas and doing the rounds of the courts. This was Kulkarni Guruji's rotation. Finally, at long last, he was transferred. The master had gone, but the village was still experiencing the fruits of his actions. Now a new master would come in place of Kulkarni Guruji. Who knew what kind of person he would be?

It was afternoon. Lunch was over. Mother put the school bag in our hands. Grandfather, coughing, was exhorting us to study. 'At least read whatever you know. Or you'll forget it all by the time the master comes.' We began to draw pictures on our slates of a parrot, a duck, a water-pot, a bucket, a tree. My elder sister Soni had drawn a fat picture of Grandfather and she now showed it to me.

Kondya Mahar had not come the previous day. Today it seemed he had come. His salutation could be heard all the way to the sofa. Grandfather was getting angry with Kondya Mahar. Kondya was our house Mahar. Because he had not come for a day, all his tasks had remained undone. Kondya was more honest than other Mahars. In our house there were two honest beings, Kondya and our dog, who were loyal to the hand that fed them. We were fonder of the dog than of Kondya. It used to roam throughout the house, while Kondya only had permission to come up to the steps. We children used to cling to the dog when we played with him. We were used to dogs. But we always had to remain at a distance from Kondya.

Once, while playing, I touched Kondya's body. That day I didn't get my next meal until I had had a bath. Grandfather had rebuked Kondya that day. 'There are small children in the house. Just because they don't understand, should you not understand as well? Mind your body when you work. Or have you gone blind?' From that day onwards, I, too, would say to Kondya Mahar, 'Don't touch me. Keep your distance.' Kondya was of Grandfather's age. An old man. But all of us used to call him 'Kondya'. Kondya was so old, but we would swear at him, and he would giggle at us. He called me the 'little Patil'. I found the same helplessness in him and in our dog.

When I saw Kondya's skin colour, his features, the tattered clothes on his body, he seemed like a man from a different village. He was not from ours. His language, his nature, his behaviour were not those of our village. From which state had he come? Were the men there descended from dogs? Kondya could never stand up straight and talk. He would sway like a dog's tail wagging at Grandfather's words. I had to see where Kondya lived. He lived in the Maharwada. Outside the village. That meant there must be a separate village, Kondya's village, outside ours. The people of that village would get up every morning and come to ask for alms. In other words, to beg. They would bring along a boy dedicated to the goddess, his face smeared with vermilion. The other day when our bull died, four Mahars came and dragged it away. Mother was saying, now the Mahars will butcher and eat it. That is why Grandfather was telling Kondya not to touch us. But how nice our dog was! We touched him. We played with him. Grandfather never got angry with us.

It was afternoon. Kondya was cleaning out the cowshed. Grandfather was swinging on the swing. Our dog began to bark. Some unknown man must have come to the house. Kondya Mahar came running. This had to be a man from Kondya's village. He was wearing good clothes, but he was a man with Kondya's face. He made a deep bow to Grandfather. Grandfather talked to him, making enquiries. This was our new master. He had come here to replace Kulkarni Guruji. He had come to our house to inform us about it.

I felt very bad that a Harijan master would now be teaching us. The Harijan master had been seated on a sack. The hospitality for Kulkarni Guruji was quite different. When he came, the whole atmosphere used to change. Mother would heat some milk for him. Now what would we do for a Harijan master? Mother poured out some water for the Harijan master from a height. I felt bad. After all, no matter what, the Harijan master was our guruji. Now we wouldn't be able to touch his feet.

The Harijan master was sitting silent. As if he had been arrested and brought here. He looked pathetic. How could such a meek teacher ever get angry with us? The master wasn't talking much. But Kondya was happy. He was feeling happy that a master of his caste had come to his village. He had put aside all his tasks and was sitting and chatting with the master. Just then our father came in from outside. Grandfather pointed at the master, coughing as he did. The master made a deep bow like Kondya. The Harijan master's coming to the village was a dilemma. First, the question of his accommodation. And how would the children of Brahmins and traders learn under his discipline?

So what if he was the master? In the end he was just a Harijan.

Because school classes took place in the mosque, gradually fewer and fewer children began to come to them. The master went on teaching. He never laid a hand on anyone. He never scolded. He had not been able to find a house in the village. He lived in a dharamshala in the Maharwada. While teaching he never asked for water. Nobody ever did a namaskar to him. The woman asking for alms in the village, or the Mahar woman who swept the road, would draw the end of their sari over their head respectfully when they saw the master and stand to one side. When we went home, we would dip in water. Only then would we go into the kitchen. On account of the Harijan master, there would be two baths a day.

It was afternoon. We brothers were sitting doing our studies. The Harijan master had not been coming for our tuition. For eight or ten days he had also not been coming to the school. Tomorrow was the time of Muharram. The symbols of the martyr would be installed. There would be a school holiday.

Kondya Mahar came to work. He was telling Grandfather, 'I hear that the Harijan master is going to ask for a transfer. He is having trouble in the village.'

Mother, serving Kondya some leftover food, said, 'Poor Harijan Master!'

When Kondya laughed wholeheartedly, he looked just like the Harijan Master.

The Harijan Master would be transferred; another master would come.

Mother asked, 'Hey, Kondya, now what caste of master will come?'

'Who knows, Mistress?' said Kondya, getting up. He took the leftovers he had been served and went away.

The Harijan Master was a good teacher. No one would be able to forget his teaching and his caste.

21

The Steps

My name is Ajay. I am from a Scheduled Caste. I have done my B.A. and B.Ed. I am the only degree holder in our village. I am approaching an age bar for both a job and marriage. There is a provision in the Indian Constitution to reserve jobs to ensure social justice to Dalits. A suitable Dalit candidate is not found; so a caste Hindu is selected and it is he who is confirmed. We are unemployed in great numbers. The government is cheating us.

It would have been better if I had not been educated. I would have been a servant of caste Hindus; I would have endured their injustices. But education has awakened my self-respect. Why should a separate hutment colony, a separate water source, a separate burial ground have been arranged for us? Our assigned place was near the steps to the temple, next to the steps to the school, at eating-places, at the houses of caste Hindus, but only next to the steps. We cannot climb these steps. I burn like a hut, inside and out, with self-respect. I become ash. Helplessness in my mind. But do things become different? No, they are just the same. They are even more vigilant to keep me enslaved.

There is a village called Rampur near our village. All the comforts of town have reached there. In fact it has become a small town. There is a high school there. Because there is no high school in our village, all our children go to the school in Rampur. Through a connection I had got a job in that school. I was to work for a year without salary. I had given my consent to this. I was the first teacher in that school from the backward classes. In spite of being a B.A. B.Ed., I had joined that school on the level of an S.S.C. Dip. Ed. The remaining teachers were from Rampur itself. Most were relatives of Shri Joshi, the administrator of the institution. Joshi's son was the head teacher. His daughter-in-law was also employed there.

One peon there belonged to my caste. His name was Nivritti. Everyone called him Nivrya. But the administrator called him 'Nivritti-Natha.' He was illiterate. He had been taught to sign his name. He used to act in a subdued manner around me.

Our high school did not have a building of its own. The Raja had a bungalow outside the village. Classes used to be held there.

Rampur was a pleasant and picturesque village in the Ramkot principality. There was a large river in the village. The village was nestled in the embrace of a hill. It was intensely green with trees and groves. When the Raja came to hunt at Rampur, he would stay in that bungalow. He would hunt all day, and at night he would stay there. In the old days there were more deer and hares there than people. Peacocks were more plentiful than sparrows. When the bus started coming to Rampur, forest life started vanishing, and now only the occasional hare could be seen. Deer and peacocks had become non-existent.

To the east of the Raja's bungalow, stables had been constructed. Today they were in ruins. The room built for a latrine was also ruined. To the west of the bungalow there were the kitchens. All the game was cooked there. Behind that there was a well. I drank water from that well. To the south was the entrance to the bungalow. At the distance of a shout from that entrance was the river. In the old days there was a lot of water in that river. Now with the drought it had fallen dry.

To the east of the bungalow was a settlement of a hundred huts. This is where people of my caste lived. Nivrya used to live here. Sturdy of body and with a coarse face, he used to roam around with the headmaster like a bodyguard. I would often have the urge to visit the Dalit settlement. I would feel like talking to my own people, getting to know them. But I would put away such thoughts in case my caste became widely known. Two boys from the settlement used to come to me for tuition.

Every Sunday the headmaster would come to the high school. Nivrya would come, too. The headmaster would stay a long time, working. Nivrya would remain sitting outside. With the headmaster's permission I lived in the school kitchens. So I did not have to pay any rent. The headmaster was happy that he had found a night watchman for the high school. Once I challenged Nivrya: 'Why don't you stay here?' He was confused. 'I did stay here at first. But not now. I feel afraid. There is a girl who walks around at night.' I was shocked at Nivrya's words. 'A girl called Jaya. She was in the tenth standard. She drowned herself in this well. Her ghost walks around at night. You haven't yet seen her.' I had been living there for so many days. I hadn't seen anything. This was just an illusion. Nivrya sat there unmoving, saying nothing. Maybe this was a way of frightening me.

I slept soundly that night. In the morning I went to the well. I took off my clothes and jumped in. Jaya must have jumped in like this, too. She must have struggled to death in this deep blue water. I at once climbed onto the steps of the well and stood there. The water has roiled and risen. The waves are seething. Drops of water are trickling down my body. Fear touches my mind.

I shake off the fear and dive into the well. I start to swim but the fear in my mind does not move aside. I am afraid that

Jaya's ghost will grab my leg and pull me down, or clasp my neck. These fears make me look at the water and recoil. I am frightened of the well. I climb out.

The next day I sit on the steps of the well and have a bath. I feel nervous while drawing water. When I lower my dipper into the well, I shiver, afraid that the ghost would grab my hand and pull me to the bottom.

I spoke alone to a boy in my class. I asked him: 'Did a girl commit suicide in this well?' Frightened, he said, 'Yes, Sir. Did you see her?' His counter-question and his frightened face. Jokingly, I said, 'Yes'. Within an hour my answer spread throughout my other students. 'Sir lives here. He must be seeing the ghost at night. How could Sir tell a lie? Now he will have to move. The boys' discussion is heard by the headmaster. He calls me. His face is swollen with rage. Nivrya is looking at me calmly as I enter the headmaster's office.

'Did you see a ghost?'

'No.'

'Then why is it being discussed among the boys?'

'I casually made a joke to one of them.'

'You are a fool. Because of your joke the school may be closed down. Now apologise to the boys and admit that you were joking. Otherwise this discussion will spread throughout the village.'

'All right.'

I apologised to the boys and explained that I had just been joking. But the students didn't believe what I said. They felt that I had only apologised because of pressure from the headmaster.

That night I couldn't sleep. It was an insult to me to have to apologise to the children. Normally I used to sleep soundly by ten every night. But that night I couldn't even sleep at twelve. One o'clock came. Then two o'clock. There was no trace of sleep. I was fed up. I came out of the kitchen. Everything was silent. There was no breeze. The leaves on the trees were still.

Not a leaf stirred. This was not greenery. This was a painted scene. I could hear the sound of crickets. There was moonlight in the sky. The night was spreading like a flood. I looked this way and that. In case Jaya's ghost came. She was very beautiful. She was in love with the art teacher. A letter from her was found. The school administration forced the teacher to resign. After some days, Jaya's body was found in the well. Now she should rise and come out of the well. I would never let her go.

I climb down into the well. I shout, 'Hey! Come here!' I hear my voice echoing. She doesn't come. I take water in my cupped palms. I take it to my lips. I see her in the water. I drink her lips. I drink her tongue, her face, her eyes along with the water. She starts to throb in my body. My body begins to shiver. Her unclothed body disentangles me beyond imagination.

I take off my clothes. I become totally naked. I gaze at my body in the moonlight. I jump into the well. The well shakes. There is a loud splash. The water seethes. I dive deep. She should embrace me now. I slowly rise to the surface. The water is roiling. Losing my senses, I start to swim. The water begins to caress my body. I shout out aloud. I want the touch of a woman. The echoes keep resonating. I get tired of swimming and come out of the well. Just then I hear the sound of bells from the village temple. These bells used to be rung for the first *aarti* at the crack of dawn. I return to the kitchens and fall into a deep sleep.

I didn't wake up in the morning. As it was Saturday, there was morning school. When I woke up, I saw the headmaster and Nivrya standing in the doorway. It was they who had awoken me. The headmaster entered. He sat down next to me. Nivrya was standing to one side. My eyes had become red. I had fever. The headmaster asked me, 'What happened?' I calmly answered him, 'I was sitting in the well the whole night. There is no ghost. It's just a rumour.' He was furious. 'But sir, because of your sleeping like this, all the students are frightened. There is a discussion going on that you are haunted by a ghost. For pity's sake, come to class.' I dressed and went to class. Everyone looked at me fearfully. 'Now Sir's days are numbered,' said their eyes.

Little by little I grew restless. I, too, started feeling afraid. I had to leave the kitchens and go and live in the village. I said this to my students in class. I wanted to take a house on rent. It could be that I wanted the house for too little. But no one agreed. To tell you the truth, this was my foolishness. How could I expect anyone to rent a house to a Dalit teacher like me? I didn't get a house in the village. However the story spread that I was afraid of the ghost and wanted to rent a house. I told my problem to the headmaster. 'Live in your settlement. Where's the shame in that? Everyone knows your caste. There will be no difference if you live there. On the contrary, your people will be happy.'

I enquired of Nivrya. I asked the Dalit children in class. I got the answer that there was no house available in the settlement. Then one day I went to the settlement myself. I went and stood in front of the gram panchayat member's hut. Just then his dogs came out and raced at me. I was upset. An old woman came out and restrained the dogs. I introduced myself and told her my problem. She gave me water to drink. After a while a crowd gathered around me. Everyone was coming to see the master from their own caste. I even got some tea.

The old woman made it known that the master required a house. One man stepped out of the crowd. He attracted everyone's attention. 'Attach four tin sheets to our back wall and live there.' I liked his idea.

My house was ready in a fortnight.

Every day, Nivrya used to set out first from the settlement. Then two students. Then I. After I went to live in the Dalit settlement, there was much discussion about it in the village. Some said, 'Master was afraid of the ghost; that's why he left the bungalow.' Others said, 'Because Master was a Harijan, no one gave him a house in the village. He has now gone to live among his own caste.' There was constant discussion among the students about the ghost, and my caste.

According to the Sunday custom, Nivrya went off to the school. The headmaster would come there, too. Today I, too, decided to go along. Although I was a B.Ed., I worked on a Dip. Ed.'s salary. If I wanted to talk to the headmaster about it, he never had time. I set out today because he had time. I wrote out an application asking that I should get the B.Ed. salary grade. I also wrote that I was from a Scheduled Caste. I went to the high school. The headmaster welcomed me with a smile.

I set out my question systematically. He listened calmly as if he had been expecting it all along. He took my application. 'All right. I'll see you,' was his way of dismissing me. I was angry at not getting an answer to my question.

'What about my salary grade?'

'If you want the job, work. Otherwise, leave.' Hearing the headmaster's ultimatum, I walked out. I had needlessly met him. On the other hand I was also in a rage. Not all the reserved jobs in our high school had been filled. And I was definitely in the reserved category. My request was not inappropriate. Even so the headmaster was angry with me. I was fed up.

After I asked for the B.Ed. salary grade, the complaints started against me. The mental harassment began. The annual exam commenced. I was working in the class as a supervisor. The children were answering the exam paper. A girl named Rupali sitting on the second bench was copying her answers. I snatched her answer sheet and copy sheet from her and told her to go outside the examination hall. The seniors heard about this. Some time later, Rupali came there with her guardians. She gave a written complaint against me—that while snatching the answer sheet from her, I had rubbed her bosom. I was appalled. I had done nothing of the kind. It was a false complaint. Someone had instigated Rupali against me. I regretted having snatched her copy paper. I went and met the headmaster. He took Rupali's side. I was helpless.

I couldn't believe that my own student would file such a complaint against me. What would the outcome be? And what if the people in the village found out? How would my students feel? I felt like committing suicide.

The school administration withheld my increment. I felt no grief about the loss of increment, but my name was being blackened. I was greatly humiliated. I complained to the Education Department, but it was no use. Their reply went in favour of the school. I was like a poisonous snake whose fangs had been removed.

The Board sent tenth standard papers for evaluation that year. I received a registered parcel from the Board. These papers were of our own school.

The headmaster called me to his house. He gave me the roll number of his niece and told me to pass her in the paper. I refused. The headmaster got angry with me. 'If you won't listen to me, then resign. Otherwise I will remove you. Your character is not so good anyway.' I stayed true to my character. 'If my niece doesn't pass this year, she will pass the next year. Her paper will hardly come to you each year. Listen to me, we are thinking of giving you the B.Ed. salary grade. The decision is yours.' I said nothing. I just walked away.

The next day the headmaster himself came to my house. He sat down. This must have been the first occasion that he had come to our settlement. He drank some tea. He folded his hands. 'Sir, please pass this girl. Otherwise she won't get married.' I was silent in thought. 'I will certainly help,' I promised. The people in the settlement were curious at seeing the headmaster in my house. The schoolchildren were hiding to catch a glimpse of him. I went and escorted the headmaster outside the settlement.

Two days later a policeman came to my house. Seeing him, the children ran away. The women locked their doors. I, too, was frightened. 'Sahib's wife has called you,' said the policeman in his thick, coarse voice. He was standing outside the door. I put on my clothes. I went out, locked the door and left with the policeman. What could the police inspector's wife possibly have to do with me? I couldn't understand any of it.

The policeman left me in front of the police inspector's bungalow. I went inside. The police inspector's dazzlingly fair wife stood before me. She told me to sit down. The policeman went away. I grew nervous. Suppose this madam made a complaint like Rupali? I felt like running away. Madam gave me a roll number and told me to pass the student it belonged to. I declined. She got furious. 'I'll tell my husband to have handcuffs put on you. How is it that you pass the headmaster's niece?' My face fell. I took the roll number. 'You must give good marks,' madam warned me. I said, 'Yes, madam,' and took my leave.

Little by little this event, too, became known to the students. Everyone started to rebuke me. They began to blackmail me. I had to pass everyone. That was the only road left to me now. I was completely trapped.

I was panic-stricken. Everything happened according to the students' wishes. Now at last I thought I was free. But the next day a detailed report was printed on the front page of the newspaper. Everyone was frightened. I went to the headmaster's house for guidance. He refused to meet me. I went back in despair.

The Standard Ten Board levied a heavy fine on me. I sold a field near the village and paid the fine. After I had paid the fine, the Board filed a police case against me. It was obvious that I would now be wearing handcuffs. All roads were now closed to me.

It was Sunday. Nivrya had gone to the high school. I took a long knife from the house. I hid it so no one would see it, and set out for the school. On the way I met the old woman from the settlement. 'Child, is it true what happened?' I told her, 'Yes, it is.' Her eyes filled with tears. Her voice trembled. 'They have caught you in a trap. May disaster befall them.' Leaning on her cane, the old woman slowly walked away. I watched her figure receding into the distance, then suddenly swung around and walked towards the school. Nivrya was watering the flower bushes. When he saw me, he became still.

'Has Sir come?'

'Yes, he has.'

'I want to meet him.'

'He has refused you permission. He told me in advance.'

'Nivrya, let me meet Sir. Just once. I only want to talk for two minutes.'

'It won't be any use. Go home.'

'Nivrya, I beg you with folded hands. Let me meet him. There has been an injustice done to me.'

'I told you, didn't I? It is of no use to meet Sir. He is busy with some important work. He will not meet you.'

'Nivrya, I will owe you a debt.'

'Sir, you are of my caste, so I will tell you. He is a man with his heart in the wrong place. It won't be any use.'

'Even so, let me meet him just once.'

'Sir, he is sitting inside with that Rupali. He won't let her go till he has used her. He had called Jaya, too, just like this. He raped the girl and threw her into the well. Jaya's family feared for its reputation. The panchnama took place right here; the funeral rites, too. Rupali is inside. Now it's going on with this girl. The two of them must be having fun. Why do you want to create an obstacle?'

'Nivrya, I will either go inside or to the police station.'

'You go inside. But don't say that I let you in. I'm going to the well to get water.'

Without a word, I hastened upstairs. Sir was sitting in a chair. Rupali was standing next to him. Seeing me, Rupali sat down on a chair. Sir was looking at me.

'Wasn't Nivrya downstairs?'

'No. He has gone to the well to fill water.'

'What do you want?'

'I want to talk to you.'

'I have nothing to say to you. Get out.'

'Sir, it was you who entangled me in this.'

'You have a mind of your own.'

'But you yourself told me to pass your niece.'

'I can tell you to murder someone.'

'And I will do it.'

'Brainless!' the headmaster snapped at me. I locked the cabin door, took out my sharp knife and stood there. Sir was shocked. Rupali's eyes filled with tears. I recklessly made attacks on their bodies with slashing movements of my knife. Sir's screams joined Rupali's cries. Sir's body was floundering. My whole body was bloodstained. A few drops of blood had splashed up onto Mahatma Gandhi's picture. I shouted at Rupali. She became quiet. Her face had become wretched. 'I want to rub your breasts,' I said. She took off her clothes at once. I told her to undress fully. In seconds, she was naked. Her body had become cold. Her gaze had congealed. I saw teeth marks on her thighs. 'Did you sleep with this bastard?' I shouted.

Desolate with fear, she inclined her head, yes. The blood on my knife had dried. I became reckless. I was beside myself. She began to cry. I held back her hair, and my knife began a rhythmic dance on her body.

Nivrya was pounding at the door. I opened the door of the cabin. My clothes were wet with blood. Nivrya's face changed. 'What is this you've done, Sir?' Nivrya's voice was trembling with fear.

'You phone the police. I am going to the well to bathe.' I took a leap into the well, holding the knife. I calmly began to swim. The water of the well seemed so full of life.

Soon I could hear shouts and cries. The villagers must be coming towards the well in great numbers. Nivrya was standing at the well and showing me to the villagers. People were calling out to me, 'Come up!' and letting loose a barrage of curses. But no one had the courage to climb down into the well. Stones had begun to rain down upon me. I stood ready to dive into the water. After a while the police reached and the crowd dispersed. But the racket had increased. The crowd had become uncontrollable.

Next to Nivrya stood the old woman from our settlement, leaning on her stick. The police were saying, 'Come out!' The old woman shouted, 'Don't come out! They will kill you!' The police drove her away, and she went off, cursing.

The police were trying to control the crowd, but it had become unmanageable. The stone-throwing was still going on. When a stone fell, I dived into the water.

As if the well had taken me under its protection.

22

Cobra's Hood

This is a story from the days of India's Independence. My grandfather had set the three-coloured Indian flag fluttering above the palace at Akkalkot. The merger of the Akkalkot principality with India had taken place. Our family had been the Patils for five villages. With Independence, our Patilship had gone, but in the first general election, my father had been elected unopposed as the first MLA of our taluka. For fifteen years continuously he was elected to that post. This year our constituency is to be declared a reserved one, otherwise my father was going to put me up to stand for election here.

My father's name is Vilas Dharmanna Patil.

At our house there was a Mahar named Kondiba. He was our house Mahar. Kondiba was prepared to do anything for my father, anything at all. In the same way, our family had cared for Kondiba and seventeen generations of his family like domesticated animals. Kondiba would massage our father, rub his hands and legs and wash his feet when he came in from outside. He would do the shopping for the house, keep an eye on the fields, pay the labourers and do sundry other work like this. He called my father 'Anna'. Kondiba's wife Kera would do the menial work for the house and find women to do housework.

After my father became an MLA, Kondya Mahar became a P. A. Whether as a Mahar or as a P. A., it was all the same. After becoming a P. A. Kondya's work increased. Khadi cloth appeared on his body. His job was to be my father's P. A., his bodyguard, his pupil; to move after him, and to announce his name. Because he did such jobs very well, my father was very pleased with him.

My grandfather was of a very traditional nature. He used to observe all distinctions and discriminations, he was orthodox in religion and liked strict discipline. 'You should not let your Mahars get above themselves. You should treat your servants like your slippers.' This was his outspoken opinion. I still remember an incident from my childhood. I was thirsty, and there was no one at hand. I didn't feel like going to the well to have a drink. I called out to Kondya Mahar. I told him to get me some water from the well. He wasn't willing. He was putting off going to the well in case someone saw him. But I kept insisting obstinately. Kondya went down into the well to fetch some water. I kept watch. Just then my grandfather materialised from I don't know where.

Grandfather had seen Kondya Mahar going down into the well. I went off. Grandfather thrashed Kondya soundly with his shoe. He had polluted the well. If Mahars polluted the wells, the goddess of wealth Lakshmi would flee the fields. A Mahar is inauspicious. Kondya was shouting. 'The young Patil sent me,' he was saying. Grandfather became furious. 'The young Patil is telling you to eat shit. Will you do it? Hey, you are a Mahar. Have you forgotten your caste? You've become over-proud.'

Kondya Mahar's son Daulya was my friend. We had both passed the seventh class together. After the seventh class we needed to go to the high school, which was at a distance of two miles from our village. This high school had been founded in memory of my grandmother. The children from five villages around used to come here to get their education. Its beautiful garden, its imposing building, its large sports ground, these used to delight the mind. The children from five villages would assemble there. Therefore its atmosphere was one of fun and games. Daulya and I would go to school together. On the road there was Andappa's well. The two of us would eat there. I used to greatly like the chutney that Daulya brought. It was spicy. I would eat Daulya's chutney. Daulya would eat my vegetables. On the way there and back, Daulya would carry my file. He would carry both our school bags. Now and then I would fight with Daulya. Then he would scold me, 'I'll tell in the village that you eat my chutney.' That would blunt my sting at once. I thought I would be humiliated if people found out that I ate a Mahar's chutney.

One day I had a violent quarrel with Daulya. I knocked him down. Daulya began to cry. That day we both missed school.

Daulya: I'll tell at your home that you eat my chutney.

Me: Tell them. What can you do? You are a human being, just like me.

Daulya: The Patil's son got polluted, eating a Mahar's chutney.

That evening my mother drew me close to her. I had refused to eat my dinner that day. My mother was pacifying me. 'We are the Patils of five villages. A Mahar's caste is a low one. They are our servants. They eat dead animals. We should not eat food from their hands. If you feel like eating chutney I will make some for you. Don't eat Daulya's chutney.'

Then Daulya's schooling came to an end. I became the only one from our village to go to the high school. My father had bought a bicycle for me.

At that time the whole village turned up to see the bicycle. I was learning how to ride it. Kondya Mahar was teaching me how to ride. I would sit on the bicycle and Kondya Mahar would hold the cycle and run after me. I would play with the cycle and Kondya Mahar would chase me like an animal. My mother had given a stern warning to Kondya. If I fell off the bicycle, he would receive a good hiding from my grandfather's shoe. Kondya took very good care of me.

When Kondya got tired, his wife Kera would run after the cycle. 'Ride slower, master. You will fall. There is a slope there,' Kera would keep shouting. I on my part was delighting in racing the cycle. The cycle reached the slope. I forgot to apply the brake. The cycle started running even faster. Kondya came running. He knew how to control animals. He came shouting 'Hai Ho Ho'. But a bicycle was hardly an animal to stop at that. The cycle and I both fell into the ditch. I was injured. Kera gently picked me up. She wiped me over with her sari. I caught a glimpse of my mother in Kera the Mahar woman.

The season of harvest. The weight of ripe jowar. Its growth had come to the stage of sweet green grain. Kera at the work of killing birds in the fields. Daulya, too, was now labouring in our fields. Flocks of birds in each field. Guarded against with slingshots. The swaying crop. I had set out towards the fields on my bicycle. It was Sunday. My father had gone to the taluka town. Grandfather had sent me to the fields. Ten servants lived there.

I proceeded embankment by embankment. At the corner, I saw some women hiding. I spurred on my cycle and raced there. Two Mahar women had entered the field and were taking the heads of grain. I saw heaps of cobs in their clothes. On seeing me, they were dumbstruck. I caught hold of them by their locks of hair and began to thump them. They were pleading with me. One of them was quite young. I was going to take them to the mansion and hand them over into Grandfather's custody. But they fell at my feet, imploring. I felt sorry for them. I let them go.

Later I saw these same women piling up heaps of grain. They themselves had taken on the task of disentangling the sheaves of grain. Each time they saw me, they would hide their giggles. I, too, found it difficult not to laugh. I would think, I ought to give both of these women another pasting.

Kondya Mahar's room was near our cowshed. He used to sleep there. The protection of our house had been entrusted to him and to the dog Motya. Both of them were loyal to the house that fed them. Kondya might be a servant at our house, but he was also an elected panch of the Mahar community. Every year on Babasaheb Ambedkar's anniversary, he would get a *patti* from my father. The Mahars of our village would observe Babasaheb Ambedkar's anniversary, but they would also drag away dead animals. I once asked him about this, and this is how he replied: 'We want Babasaheb. But we also want the village. Just because Buddha has come into our house, that doesn't mean that we should throw away the tradition that has come walking to us like the basket on our father's head. We will worship both. After all, a Mahar's life is determined by his basket and his staff, isn't it?'

This year, our area had been announced as a reserved constituency. My father had enjoyed his post as elected representative for fifteen years. His words carried a lot of weight in politics. Five villages regarded my grandfather as a god. My father had decided to have Kondya elected. Kondya was a Mahar yes-man. He was our house Mahar.

Kondya was sitting and pressing my father's legs. My father was explaining the whole matter of the election to him. He was going to spend money on Kondya. Kondya was saying, 'All right, Anna,' 'All right, Anna'. My father decided to fill out Kondya's application and Kondya went off to wash and water the animals.

That evening my father, Kondya, my grandfather and I went to the taluka town to complete the application form. My father took out his jeep. There were only two such jeeps in the taluka: one with us, and one with the Raja of Akkalkot. We went to Akkalkot and had an audience with the Akkalkot Swami. We took his blessings and then filled out the form. We distributed pedas. What joy for my grandfather that his house Mahar was to become a member of the Assembly!

We learned that Daulya had also filled an application form for the election. Since his wedding he had been living at his father-in-law's house at Akkalkot. His father-in-law was a leader in the Republican Party of India. He had a wood warehouse. For the past ten years, Daulya had been living in his house as a resident son-in-law. He even had two children. When we learned that Daulya had filled in a form, the fire of anger spread from Grandfather's soles right to his head. Daulya's mischief filled his whole vision.

Grandfather himself went to Daulya and told him to withdraw his application. I, too, went personally with Grandfather. We persuaded him, take fifty thousand rupees, but withdraw your application. But he wouldn't listen. To someone whose word had never been broken, like my grandfather, this could not be borne. That very night he attacked Kera and Kondya with his bullwhip. My father intervened, so the whole matter cooled down.

Grandfather was bent upon revenge. He was burning with vengeful thoughts. Daulya had been forbidden entry to our village. Even so, we heard that Daulya, with a gang of twenty-odd young men, had entered our village. Grandfather came shouting out of the mansion. In moments the whole village assembled, and we were moving towards the Mahar settlement, ready to jump on it.

Daulya's gathering had run amok; a few huts were ablaze. Shouts and cries had risen to the skies. There was loud wailing all around. I, too, was out of my mind. I was flogging whoever I could see with my whip. Even women and children did not escape my reach. Grandfather stood at the edge, while we created mayhem. Daulya however had remained unhurt and escaped; he was running away from the village. Someone gave us the news, and we started to chase Daulya. We were all bent on revenge. Daulya was running ahead, and we behind him. It was the chase of a rabbit by hunting dogs.

Daulya, his life in his hands, was running helter-skelter, and we were chasing him with rods and machetes in our hands. Everyone was shouting. Daulya was running for his life. We, too, had gone mad. Near Andappa's well, Daulya collapsed. Where Daulya and I used to eat our meal. And I used to enjoy his chutney so much. By the time I reached Daulya he had been attacked by many. He was covered in blood. His body was struggling. His limbs were trembling. Daulya's gaze, however, was fixed on me like that of a cobra. Whenever in the past Daulya and I had fought, on each occasion Daulya would look at me just like this.

Today, half a dozen years later, as we step out of the court, these memories will not budge from in front of me. Grandfather was standing outside the court with a box of pedas. We have been cleared as innocent. Grandfather had passed a 'covered fist' to the judge. At that moment I remembered the Daulya who had refused money. My father, I and MLA Kondiba Kamble sat in the jeep. Grandfather was distributing pedas.

I looked at Daulya's wife who was coming out of the court. I saw the same look as Daulya's in her eyes. That gaze still continues to pursue me. I run, but thousands of small venomous cobras come after me to bite me. How many cobra fangs these court walls must have summoned forth!

23

The Procession

Devgarh is a rural area close to the district town of Nagar. The children from Devgarh used to go to Nagar for their education. The city bus came right up to the village. The people of the village used to go to Nagar to do their shopping. Many children from Devgarh studied, but very few of them went to college. The five or ten students who went to college were all from the village. The children of Bhimnagar, on account of their circumstances, used to leave school halfway through.

The Dalits could not afford to put their children all the way through school, so school ended incomplete for them. With only half a school education, they were of no use to employers. It was better for them to do village tasks, so that they could be of help in running their households. Children would be ready for work right from their childhood. So it seemed more profitable to harness the children to village work than to put them in school. Rather than going to school, Dalit children used to wander around like animals.

Divakar studied in great poverty. He passed his S.S.C. He was the first boy from Bhimnagar to go to college. The chest of Kashi, Divakar's mother, had swelled with pride. Since her husband died, it was she who had brought up Divakar and educated him.

Now that he was to go to college, the people of Bhimnagar arranged a felicitation for him. Jyotiba took the lead and raised contributions. He gathered money from house to house. Contributions also came in from neighbouring areas. Jyotiba was gathering funds so that Divakar's education should not come to an end. This felt strange and rare to the Dalits, too. Many people were helping out for Divakar's education. Kashi was just two fingers' length away from heaven. She had the joy of having fulfilled her duty. Soon after Divakar, one boy after another started to progress in education. They began to study. The dream of being as great as Divakar flowered in every hut.

Devgarh village was close to the district town. Therefore, conveniences like electricity, a school, a dispensary and a post office had already become available. The village's old countenance was rapidly changing. But caste consciousness remained. Electric poles came to Bhimnagar, the breath of education touched it, but the old distance between the village and Bhimnagar remained. The world rapidly came nearer, and each rural area became joined to a town. But the caste distance between Bhimnagar and the village was not destroyed. Every year Devgarh experienced a shortage of drinking water. In fact, in the summer there was a painful dearth. There were two wells in the village. At one of them, the caste Hindus filled their water, and at the other the untouchables filled theirs. Every year there would be quarrels over drinking water. The village goons would throw dirt in the Dalits' well. They would sully the drinking water. On one occasion a dead dog was found lying in the well.

Rebellion grew in Bhimnagar. The people of Bhimnagar were tired of this oppression. But to whom should they complain against the village? If they left this village, where would they go?

The news reached Divakar that the villagers had thrown a dead dog into the Dalits' well. A new confidence had broken out in Divakar on account of his education. He felt ashamed of his village. Divakar told all his fellow hostel mates about what had happened. Strong feelings of unrest developed among the Dalit students. Each of them began to talk the language of revenge. They all came together. They hired bicycles and reached Devgarh.

Over a hundred cyclists roamed around the village, giving voice to dissent. There was a small assembly in the central square of the village. It gave expression to its anger against the terrorist tactics of the villagers. Devgarh had become panic-stricken. No one could impede the Dalit students. They entered the village temple. They went to the caste Hindus' well and drank water. A form of fear spread in the village. The ringleader of this whole programme of events was Divakar.

Bhimnagar's Dalits felt satisfied. Their strength was not inferior. If injustice were done to them the rest of the world would respond. These were no longer the days of old. There was no reason to fear the villagers. These were the topics of discussion. Jyotiba was telling all this to the people of Bhimnagar. He was teaching them. A new movement had begun in the settlement. Sparks were being lit in the minds of the Dalits. A new situation was slowly being born.

The Dalits had to unite. They had to fight injustice from a united front. Unless the Dalits came together, they would not be able to fight. And without a struggle, they would not develop self-confidence. So Divakar decided to unite the Dalits of Bhimnagar. Jyotiba had begun to celebrate Ambedkar Jayanti in the village, but there was no procession for it. Divakar announced his intention to start having a procession. Everyone set to work.

A collection was raised. Thorough preparations were made. A large mandap was raised. Widely known troupes of singers were invited. A big statue of Babasaheb Ambedkar was brought from Nagar. Bhimnagar glowed bright with electric decorations. Everyone enthusiastically cooperated to increase the splendour of the Jayanti. An atmosphere of joy and excitement had spread in Bhimnagar. Dalit people had assembled from nearby rural areas. Everyone had put aside their jobs and stayed home. Bhimnagar was fully decorated.

Shivaji Jayanti was being celebrated in the village. Sometimes the Ganesh festival clashed with Muharram, and sometimes Ambedkar Jayanti with Shivaji Jayanti. So the village goons would see an opportunity and create havoc. Now, because Ambedkar Jayanti had coincided with Shivaji Jayanti, there was a perverse atmosphere in the village.

The villagers had made preparations with the aim that the Shivaji Jayanti celebrations should be better than those for Ambedkar Jayanti. A huge mandap had been set up in the main square of the village. A beautiful statue of Shivaji Maharaj was seated in it. Beautiful decorations had been set up. Recordings of songs played night and day. At various places in the village there were electric decorations.

In the evening the procession to display Babasaheb Ambedkar's statue set out through the village, accompanied by music. At the head of the procession there were lezhim players on foot. After that came the young men making announcements. Divakar was fully coloured with blue gulal. The colour blue had been thrown on everyone's bodies. Jyotiba's face had been smeared with blue. From time to time, someone would throw blue all over Divakar. Seeing Divakar all bathed in blue, Kashi felt happy.

The procession was halting in every square. Displays of wrestling would take place there. Lezhims would be played with. Then the procession, making announcements, would move ahead. At the end of the procession there came a decorated bullock cart. The statue of Babasaheb Ambedkar had been placed in that cart. Behind the cart came Dalit women and children, singing songs about Babasaheb. The Dalit people, who daily moved around so humbly in this village, today moved along joyfully singing and dancing and making proclamations. The Ambedkar Jayanti procession now reached the main square of the village. In the square young men from the village were on purpose playing lezhim. The huge drum was being beaten loudly. The playing was at a peak. There was no room for the procession to move forward. Therefore the procession halted. The young men of the village suddenly stopped playing the lezhim and refused to make way for the procession. Basically they wanted to obstruct the Ambedkar Jayanti procession. Divakar and Jyotiba made a request to the villagers: 'Give us space for the procession. Once it has gone ahead, you can play the lezhim once again.' The chairman of the Shivaji Jayanti blew off Jyotiba and Divakar's request. 'Take back your procession. We will not stop our play.' This was the stance the villagers took. 'The procession will stop here until you have finished your play. Then we will take the procession ahead,' Divakar explained. The villagers were not willing to accept that either. Little by little, they began to gather around Jyotiba and Divakar. All of them were stained with vermilion gulal. Divakar told the Dalits to sit down on the street. The villagers obstinately insisted that the procession be ended and turn back. Divakar and Jyotiba refused. Then shouts of 'Jai Bhavani! Jai Shivaji!' ensued and the procession was attacked. Confusion and cries began. People began to run helter-skelter. Kashi was badly injured. Divakar and Jyotiba were wounded. Babasaheb's statue was broken into pieces.

When Kashi regained consciousness, she began to see frightful countenances smeared with vermilion gulal. She grew terribly frightened. Divakar tried to restore his mother to full consciousness. The police came and arrested the villagers. The news came in the papers. The names of Devgarh and Divakar became famous.

Divakar became crazy with the thought of being a leader. He began to have dreams of being a political leader. Elections to the State Assembly were just around the corner. Every party had built up their organisation. Divakar, too, filled out an application for the election. This was an election for the reserved constituency. Divakar announced his candidacy for the Republican Party of India. The Republican Party was the official party of the Dalits. It was heir to the thought and struggle of Babasaheb Ambedkar. Divakar was excellent in every respect among all his competitors. He had a name as a political worker. For the past decade he had been working hard in the social movement. His name had the aura of fame and respect, but his caste had eclipsed and swallowed them up.

The party in power had given its candidacy to Dajiba. Dajiba was a flunkey to caste Hindu leaders. The true fight would be between Dajiba the candidate of the party in power, and between Divakar.

The Mahar caste was a bitter one. Belligerent and abusive, it had been awakened by Babasaheb Ambedkar's thought. The Mahars educated themselves. They formed associations. They engaged in struggles. That is why the Mahar caste was well ahead of other Dalit castes in all fields. It also got the benefit of all this. In comparison to the Mahars, other Dalit castes appeared backward.

Caste Hindu society was upset at the aggressiveness of the Mahars. They disliked them. Because Mahars do not vote for caste Hindus, they in their turn do not select them as their candidates. Caste Hindus select candidates from other Dalit castes and put them up against Mahars. However suitable the Mahar candidate is, he loses the election. Babasaheb Ambedkar himself had been defeated in this manner. So how was Divakar going to defeat his opponent? The results were announced. Dajiba had won with a large majority. Divakar had even lost his deposit. Dajiba's victory procession started. That day some stones had fallen on Divakar's home, and in a few villages of the constituency the villagers had rioted in the Maharwada. The Mahar community was thus being singled out and pounded. Many backward communities were going along with the caste Hindus against the Mahars. The Mahar candidates had been pushed aside in every sphere of activity.

Dajiba's victory procession ended. The public meeting began. Leaders thanking the voters. Politicians giving assurances to voters. Activists dreaming dreams of gaining power. The common people applauding. The crowd that had gathered because a man from their caste had won the election. Standing some distance from the crowd were poor women. Understanding nothing of all this, they gazed speechless at the crowd.

Within seconds, a fire broke out. Because of a short circuit, the entire mandap was consumed by flames. With one mind, people ran around screaming and were in confusion. Every man was trying to save his own life. Because of the unexpected fire, everyone ran wherever they found an opening. As they were running without restriction, out of fear of death, a lot of crushing and crowding ensued. Twenty people died in the stampede. Countless people were injured. Agonies of grief were heard all around.

Divakar, introverted on account of his defeat, was contemplating. It was not possible to govern this country on the strength of one caste. This country was divided into many castes. In order to win an election, one caste would have to rely on another. Therefore there was no alternative to a broad agreement in society. The caste Hindus did not give their votes to Dalits. If all the Dalit groups became one, it would be possible to fight against caste consciousness. Buddha, Phule, Kabir and Ambedkar had come and gone. But our society had remained the same. How would we be enough for it? Divakar was being flattened to the ground inside. Disappointment had encircled him. A by-election was announced. Divakar made a compromise. He asked for a ticket from the party in power. He filled out an election application form as a candidate for the party in power. Divakar had changed his profile for the chance of acquiring power. He was convincing himself about this. His character was one of truth and breadth. He was explaining to himself that because of this the movement would gain a new direction. The Dalit activists had gone against Divakar. The opinion had spread throughout their society that Divakar had sold himself to the party in power. And a storm had arisen in the party in power on account of Divakar's candidature.

The Dalits within the party in power had taken a stance against Divakar. 'We have been in the party for years,' they said. 'Instead of giving a ticket to us, you are giving it to an outsider who does not have any loyalty to the party.' That was the rebellious stance they took. The elections took place. Divakar was elected with a huge majority. Divakar's victory procession started. Bhimnagar was decorated to welcome Divakar.

There was no limit to Kashi's joy. Divakar's car came. Behind it were a fleet of cars, announcements, a fireworks display, the sky-splitting sounds of a shehnai troupe. Without going home, Divakar went straight to the village. He paid a visit to the village goddess. People were delighted that their candidate had won. The same people who had opposed the Ambedkar Jayanti procession were now singing praises of Divakar. His whole body was vermilion with the powder thrown at him.

The procession was going slowly towards Bhimnagar. Divakar was longing to meet his mother. The whole of Bhimnagar was standing with its eyes fixed on the route of the procession. Kashi and Jyotiba were in front of everything. Announcements could be heard. Also the sound of fireworks and musical instruments. Bhimnagar was crazed with joy. The uncontrollable bulk of the crowd was sliding towards Bhimnagar. A saffron cyclone was roaring up, and broken-down old Bhimnagar was standing like a small child to welcome it. Confusion too great to measure, a horrifying saffron mob of maddened, excited and violent people making a frenzied noise that burst the eardrums. Bhimnagar was shocked. The Dalits were terrified. They were paralysed with fear. Seeing the saffron crowd dancing towards her, Kashi was reminded of the attack that took place on their Ambedkar Jayanti procession. Kashi was losing consciousness. She broke out in a scream of terror. In an instant the Bhimnagar that was had disappeared. Everyone took their fate in their hands and fled.

Kashi had collapsed unconscious to the ground. Jyotiba was trying to restore her to consciousness.

The procession was proceeding slowly towards Bhimnagar in a delirium of celebration.

24

Cow Slaughter

Mhadba sold his cow to the butcher Yakub. He had meant to sell the cow for a long time. She did not give any milk; she was barren. So what was the use of keeping such an animal at his house? Mhadba sold his cow because selling her would bring him a little money. Yakub paid the money and took the cow's halter in his hand. Yakub felt happy. He had found an animal for the Wednesday market. Selling a live cow would bring him five hundred rupees. But slaughtering her and selling the meat would bring him a hundred or hundred and fifty rupees more. Today the number of people who ate the meat had increased. There was a new saying, wasn't there? 'If the Mahars have made books more expensive, Brahmins have made meat more dear.' People who never read had started reading books, and the caste that didn't eat meat had begun to eat it.

Yakub pulled the cow out of the cowshed. It began to bellow. The animals in the cowshed were looking silently at the departing cow. The cow's stall looked empty. Mhadba's eyes filled with tears. The master's wife fed the cow a final bhakri. The children of the house fell at the cow's feet in obeisance. Yakub pulled the cow out further. Mhadba pushed the cow forward. The cow crossed the threshold of the house and stepped out.

Yakub was proceeding with the cow. Yakub's son Hussain was walking behind the cow. He was urging the cow forward. Yakub was happy. He glanced at the cow every now and then. The animal had not been expensive. It would sell well. It would be enough if he got even a hundred or a hundred and fifty. He would be able to buy the children some clothes at Muharram. Yakub was thinking all this as he pulled the cow along. And the cow went quietly behind him.

Yakub was going happily along the road with the cow. On the way he met Gana Mahar. He saw the cow and halted Yakub. 'You got a fine animal there. For how many rupees did you clinch the deal?' he enquired. Yakub laughed as he answered his question. As he departed, Gana said, 'Keep the cow's tongue for me. Don't sell it to anyone else.' Yakub was happy to have acquired a customer.

Shekhar accosted Yakub. Shekhar's friends also came to his aid. They caught Yakub and took the cow into their possession. Their emotions were inflamed at seeing a mother cow in a Muslim's hands. They berated Yakub. He resisted them. A quarrel broke out between them. Shekhar's anger became uncontrollable. He took hold of Yakub by the collar. A street fight began. Men came out of the Muslim mohalla. The Hindus gathered, too. Fisticuffs started. Blood was spilt from one or two people. The atmosphere was ruined. The quiet cow, too, bellowed.

Shekhar brought the cow back. He tied her to a tether. He reprimanded his father. He hadn't liked this deed of his father's. He was seething with anger. 'Baba, you have committed a sin by selling our mother cow. Oh, what did it matter that she was barren? Would we have sold our barren mother? You are committing the crime of selling our mother.' Mhadba was very annoyed. All the Hindus had gathered and were pinning his ears back with complaints. That such an incident should occur at the home of Shekhar, one of the most hard-bitten Hindutvavadi activists, was not tolerable to other activists.

The activists were furious. Shekhar's leadership was in peril, which was why he had cornered his father.

'The cow is a mother. In Hindu culture, a cow is considered pure. Not only that, but her urine, too, is considered pure. Three hundred and thirty million gods reside in her. The cow is a useful animal. For farmers, the cow is Kamadhenu—the sacred cow that fulfills all wishes. The cow gives milk. She gives birth to calves. The cow is pure. Violence against such a cow must stop.' Shekhar was giving a speech in a loud voice. An assembly had been planned in the village against violence towards cows.

'The cow may be pure to you. But we like cow's meat. The cow is our food. What kind of ban is this on our food?' This was the kind of conversation that went on in the Muslim and Mahar quarters. But no one was speaking out against the village. 'You slaughter the cattle in secret. We'll eat the meat in secret.' This, too, was being said. 'The slaughterhouse must be closed down.' This was the demand the Hindus were putting forward. The police had come into the village. In the forty-five years since Independence, this was the first time the villagers had seen policemen moving about in the village. Because of a cow, the village had become a topic of discussion in the state. Because of a cow, Shekhar's name was on people's lips. Seeing the rebellious stance he had taken against his own father, the district political world had accepted him. Mhadba had understood his own mistake. He now agreed that, 'A cow means a mother.'

The village's affairs proceeded smoothly. The police went away. Yakub brought in animals at night from outside the village. He would slaughter them at night. The villagers had slowly started to forget. Those who ate beef were eating it. Every day a cow's throat was slit. The cow's bellows were being buried under the blade of a sharp knife. Shekhar had acquired new responsibilities. He, too, was doing his work with hope. A new atmosphere of harmony was present in the village.

The village woke up to the sound of the morning bells. The sound of the temple bells spread throughout the village. People used to wake up and set out for the temple. There would be the first aarti of the day in the dawn chill. Everyone would gather for the morning puja. Every dawn, purified by prayer, they would be terrified by the bellowing of the cattle in the slaughterhouse outside the village.

On hearing the sound of the temple bells, Yakub, too, would awaken. Hussain would take the knife. The village would have gathered in the temple. Yakub would tie the four legs of the cow together. He would throw the cow down. It would struggle. Yakub's household would come to his help. Hussain would hand Yakub the knife. Yakub's wife Malan would bring him a copper vessel full of water. Yakub would give the cow its last drink of water. The cow would bellow. The hymns would cause the cow's eyes to brim. The inner sanctum of the temple, exalted with the hymns, would make one's throat fill. Yakub would examine the knife. He would place it on the cow's throat. Summoning all the strength in his body, he would wield the knife. Spurts of blood would fly. The cow's bellowing would spread and fill the dawn. The cow would writhe. Little by little, the cow's body would grow cold. As the dawn aarti finished, everyone would eat their share of the prasad and go home. The cow would go to heaven. Yakub would skin the cow. He would put the hide to one side. Slowly the sun would rise. The sun's rays would get stained by the cow's blood. One by one, customers would come. The cow from the cowshed would cook on the stove. It would bellow. Once more, the dawn aarti. Once more, the bellowing.

Shekhar announced a fast unto death for the demand that there should be a law prohibiting cow slaughter. Again the atmosphere took a different turn. The discussion overflowed. Newspaper columns began to fill. Opinions began to be laid out both for and against cow slaughter. 'Our country is a secular one. Such a law cannot be passed in a secular country.'

This, too, was heard. The movement took on an ugly nature. Shekhar began his preparations for the fast.

The barren cow in Shekhar's house had died. Shekhar felt very bad. He had to set out today for his fast. Mhadba sent a message to Gana Mahar. Gana Mahar brought along four men. They tied up the body of the cow. They lifted her. The cow had been given into the custody of the Mahars. 'If Mother had died, would you have asked the Mahars to drag her away?' Since he would otherwise miss his train, Shekhar set out for the district headquarters to begin his fast. Gana Mahar brought the cow outside the village. They put it into a dark wood. Gana put his knife to the cow's throat. He skinned the cow. He took the hide into his possession. Then other men came. They took the cow's meat. Then came the dogs. They bit off pieces of bone. After them came the vultures. They pounced on the cow's skeleton. Now came Yakub. He took the cow's bones and sold them. Truly, how useful an animal the cow was! Shekhar withdrew his fast. He was going to get a ticket for the Lok Sabha election.

Every day, dawn would appear. The priest's hands would be stained with *tirth*, and Yakub's hands would be purified with cow's blood.

25

The Mausoleum

That night the sky had filled with clouds. The wind was blowing in gusts. Lightning bolts were flaring out from time to time. Anyone could have said that it would rain that night. The advent of rain had become certain in the atmosphere. The whole village of Pimpri Deshmukh in Parbhani District was making for home for fear of the rain. Cooking fires had been lit. Worn-out men were settling on the ground. The village's bhajan-singing group was assembling one by one in the temple.

Since the attainment of Independence, there had been ten parliamentary elections, but the orthodox atmosphere of the village of Pimpri Deshmukh had not changed. The history of this country was itself like that. Kings changed, kingdoms changed, but society here changed at its own pace. People were the way they were. In this village, Dalits were still not allowed to enter the temple. They were not allowed to fill water at the caste Hindus' well. Just as termites attack books, some man takes birth, breaking through the traditions of thousands of years.

The village had grown absorbed in bhajans. Religious observance had given them status. Their god, too, was disloyal to human beings. He weighed caste Hindus in one set of scales, and Shudras in another. He gave all rights and privileges to caste Hindus. Society was tightly bound in religious rules. Every page of the religious books bore orders to insult and torture Shudras. One felt like shitting on every page of those religious books. These mantras should be soaked in one's urine. It was these mantras that denied our humanity. So we deny those mantras. We put our foot shod in a boot on the head of a god who considers us impure, and say to him, 'You pimp! How many of our Rukminis have you despoiled? How many of our women have you kidnapped? How many of our Parvatis have you killed? You have turned us into bulls. Hey, how many sham guises do you have? A poisonous snake moves around your neck, and in front of you, the bull Nandi—but not any of us. Hey, you can safely digest venom, but not our entry into temples. We feel like tearing you out root and branch. What kind of a god are you? One that instils hate between man and man. We feel like applying bullwhips to the genitals of all priests and throwing them out. You pimps, how many idols of stone will you pamper while you keep on denying human beings?' These thoughts were buzzing in Kotwal Ambadas Sabne's head like a honeycomb swarming with bees. Ambadas Sabne was the kotwal of this village. A Dalit kotwal had to serve the village. He had to labour for the caste Hindus. He could not flout the norms of any community. If societal norms were breached, there were the *panch*, the gods, and rules of right and wrong. With what crafty and devious machinations the religious books were filled! Those religious books had caught leprosy!

The bhajani mandali was singing hymns in the temple. A few of the village goons had also assembled in the temple to look at the women in the bhajani mandali. The priest, arranging his *pancha* around him, was coming in and out. The mridangs were resounding. Clashing cymbals kept the beat. Everyone's voices had found a melodious balance. The sound of the veena mingled well with the notes of the harmonium. Mhorkya was gesturing as he sang. The woman who was singing the *goulan* had drawn her saree tight over her chest, so the gaze of the *ektara* player went to her bosom. She had no bosom. The priest's breasts, if measured, would prove larger than hers.

The sky began a drumbeat. Large, round drops of rain began to fall. People on the street started to seek shelter. This rain would fall all night. Nails should be hammered in at the doors of the rain. Today the rain had taken on a dreadful form. The next day a statue of Dr. Babasaheb Ambedkar was to be installed in Bhimnagar. The whole settlement had collected money. A stone statue had been sculpted. Tomorrow was to be a festival day for the settlement. Tomorrow the settlement would sing and dance. They would instal Babasaheb's statue. Kotwal Sabne had taken the lead for installing the statue in the settlement.

Kotwal Sabne had experienced self-respect. He lived in the village with self-respect, but the self-respect of Dalits rankled with caste Hindus as if it were the raised hood of a cobra. The village did not approve of Sabne's living with self-respect. It envied his good clothes. Dalits should wear dirty, tattered clothing. They should live subserviently in the village. They should live in huts. They should not build good houses. Sabne was a challenge to all this.

The installation of a statue of Babasaheb in Bhimnagar would give birth to a rebellion against Babasaheb himself. The village had come to think about Babasaheb just as King Kansa thought when his sister Devaki gave birth to a son. The village Patil had already pinned back Sabne's ears for a scolding about his deeds. The village had already had a few meetings about the issue of the statue's installation in the Dalit settlement. The village was opposed to the statue. A statue of Babasaheb was not just a statue. It was a volcano of self-confidence. How could the village afford to have that volcano simmering away just outside the village limit? How could the Dalits continue to live at the level of the villagers' shoes? How could they go on enduring servitude? As long as Dalits remained unconscious of their slavery, the village's reign was intact. Now the village was realising that the sand was slipping under their feet. There was fretting and fuming in the village now.

The rain gained strength. There was a crackling bolt of lightning. Kotwal Sabne, getting wet, came to the shelter of the temple. In the temple people were remembering and invoking the name of god. God was being made happy. Lamps were lit. The face of god was glowing in the pleasant light from the large hanging lamp. The inner sanctum was heavy with devotion. Kotwal Sabne's feet touched the first step of the temple, and the essence of god was rocked from the steps up to the pinnacle. There is no death for those who seek sanctuary. These Hindu gods are very generous. They protect their devotees. God will mill the flour for some Janabai. He will draw the cattle for some Chokhamela. If some Draupadi's clothes are being pulled off her, he will provide fresh clothes. But when hands are laid on a Dalit woman's clothing, he will remain as he is. Kotwal Sabne had come to god for shelter. On seeing Sabne, the cymbals halted, the veena was rocked, and the ektara began to tremble. The recitation of *owis* stopped; in their place arose curses. In a moment the bhajani mandali fell silent. Its exaltation fled. The sacred chant of god's name was destroyed. Seeing that Sabne was entering the temple and polluting their pure god, the priest's body cloth began to tremble. The Patil was disturbed. A few respected goons were enraged. One step of Sabne's had blackened the devout atmosphere of the temple.

Sabne was standing firmly by the temple door. Just as if a crackling bolt of lightning from the sky was standing holding the door. In the temple, god, and in the doorway, Kotwal Sabne. Within the sound of the rain, the village had become dead silent. Kotwal Sabne stood there calmly. The goons arose. The Patil followed them. The temple was taking a different turn.

The goons caught hold of Sabne. The cymbalists came running. They all caught hold of him. They knocked him down. They started beating him. The priest was banging away at the bell. The villagers had gone wild and were banging away at Sabne. Sabne was shouting. It was raining stormily. Sabne was groaning. The goons were mad with fervour. They beat Sabne with kicks and blows. A bolt of lightning fell on the pinnacle of the temple, and a murderous silence began to inhabit it. In the heavy rain, they started to make for home one by one. The priest, too, left god alone, and went home in the rain. The temple emptied out. There were now two corpses in the temple. One was of Kotwal Sabne. The other was of god.

The rain was coming down in sheets. Lightning was flashing and crackling. The nanda-jyot that burnt in the temple was still alight. A solitary mouse was running here and there in the inner sanctum. The walls of the temple had begun to leak. A storm came. Hail fell. The darkness deepened and an enormously loud lightning bolt fell. There was a noise loud enough to keep the village awake at night. Cracks appeared in the temple walls from its pinnacle to its steps. A bastion of the temple crumpled and fell.

First thing tomorrow, the priest would come and make an announcement: 'Sabne came to take a darshan of the god. He was so exalted with devotion that even when the temple wall collapsed, he did not run away. He was beloved of the gods. He has gone to god's home. He has become a saint.' The village will gather. Money will be collected. A mausoleum will be built for the saint Sabne, like Chokhamela, and the same murderers will gather to sing bhajans.

26

Sir, I Salute You

The enormous temple of Vitthala. The daily crowd of people seeking to acquire merit. The shops that survived by selling flower garlands, bouquets, incense sticks, abir and gulal. Processions of prasad on every side. The victory cries of boon-seekers. Players on cymbals and drums who had come there from afar. Their stony eyes in which god had blossomed. Those songs of devotion made weighty with the worship of Vitthala and Rakhumai. The pujas scattered like dewdrops on the faith of the devotees. And the puja of the priests which had this faith as its base. The very different economics of this temple.

This town resounding to the drumbeat as if the sound of the drum was thrumming out of the very soil. Men bleached out by gunny sacking. Foreheads anointed with an excess of gulal. Ears purified by the ringing of the name of Hari. The gaze of eyes joyfully fulfilled by the immense crowd of devotees. The vow moving forward through the line of worshippers. Vitthal perched on the minds of policemen harassed with carrying out their duties. Or Vitthal hidden in the hearts of the *badvas* who made haste to hand out prasad to the devotees.

The suitability of worshippers assessed by the flower garlands they offered. The size of the donation determining whether they got blessings full-mouthed. And the river

Chandrabhaga flowing at a distance from all this. The shadows of sin that had flowed away into the hot desert sand, spilling from an overfull vessel. This vessel was neither on this bank nor on the other. It was stationed in the centre, in Vitthal. The cries of victory on their lips had been smothered by the water. They had received a water burial at the bottom of the Chandrabhaga. Some young men would come along at some time, as in Tukaram's songs. But as of now, they are merely an item in a newspaper.

Outside the temple of Vitthal was the mausoleum of Chokhamela. He was a scion of the dwellers outside the town. In the path of Bhakti, all are equal. Chokhamela, Sena Nhavi, Gora Kumbhar, Savta Mali, Jani, Rohidas: it is on account of their unprecedented devotion that the dark presence of Vitthal acquired its popularity.

Vitthal ground flour for one person; he drew animals for another. This enormous heart would work itself to the bone day and night for his devotees. I was sitting near the mausoleum of Chokhamela. Chokha the Mahar was a devotee of Vitthal. His devotion became immortal. Following the great example of Chokha, new Chokha Mahars were born from village to village. Carrying the flag of Vitthal on their shoulders, they began to join in the pilgrimage to Pandharpur. People from a variety of castes and places take part in Vitthal's pilgrimage. The pilgrimage goes to Vitthal's court. All of them take a darshan of Vitthal according to their capacity and station in life. Forgetting their caste and identity, the pilgrims make a run towards Vitthal. It is only after returning to their villages that they go back into the bounds of their caste.

Chokha Mahar was a saint of the dwellers outside the village boundary. He, too, served Vitthal with all his heart and mind. Although Chokha was one of the Mahars, he was a beloved devotee of Vitthal's. Vitthal had a measureless affection for Chokha. Vitthal, who never discriminates between his devotees, is profound. 'Say *Pundalik Var De Hari Vitthal. Shri Dnyandev Tukaram, Pandharinath Maharaj ki Jai!'*

Vitthal dragged away animals. Dragging animals is Mahars' work. They must do it honourably and with honesty. Devotion to one's duty is true worship of God. Dragging away animals is not bad work. No work is bad. One remembers that Mahatma Gandhi cleaned latrines.

We must do the work that has come down to us by tradition. Along with that we must pray to God. God helps us; he drags animals, he does the washing, he grinds the flour. Keeping the image of Chokha Mahar in their view, my ancestors had sworn their fealty to Vitthal.

Johar, mai baap, johar,
I am the saint's house Mahar.

We were, in fact, house Mahars to the Patil.

Vitthal's Mahar. The saint's house Mahar. The Patil's Mahar.

Whatever may be the case, this town was a sacred place. It was the abode of moksha. The sins of many were washed away. People gained merit. Thousands, hundreds of thousands of people came there, driven mad by their devotion to God. I recall the March to Dandi. It was a demonstration for a handful of salt, a movement begun against hundred and fifty years of servitude foisted on us. I also remember the movement begun at the lake in Mahad. This movement launched for a handful of water was against the caste society that had persisted for thousands of years, and for equality. I can see those processions, those pilgrimages. But the endless night in the country has not ended yet. Even so, the efforts of those thousands of people go on drying up in the desert.

Live on, just as it has been ordained forever.
Let it call your attention; take comfort from it.

Vitthal dragged dead animals. Dr. Ambedkar said, 'Don't drag dead animals', and our houses burned.

The storm of the Ambedkarite movement had reached the doorstep of every hut in the villages. The previous year we had celebrated Dr. Ambedkar's anniversary in the village. We all left the Hindu religion and became Buddhists. Our Maharwada was now called Bhimnagar. We were now known as NeoBuddhists in official circles. We were still living outside the village limits. Even though we were converts, the roof over our head remained the same. There was also no change at all in our poverty. But this much is true: we had acquired manhood.

It was morning. Somebody's animal had died in the village. A message came that a Mahar should come and drag it away. The Mahars refused to drag it, and the villagers had set fire to their huts. Our house was burnt down, too.

'We are Buddhists now.'

'Who told you to become Buddhists?'

'Who told you to keep us outside the village?'

We had gained the strength to answer question with question. The days of mutely swallowing our own spit had ended. We had freedom. We had rights. We had gained acceptance as men. This was an unacceptable truth. That's why our house was burnt. We went silent. Because the question of our daily bread had not yet been resolved.

We left the village, we left our homes, and we left the rural area and went to the town. We came here with the hope that here we would get the protection of the law.

The saint Chokha's memorial is a support to our life. Pious people come here to have a darshan of Vitthal. I do the work of guarding their footwear. I get twenty-five paise for each pair of sandals. I give them a token. I look after their slippers. Guarding the footwear of pious people is a meritorious act. Some of those pious people quarrel with me. They leave their slippers somewhere else. Until their slippers are stolen, they will not appreciate my worth.

In my childhood I used to come to this temple. I used to filch a handsome pair of slippers, put them on my feet and leave. My little brother used to help me in this work. If a man dressed in a suit approached, I would keep watch on him. I would see where he left his slippers. Once he entered the temple, I would quietly go near the slippers. I would look to either side, adeptly put on the slippers and walk out in great style. Later I would sell the stolen slippers, boots and sandals, pricing them a little lower. I used to run the house in this way. Now I do the work of guarding footwear.

Today, since we have the festivals of Ashadi and Kartiki *ekadasis*, my business is going well. I get some money from it. This is the mercy of Vitthal. People who have studied and got M.A.s and B.A.s are without jobs. One should lead one's life honestly guarding other people's footwear, all the while chanting, 'Hari, Hari.'

Some time later, the police came dragging a woman. She was pregnant. The police were cursing her. She was crying. She had stolen some woman's mangalsutra. There would always be a handful of thieves at a religious occasion. How could Vitthal be concerned about everyone? We must guard ourselves against pickpockets. And if they didn't pick pockets, how would they live? The police were beating up the mangalsutra thief. Then they took her to the police chowky.

The crowd of people was like a swarm of ants. The atmosphere was stirred up by the noise. Gulal was being flung into the air. The pilgrims were dancing to the beat of cymbals and drums. The chanting of Hari's name made the mind ecstatic. The beast in men's minds had fled. Man now belonged to God.

'Oh, lady! Leave your slippers here.'

'How many paise?'

'Twenty-five.'

'No, we'll leave them somewhere else.'

'Their slippers ought to be stolen.'

I would take other people's footwear into my care. I would give them tokens. I would accept those tokens and give back people's footwear. Business was going well. It was getting difficult for me to look after so many items of footwear. No food since morning. The afternoon was coming to a close. My mother had still not brought my lunch. If my father had sat here for a little while, I could have had my lunch and returned. But, keeping me hungry, my father was enjoying roaming around and mingling with the pilgrims. He was always more interested in the pilgrims than in his own family.

After some time, the police caught a man and brought him there. The police were belabouring him. They were calling him a slipper thief. It was my father. I was frenzied. I could understand nothing. I was throwing all the footwear that I had with me. The crowd of worshippers was in turmoil. I had become uncontrollable.

27

Vows

The sun was cooking my body to a roasted crisp; the wind was roaring like a monster. All the people were occupied with wandering to support themselves. The eyes of the sky had turned white. Somehow or other, people were grinding themselves, doing famine work. The torture that dumb animals were going through was painful to behold. In order to survive, people were going off in all directions, changing their places of residence. The whole village was desolate. The love that mothers felt for their children had lessened. What godforsaken times had come upon everybody! 'If God takes something in mind, no one else's word counts.' Sin had increased; that's why it didn't rain. The prediction the priest had made in the last festival had come true.

Mahishasuri was a true goddess. Vows made to her were fruitful; boons were granted. Childless people had children. If there was fighting in the house, she would sort out that misunderstanding. She could turn five into fifty. If their character was good, nobody would go away empty-handed. Some way would arise out of the current famine. How long could Mahisubai go on watching her own children suffer?

Parshya had come to the village after ten years. At Mahisubai's festival, the people were going to make Parshya take the vow of the *dhadka*. Parshya left the village during a time of drought. Mumbai showed favour to him. Parshya had earned affection by labouring like a beast of burden. Parshya's wife Subhadra had taken jewellery. Otherwise her life would have been spent cleaning houses in the village. She would not have remained *raya*. So what if he was cleaning out shit in Mumbai? He had returned to the village in style. Was there just soil in the countryside?

The next day there was to be a festival. Relatives and guests had begun to arrive. The area of the temple had started to swell. The village Mahars had thoroughly cleaned the courtyard. They had used paint, too. Women were plastering the floors of their houses from side to side and up and down with fresh cow dung. Washing and bathing was going on, too. Everything was being cleaned and purified so that no pollution would remain. Parshya's mother had brought a pot full of cow's urine and kept it in the house. From house to house elderly people were keeping watch to ensure that the garments of strange people did not touch anything important. The next day Parshya's mother was to make her prostration to the goddess. She had bought a goat as high as her waist. She was going to perform a sacrifice of that goat. The house was full of guests.

The next day Mhasha was going to perform the dhadka, so Parshya was anxious. He remembered doing his dhadka the previous year. He remembered his head all covered in blood. Parshya had come close to death but had been saved, thanks to his mother. Parshya's uncle did not take the dhadka, so his vow had been broken. Parshya felt afraid of having to take the dhadka. Who can go against God's will? It is He who brings all to birth, and it is He who causes them to die.

The festival had gathered at Mahisubai's temple. Worshippers and enthusiasts had formed a crowd.

Shops selling coconuts, turmeric, kumkum, incense sticks, flower garlands and offerings of bordered blouse pieces had been set up near the temple. A swarm of people had flown to them. Surrounding them were bullock-carts from villages all over. Beneath each bullock-cart was a goat, a chicken or a buffalo brought there to be sacrificed to Mahisubai. Everyone was wrapped in his own self-satisfaction. Cooking fires made of three stones had been lit on every side.

The Patil of the village and four Mahars had set up near the temple. The festival was reaching its full height. It was unbearably crowded. Goats were sacrificed. Numberless chickens were cut. There was a slush of blood in front of the temple. On the door of the temple bloody palm-prints had been slapped. The musicians could be heard. The devotees were crowing and parading. The women who had been possessed by the goddess were dancing in the temple courtyard. Heaps of incense ash and coconut were lying around. There was a long queue for darshan. The police had their hearts in their mouth. How long and how well could they control the crowd?

The dhadka was to start in a little while. Parshya had made his boy bathe and drink something. He explained to him how to take the dhadka. 'You must not take the dhadka too hard. If the dhadka is too hard, it injures the brain. One's understanding is destroyed. A man could die. So you must take the dhadka in such a way that you will not upset Mahisubai. Don't forget the invocation to Mahisubai.' Parshya was explaining everything this way and that to his youngest offspring. And Mhasha was not listening with total concentration. 'A dhadka like this—is it a *bidka*?' he said, fed up. At this, Parshya roared out loud, 'Don't talk like that! Or Mother Mahisubai will take care of you! Don't blaspheme against the devi or you will die. Say *Toba, toba* at once. You must sacrifice the goat. After that a mutton curry should be cooked and offered before the goddess. Then the visitors should make their offerings. Then and only then you should dine. Then you should watch the dhadkas.'

People were putting up flowers on the goddess. They were setting light to oil. Women were holding the hands of their little children so they should not get lost in the crowd. 'You picked my pocket, you pimp!' people were shouting at a poor man as they fell upon him. The police got hold of him and took him away. People who had made vows came dancing, with music playing.

The time came for the dhadka. The procession was approaching, accompanied by loud music. In front was the priest, calling out, 'Mother, come. Mother, come,' and throwing around limes, turmeric and lime leaves. Married women were holding lamps with five wicks. The men who were to take the dhadka, wearing garlands and so on, were walking towards the goddess's temple like sacrificial goats. Behind them was a crowd of people. A confused scrum was taking place before the temple. Men were performing the run towards Mother Mahisubai. The drummers sounded louder and louder. They were throwing coconuts against the walls of the temple. Confusion abounded everywhere.

Parshya, his mother, Subhadra, Mhasha and their kin were standing to one side. There was a garland around Mhasha's neck. They had worshipped the goddess with live coals and incense. Subhadra had prostrated herself before Mahisubai, spreading out the end of her saree in supplication. Parshya's mother had done a great deal. An enormous crowd had spread everywhere. The dhadka ceremonies were about to begin.

Anxiety was burning in the hearts of those who were about to take the dhadka. The previous year Genudada had taken the dhadka and lost his wits. Women and children were watching, astonished. Yesu had come drunk on alcohol to take the dhadka. His arms and legs were trembling. People had climbed onto trees to watch. The priest, the Patil, the Mahar village worker and the police were there in readiness. The blood of the sacrificial animals had been spilt at the temple. Now the blood of the Mahars was about to splash there. The caste panchayat of the Mahars had worshipped Mahisubai with all dignities. Mahisubai gave a good omen in reply. The famine would go away. Disease would stop. Everyone chanted the praises of Mahisubai.

Yema was to take the dhadka for the first time. Yema began his run from about twenty-five feet away. The drums grew louder. The priest scattered ash from the goddess's sacrificial fire. The priest chanted, 'Mother, Mother, run to me!' Yema was going to fulfil his vow by taking his dhadka against the wall of the goddess's temple. He would collide with the temple like an animal. Put his life in danger. This was a custom with a tradition of years. Mahars had been observing it for years without any fanfare. As the saying goes, 'If you rape a dumb woman, she will neither shout nor make a noise.'

Yema began to run. He hit his head on the wall with a resounding crack. And, holding his head, he abruptly sat down. The village Mahar took him to one side. The priest applied some of the sacred ash. People poured turmeric onto his wounded head. Ten people gathered around Yema. People were beating frantically on the drums. The priest was shouting. He was dancing with a lime held in his mouth. He was chewing lime twigs with a squelching sound. People were in an uproar. Everywhere there was awe of Mother Mahisubai. Married women holding lamps with five wicks had stopped beneath the banyan tree.

Now it was Bhimsha's turn. Bhimsha started preparing to take the dhadka. His mother showered flowers upon him. She applied sacred ash. She touched the backs of her fingers to her ears to protect him from the evil eye. She prayed to Mahisubai. The sound of the drums grew louder and louder. Bhimsha began to run. The whole crowd was looking at Bhimsha. Bhimsha knocked his head against the wall and fell to the ground. A few people drew him to one side. The priest applied sacred ash to him. The priest also applied turmeric to his head. Bhimsha's teeth were clenched. The drums were sounding without cease.

Seeing all this, Parshya's throat became dry. He looked at his son.

Mhasha prepared to take the dhadka. Parshya joined his hands in prayer to Mother Mahisubai. Parshya's mother made a deep obeisance. Subhadra was gazing wide-eyed. She was muttering, 'Toba! Toba!' Her eyes had filled with tears. Saying, 'You are the one who gives life. You are also the one who takes it away. Keep my children in your womb,' Subhadra folded her hands to Mahisubai. The devotee danced differently. His face smeared with vermilion looked ghastly.

Mhasha started to run. The crowd was looking at him. Mhasha took the dhadka and silently crumpled to the ground. A few people moved him to one side. Mhasha's limbs were trembling. The whites of his eyes showed. Spurts of blood were flying from him. The priest was applying sacred ash to him. The devotee was filling his wound with turmeric. The drums were playing. People were in shock. The dhadka had taken place at the height of the run. Parshya's limbs were melting under him. Subhadra could understand nothing. Mhasha was not speaking. He was not crying. Subhadra entered the crowd. And many streams of tears began to flow from her eyes. 'Don't cry,' the Pothraj was saying to her. 'You will commit a sin. Be silent. Mahisubai is doing all this,' the priest was babbling.

Mhasha's legs spasmed and he gave up his life. The drummers were still sounding. Subhadra went running and began to knock her head 'Bang! Bang!' against the wall. Streams of blood began to flow from her head. The entire crowd became panic-stricken. 'Bring my son to life. You are the image of truth. Or else I will take my life.' Saying this, Subhadra took the dhadka and collapsed to the ground. Her body was bathed in blood. A few people moved her to one side.

Men are supposed to take the dhadka. If women take it, that brings disaster to the whole village. Now everyone was worried about what was going to happen to them. The whole temple was appalled and terrified. Seeing the bodies of

Subhadra and Mhasha lying dead, Parshya's emotions were torn to pieces. Subhadra's and Mhasha's bodies lay before the temple like sacrificial goats. The drummers were sounding. Barmya prepared himself to take the dhadka. Everyone was doing the sacred run of Mahisubai.

Garlands and coconuts were lying in heaps. On the far side, women were dancing. The priest was cutting limes into pieces and throwing them in every direction. A caste panchayat had been set up in the courtyard of the temple. The lamps of the married women were overflowing. The priests scattered sacred ash all around. The village worker was marshalling the crowd.

Barmya was running to take his dhadka. Each one gets gifts according to his deserts. Unless there has been an error, Mahisubai does not get angry. God makes no distinction between the five fingers of his hand. Parshya must have committed some mistake. Parshya's mother was at a total loss. She was desolate with the fear of a sin. She was confused. She felt as if the sky had fallen on her. She was growing more panic-stricken moment by moment. But Parshya was beside himself.

Barmya was running for the dhadka. And Parshya, too, pushed through the crowd and started to run. The priest came in his way. Parshya shouldered him aside and slipped into the temple. The priest blocked him. Parshya took hold of the lock of hair on his head and sent him sprawling. Parshya went into the temple. The village followed him. Parshya climbed up on the goddess's head and began a stamping dance. Both his feet were full of vermilion. As if Mahisubai's head had been reduced to smithereens under Parshya's feet, and his feet had been soaked with Mahisubai's blood. The priest was speechless. The village worker caught hold of Parshya and pulled him down.

The hubbub outside the temple had increased. The dhadka had come to a halt.

The priest's mouth had gone dry. The women possessed by the spirit of the goddess were back to their usual selves. The sound of the drums had ceased. The married women had fled. The crowd had thronged the place. Women and children had taken their lives in their hands and gone to their own homes. The people had created an uproar in front of the goddess.

The village worker lifted Parshya up and brought him out of the temple. People could see his feet, all covered with vermilion. And Parshya, like a man demented, was shouting out curses at Mother Mahisubai.

28

Sunflower

Trimukh was tiring like an ebbing flood. Each step he took in front of him freed itself and fell, like a comet freeing itself from the force of gravity. His gaze was being uprooted from him and falling, like a collapsing tree. His stomach felt as desolate as a ruined sanctuary.

Trimukh was a boy of about fifteen years. He had set out for Banaras. Walking silently. Carrying his mother's bones. His village had receded far behind him. He did not even know how much further Banaras was from him. He had no money with him, nor food and clothing. What did he have at all besides these? It was only the filial duty of throwing his mother's cremated remains into the river Ganga at Banaras that had made him set out. Crossing village after village. He was told that he would reach the railway station in two days. He had not yet ridden in a railway train. He had never even seen one. The railway, Banaras, his mother's bones: all these things were choking his heart like a dam about to burst.

Today Trimukh was tired out by the incessant walking. His hunger and thirst were making him desperate. He could hardly eat his mother's bones. He was exhausted. The tattered clothes he was wearing, the dishevelled, overgrown hair on his head, the dirt accumulated on his body, his concave stomach, his sunken eyes, combined with the bundle of bones he was carrying, made his appearance disgusting.

Trimukh was the son of the Mang called Sambha. His stomach was hollow with fear of his low status. His caste followed him about like a demon. He couldn't forget his inferiority complex. His caste had hollowed him out. His humanity had died a long time ago. The only thing that remained in him was his disgusting caste. There was pressure of his caste on his mind. He couldn't cross his limits.

'I am a Mang' was all he knew. He had often remained hungry, but had not stepped above his station in life. He had not wished to commit the sin of acting against the religion that had been handed down to him. He was diffident. He was fearful. His caste had made him helpless. While walking in the streets or travelling around villages, he acted as if he was balancing the weight of his caste on a high wire.

Someone had thrown some spoiled rice at the side of the road. Dogs were eating that rice. With a leap Trimukh sat down by that heap of rice. The dogs ran away. He started eating that spoiled rice. Just as fire laid siege to skyscrapers twenty-five stories high, hunger had laid siege to him. Each cell of Trimukh's body had become a ravening hunger. Trimukh's hunger had become as monstrous as a bursting dam.

Before the mansion in front of him, Trimukh saw a new bride doing a puja to the sacred tulsi plant. His thirst reached the tulsi plant like the hand of a thief. The roots of his thirst were becoming madly clasped to the roots of that tulsi plant. He slid towards the door of the mansion like a lizard.

The dogs were barking at Trimukh. That house, too, seemed to be rejecting him in the guise of a dog. The animal in that dog had died a long time before. All that remained was a domesticated human. After completing the tulsi puja with complete devotion, that new bride had gone inside. Along with her newly washed hair, the straying end of her saree, her rounded hips, Trimukh's view of her vanished into the house.

In a little while, a household servant came out. He yelled at Trimukh.

The tulsi was a tame pigeon.

The dog was a domesticated man.

The household servant was a trained animal.

Even in that bright sunlight, who knows how Trimukh's shadow disappeared into the shadow of the mansion. Trimukh was becoming distracted in the scorching heat. He had lingered in the shade of that mansion. He was reminded of the mansion owned by his master.

The thing that stood out most in his village was the mansion of Shivaji Patil. Trimukh's father was Shivaji Patil's Mang. Shivaji Patil had looked after Sambha Mang. Sambha Mang had grown up with food and shelter from Shivaji Patil. Shivaji Patil had given a loan and arranged a marriage for Sambha. The loan had not yet been paid off. Sambha's wife had passed away, and Sambha had been rotting in jail for the past five years. Shivaji Patil had an immense bearlike strength in the region, but in the village elections Sarjerao had defeated the Patil's party. In the elections, the Maharwada had voted against the Patil. Sarjerao's party had been elected, and the Patil was unhappy.

In order to avenge his defeat, the Patil collected about fifty goons and launched an attack on the Maharwada. They had burnt a few huts. They had killed Dagdu Mahar. The Maharwada had been destroyed. The backlash for this atrocity had registered itself everywhere. Many cases had been filed, and the post of Patil had been lost.

That post had gone to Dagdu Mahar's son. Shivaji Patil was enraged at the insult. The worth of his status and his ancestry had been reduced to mud. The ignominy had bound their muzzles into silence. The Patil was blazing with vengeance. That the Patil's post should go to a Mahar's family was in any circumstance an inflammable matter for him. 'A Mahar has become the Patil': that was a pain he could not endure. He was being killed by it, though alive.

Shivaji Patil gave Sambha Mang a contract to kill. Sambha had to honour his instruction. Shivaji Patil's favours to him were such that they could not be repaid. For Sambha, to disrespect the word of the Patil was a sin. He was ready to give his life for his master. His creed was that his master was the road to moksha for him. 'Sambha, I don't care if I lose all my fields, I'll pay your bail and get you out. I'll look after your wife and children very well. Don't worry about it. Just remove this thorn from my way.'

Sambha murdered the son of Dagdu Mahar in broad daylight. He cut off his head, bound it in his upper garment and flaunted it in the Patil's honour. A tremendous wave of fear shocked the village before departing.

The Patil was looking after Sambha's wife and children. Saraja used to work herself to death in the Patil's fields, and the Patil would feed her. Trimukh looked after the animals. The Patil raised him, considering it his fate. Day after day came and went like the breeze. She was like the animals in the Patil's barn. She lived night and day, in daylight and dark, by the Patil's hands and feet. The Patil's words, his spit, his gaze, his wishes, had become the unbreachable boundaries of her life. After Sambha, she was totally in the Patil's custody. She would do whatever the Patil told her and eat whatever he gave her.

Saraja became pregnant by the Patil. The whole village was up against the Patil. This had been so for thirteen months. Saraja's belly was growing larger day by day. Her calves were swelling like the corn in the crop. The Patil's sleep had become a torment to him. Sambha's murderous hands stalked him day and night.

Saraja died of snakebite; the Patil performed her last rites.

Trimukh slowly began to slither like a snail towards the bathing pond. He set down the bundle of bones and took some water into his cupped hands. He raised his hands to his lips. The water smelled like soap.

Just then, some small children came running there. They began to harass Trimukh and started to throw pebbles at him. After some stones landed on his forehead, Trimukh shook his head. His head felt lighter just as a stove grows lighter after it has run out of kerosene. He staunched the welling blood and screamed. The children began to laugh out loud. They found his strange screams amusing.

Trimukh came to the outskirts of the village. The sun was blisteringly hot. Trimukh cried out like a strange bird. He leapt about a few times. He threw the dust around and began to run. Just as dried leaves fall from trees and fly away with the wind. Memories of his mother were settling on his heart like a flock of birds. The Patil's words were ringing in his ears: 'Take your mother's bones to Banaras and throw them there. Her dead soul will find peace. You are her son, aren't you?'

A desolate moorland dancing with mirages. A route that, like a serpent, did not come within reach. A time that choked the throat of a dove. A totally hushed environment. A hot sun that fell harshly on the head. And a completely harassed Trimukh. He was trampling his way, sunstruck and thirsty.

Trimukh lay motionless under a tamarind tree along the way. He began to eat the tamarind leaves that had fallen to the ground. He began to swallow the sour juice from them. His stomach was not responding at all. The sour taste was causing his tongue to shiver. His mouth was trembling. Trimukh vomited a couple of times. A thousand black waves of unconsciousness were galloping over his body like mounted horsemen. Taking his mother's bones as a pillow, Trimukh lay down and closed his eyes. Languor took possession of him.

Trimukh got up. The day was declining towards sunset. Now he must reach close to the next village. He began to walk with a new strength. He could hear the festive sound of the shehnai. His hopes had begun to rise. In the next village there must be a public feast at the home of some Patil or sarpanch. He would at least get some food there. He was walking with that hope, and his stomach had long since gone into the village and was roaming around it from house to house.

Outside the village, in Bhimnagar, a celebration of Dr. Babasaheb Ambedkar's anniversary was in progress. All the Buddhists had gathered enthusiastically. A Dalit activist was passionately giving a speech. Trimukh had become an inseparable part of that intensity. He got a meal there. At night, he slept in that very same enclosure.

The next morning, he set forth again on his journey. That day he would reach the railway station in the nearby town. He would see the railway station. He would sit in the train without a ticket. He went forward step by step.

Trimukh left Bhimnagar. Outside the village he found the thighbone of some animal. He went on walking like a man with a contagious disease. Then he found an animal's rib. Trimukh began to collect animal bones. Animal bones and his mother's bones had accumulated with him. He went further ahead. Outside the village there was a hut. An old crone sat coughing in the hut. Buying bones was her business. She was very tired. On account of her age she could not see too well. Her only son had set out that morning on his bicycle to buy bones in rural areas.

Trimukh gave that old woman the animal bones. The old woman evaluated the bones. To Trimukh's eyes, the old woman's hands stood before him like those of the goddess of justice, holding the scales. The weight of the animal bones was proving insufficient. The Banaras in Trimukh's mind went up and down like the weighing scales. Trimukh put his mother's bones into one of the scales, and Trimukh was given one rupee. He would have reached the railway station by that evening. He turned around and looked back. Bhimnagar could be seen at the distance of a shout. Trimukh set out in the direction of Bhimnagar. Like a sunflower at the pace of a thousand storms.

Trimukh wanted to donate the rupee he got from selling the bones to the fund collected to set up Dr. Babasaheb Ambedkar's statue.

Glossary

abir: a black powder that is used during rituals and also flung in celebration

adda: a meeting-place; a hangout

badvas: temple priests

balute: the share of the harvest traditionally given to the Dalits of the village

Bamanwada: the quarter occupied by Brahmins

bhakri: unleavened flatbread usually made from millet or rice flour. It is thicker and stiffer than the chapatis made from wheat flour. The dough is flattened between the palms, not rolled out.

bhajani mandali: a group that assembles to sing Hindu devotional songs

bhikshu: a monk

Bhimnagar: Bhimrao Ambedkar was a leader of Mahars who waged a lifelong struggle for the uplift and emancipation of Dalits. To honour him, Mahars changed the name of their dwelling from Maharwada to Bhimnagar.

Chambhar: an untouchable caste in Maharashtra which is known as Chamar in north India

dhadka: a ritual performed because of a vow, in which the devotee runs up to and dashes himself against a wall

ekadasi: the eleventh day of each fortnight of the Hindu lunar month

ektara: a lightweight musical instrument carried about and played by plucking its single string

Gard: brown sugar; a person towards whom others are powerfully attracted or drawn much like an addiction

goulan: a milkmaid; folk song based on Krishna and his gopis sung by devotees

gulal: a scarlet powder which is flung around on joyful occasions, often during processions, covering the clothes, heads and faces of all those around with bright colour

haldi-kunku events: social occasions to which women invite their women relatives and friends. The hostess ritually applies turmeric and kumkum (i.e. haldi and kunku in Marathi) to their foreheads and gives them small gifts and refreshments.

Jai Bhimwala: a Dalit Buddhist. Thus called because they greet each other with the salutation 'Jai Bhim', in honour of their leader Dr. Bhimrao Ambedkar.

kumkum: the red powder that Hindu women (and sometimes men) wear in a dot on their forehead.

lezhim: a musical instrument consisting of a rod and a string of miniature cymbals, which is played by holding the rod in the left hand and rhythmically clashing the cymbals. This is done while performing a vigorous dance.

Mahar: an untouchable caste in Maharashtra. A 'house Mahar' is a member of this caste who serves one or two houses in the village; a 'village Mahar' is one who serves an entire village.

Maharwada: the settlement outside a village where Mahars were (and still often are) forced to live

Mang: an untouchable caste in Maharashtra

mangalsutra: the necklace worn by married Hindu women as a token of their marital status

mantrik: an exorcist

mhorkya: the principal singer in a group of singers

nanda-jyot: a large lamp in a temple

owis: short verses

pancha: thin hand-woven towel

panchanama: enquiry into an incident such as a death

patti: subscription money

pothi: a book printed so that it opens vertically and not horizontally. The format is commonly used for sacred books

raya: radiant, glowing

Satyakatha: a Marathi magazine which publishes mainstream Marathi literature

shabnam: a carrying bag used perhaps for books

shakha: a branch of an organisation. Now commonly refers to local offices of the Rashtriya Swayamsevak Sangh (RSS) or the Shiv Sena

shakuti: a spicy meat curry

shanti ceremony: a ceremony performed to calm and dispel any evil influences

shehnai: a musical instrument played by blowing; part of an ensemble that plays on auspicious occasions

sthitapradnya: being totally unattached to the results of one's endeavours

talati: an official in a village who deals with matters such as land records and revenues

tambya: a small copper vessel used to fill with water

tipri: a stick for beating a drum

tirtha: the liquid from the washing of an idol with water, milk, curd and honey, spooned out into the palms of devotees after a ritual of worship, and drunk as a form of communion with the deity

tirtha prasad: a combination of tirtha and the food offered to the deity during a ritual of worship, which is later distributed among the devotees

Yeskar: an untouchable who patrols the village at night

Yeskar's bhakri: the bread that the Yeskar begs for from every house in the village in lieu of his services